There was no doubt in her mind—it was the same man who'd rescued her

"Andrew," she called to him.

"Let's start this off by introducing ourselves." He held out his hand. "I'm Andrew Wallace."

"Yes, yes. I know very well who you are. We just spent the night together."

That caught him off guard. "No."

"Oh, yes."

"No, I mean—" He raked his fingers through his hair. "Believe me, I'd have remembered if we had."

He looked sincere, Sydney realized with a stab of fear. What on earth was going on here?

Dear Reader,

Evelyn A. Crowe's legion of fans will be delighted to learn that she has penned our Women Who Dare title for November. In *Reunited,* gutsy investigative reporter Sydney Tanner learns way more than she bargained for about rising young congressman J. D. Fowler. Generational family feuds, a long-ago murder and a touch of blackmail are only a few of the surprises in store for Sydney—and you—as the significance of the heroine's discoveries begins to shape this riveting tale.

Popular Superromance author Sharon Brondos has contributed our final Woman Who Dare title for 1993. In *Doc Wyoming,* taciturn sheriff Hal Blane wants nothing to do with a citified female doctor. But Dixie Sheldon becomes involved with Blane's infamous family in spite of herself, and her "sentence" in Wyoming is commuted to a romance of the American West.

More Women Who Dare titles will be coming your way in 1994. Patricia Chandler and Tracy Hughes have two great, daring stories lined up for you in the spring. And watch for titles by Vicki Lewis Thompson, Margaret Chittenden and Margot Dalton this month and next as we begin to draw the curtain on '93!

Marsha Zinberg,
Senior Editor

Reunited

Evelyn A. Crowe

Harlequin Books

TORONTO • NEW YORK • LONDON
AMSTERDAM • PARIS • SYDNEY • HAMBURG
STOCKHOLM • ATHENS • TOKYO • MILAN
MADRID • WARSAW • BUDAPEST • AUCKLAND

ISBN 0-373-70570-0

REUNITED

Copyright © 1993 by Evelyn A. Crowe.

ABOUT THE AUTHOR

Evelyn Crowe worked for twelve years as a media director in an advertising company before turning her hand to writing in 1983. Her decision to change careers was a stroke of good fortune for both Harlequin readers and for herself. "I love to tell stories," she says simply, adding that storytelling and reading have been a big part of her life for as long as she can remember.

Evelyn makes her home in Houston. When she needs a break from the printed page, she goes antique hunting or hiking.

Books by Evelyn A. Crowe

HARLEQUIN SUPERROMANCE

112—SUMMER BALLAD
160—CHARADE
186—MOMENT OF MADNESS
233—FINAL PAYMENT
262—TWICE SHY
294—A WILD WIND
362—WORD OF HONOR

Don't miss any of our special offers. Write to us at the following address for information on our newest releases.

Harlequin Reader Service
P.O. Box 1397, Buffalo, NY 14240
Canadian address: P.O. Box 603,
Fort Erie, Ont. L2A 5X3

CHAPTER ONE

SHE WAS LOST. Utterly, hopelessly lost. And to make matters worse, the daylight had so suddenly been swallowed up and turned into a nightmarish darkness that it nearly robbed her of her breath. That abrupt darkness was the most frightening—a total pitch-black nothingness, a void that sucked the shadows away and left her feeling as if she were the only living person on earth. Thunder boomed overhead, not just loud, cracking claps, but ground-shaking thunder, the kind that made her bones vibrate. The wind howled like a banshee on a rampage. And the rain . . . God, the rain. It pounded against the car's windshield like a million hammers, making the wipers about as effective as trying to stop a flood with a teaspoon.

Sydney Tanner grabbed the steering wheel harder, squeezing it until her knuckles turned white. She leaned forward, straining to see the road through the meager beams from the car's headlights. The two-lane blacktop didn't have a white dividing line, so she didn't know whether she was on her side or driving down the middle. She wanted to stop, let the storm pass, but when she'd tried to pull off the road a few minutes ago, she'd managed to yank the wheels back just in time to avoid sliding into a steep ditch full of turbulent water. The road had no gravel or dirt shoulder.

She reminded herself that this was all her own fault. If she hadn't made the fatal mistake of stopping at one of those mom-and-pop gas station/grocery stores to use the rest room and have a Coke, she wouldn't be in this situation. If she hadn't started up a conversation with the old man at the cash register and casually asked if there was a shorter route to Wallace, Texas, other than the main interstate, she wouldn't be in this mess. If she hadn't listened and taken the infamous shortcut... But she had, and the feeling that she'd turned onto the wrong road was too strong to ignore. Now she couldn't stop, and going on was suicidal.

Sydney couldn't understand how she'd gotten lost in the first place. She had a knack for reading maps and memorizing every turn, every road marker. Plus, she had what her father called an "inner compass"—a sense of direction that could put a flock of migrating birds to shame. She never got lost!

How had she missed the signs of the approaching storm? Had there been any? She couldn't believe she'd been so unobservant. One minute it was three o'clock on a typical, scorching summer afternoon and she was turning onto the old blacktop farm road, the next minute the bright Texas sun was gone. She'd caught sight of the black velvet curtain of clouds in the rearview mirror, but before she could do anything—Lord only knew what—those menacing clouds had rolled above her. Then the wind had begun to beat at the trees with a savage fury, sending leaves and branches in a whirlwind around the car. Texas was legendary for its unpredictable weather, but this was weird. What spooked her the most was the thunder. It shook the ground so hard she could have sworn the car actually jumped with fright. And then there was the fact that there was no lightning, only the thunder, wind and rain, and her alone on a road that led to who knew where.

Sydney tore her gaze from the road, glanced down at the speedometer, then quickly looked back at the road. Five miles an hour and she couldn't see worth a damn. The irrational thought popped into her mind that if she hadn't taken the shortcut, the storm wouldn't have caught her. She had no one to blame but herself. But that wasn't totally true. Her editor had a large bony hand in this mess, and if she made it to Wallace in one piece, she was going to call the weasel and tell him just what she thought of his bright ideas. What was it he'd said? "You're from Texas, Syd. You know the lingo, the way to dance around the good-old-boy network and still get the job done. You wouldn't be just some hotshot reporter from the *Washington Post*. Senator James Darcy Fowler will welcome you like family."

Bull! Senator Fowler would have agreed to the indepth interview if she'd had two heads and hissed her questions like a snake—that was the nature of politicians. She shouldn't have been so eager, so willing to take on the assignment. Sydney rubbed her tired eyes with a hand that shook from the death grip she had on the steering wheel. She scolded herself to keep her mind on the road, pay attention to what she was doing. Instead, her mind seemed to drift along other paths as if the danger she was in was of little consequence.

She'd been working too hard, she told herself, that was the problem. She had been exhausted when her boss hit her with the assignment and caught her in a weak moment with visions of home, family and all the secure comforts those early childhood memories offered.

"Who are you fooling, my girl?" she whispered. "You haven't had a moment's peace in that house in years. So you jumped at the chance to take the job. Were even willing to use up some of your two-week duty vacation with the *family* to do the interview. Hell, you almost kissed the top of the old warthog's bald head when he gave you a legit excuse not to go home so soon. And, of course, he'd beamed like a smiling jackal when he saw a way of using up your time instead of the paper's.''

Sydney realized she was talking to herself again, something that had been happening more frequently lately, and she shook her head. That was another reason she wanted to come to Texas. It was time to leave Washington, and she wanted to circulate her résumé around Dallas and maybe Houston. The Washington political scene that had drawn her away from Texas had lost its glitter. If she had to cover one more political meeting that ended in grown men acting worse than children, or hear one more politician mouth another hypocritical promise, she'd barf.

Sydney pried one hand off the wheel again, wiped it on her thigh and flexed her fingers, all the while cautioning herself to concentrate on the road. She frowned, squinted through the darkness and silently warned herself once more that a wandering mind could put her in the ditch. The problem was, she decided, that she was scared and realized that the fear was unrelated to her predicament. Something kept nagging at her—a feeling, a sense of wrongness. Her heart was pounding, her mouth suddenly dry. She felt funny inside, as if she had the shakes, but she wasn't shaking. The storm. That was it. She rubbed her tired eyes again and gently applied the brakes to slow her already snail's pace. The eerie thunder, the absence of lightning, her exhaustion—they were all playing tricks on her mind.

Suddenly, the sky was filled with a blinding blast of light. Sydney flinched and her eyes squeezed shut. But in that millisecond before her eyes closed, she saw a man standing in the middle of the road, directly in front of her. She frantically stomped on the brakes, but the tires refused to grip the slick blacktop. The brakes locked, and the car began sliding toward the side of the road.

She grappled with the wheel, fighting to steer into the slide, all the while expecting to feel the thud of a body impacting the car, but there were no sounds other than her hard gasps for breath. One second she was angled sideways across the road, the next, the car slipped off the road, front end first. Before she knew what was happening, the hood hit the bank of the ditch, throwing her forward. Her forehead bounced off the top of the steering wheel. The rear of the car quickly followed the front with an ominous sucking and grinding sound as it slid down the embankment and finally smashed into the side of the ditch. Her mother always accused her of being hardheaded, but this time the car's window proved to be more than a match. Her head snapped against the unyielding glass. She immediately saw a frenzy of bright pinpoint lights, and a second later they were extinguished by her howl of pain. Then everything went black....

When Sydney came to, she was fully aware of what had happened. Careful not to touch her head, and avoiding any quick moves, she eased into a more comfortable position, trying to take stock of her situation. The well of darkness still surrounded her; she didn't think she'd been out very long. She took a breath, blinked, closed her eyes, then opened them again. From the crazy angle of the headlights' beams she could see that the storm had played itself out. The rain was only a steady pelting on the windshield, and the wipers thumped noisily back and forth, their irritating sound keeping perfect time to the thumping in her head. There was a metallic taste in her mouth, yet she hadn't bitten her tongue. Then she realized what the taste was. The inside of the car was filled with gasoline fumes.

Suddenly all she could think about was fire. Panic spurred her into action. First the engine, she told herself, then couldn't remember what she was supposed to do. Just thinking hurt, but she knew she had to do something fast. She switched the engine off and was about to turn off the headlights, but hesitated. She just couldn't bear the thought of being in the dark. A soothing silence descended and warmth seeped into her body, making her relax. If it hadn't been for the pain in her head and the ache in her shoulder where she'd been thrown against the door, she could have laid her head back and gone to sleep. God, how she wanted to close her eyes and take a long nap. She was about to succumb to the urge when she became aware of a cold wetness around her feet.

Her mind was so woozy it took her a minute to think about the problem and sort it out. The feeling of cold wetness crept up to her calves. Reason it out, she told herself. If the ditch was full of water and the car was on its side, it was logical to assume that the car would fill also. Visions of drowning sent a jolt of adrenaline surging through her. Muscles that had been rubbery with shock suddenly came alive.

Sydney fumbled with the seat belt, panic making her fingers clumsy. When the metal clamp snapped free, she crawled into the passenger seat, toward the door handle on the other side. Finally, clawing for anything to grab on to, her numb fingers grasped the handle. The angle of the car had made the heavy door about three times its actual weight and impossible to open. Water was lapping at the rim of the driver's seat. How long did she have before the car would fill up completely, or worse still, slip farther into the ditch and be swept away? She wanted out now, and she pounded on the window, screaming for help until she realized no one was out there. She was irrational, alone and scared silly. *Calm down, Syd. Take a deep breath. Think!*

"Of course, of course," she whispered, and pressed the button for the electric window. Nothing happened. She almost cried with frustration and fear, but bit down on her lip until she realized what was wrong. Reaching around, she turned on the ignition, pressed the window button again and held her breath as it slid smoothly down. Cold rain splattered against her face, and for a second she savored the feel, the sweet smell of freedom. But then she reminded herself that she wasn't free of danger yet. She was just about to dive out the window when she remembered her purse. From years of habit, because she always kept all her notes with her, she was never without the oversize purse. She yanked at the strap and finally worked the big leather bag out from under her. Slinging the strap over her head, she grasped the edge of the door, got some leverage with her feet, then went headfirst out the window....

Sydney came to, dazed and confused. It took a blurry second to recall everything. *I must have blacked out,* she thought. Carefully, she eased into a sitting position. The movement made her dizzy; her head throbbed. She was sitting in the rain on the side of the road. The car was a wreck. She was alone, lost, cold, scared, and dammit, her head hurt like the devil. She sniffed, self-pity threatening to engulf her.

"Well, my girl, this is another mess you've gotten yourself into," she whispered. "And what's to be done now?" At least she wasn't in total darkness. The car headlights were still on, even if they were pointed partly at the ditch and partly out into the thick trees at the side of the road. As she stared hopelessly into the misty light, she thought she saw shadows moving among the trees. She quickly told herself, in spite of the hard shiver that trickled down her back, that it was only her imagination.

After a moment she realized she couldn't continue to sit on the road like another accident just waiting to happen. Then again, she didn't have the foggiest idea what she should do. The rain had slowed to a steady drizzle, her hair was plastered to her scalp, and she was soaked to the skin. She closed her eyes and was not surprised when her mind went blank as she tried to think of a way out.

"Are you all right, ma'am?"

"What the hell do you think? Of all the stupid..." Her voice trailed off to a whisper. She was almost afraid to open her eyes, afraid she was hallucinating. When she did brave a peek, she winced and jerked up her arm to shade her eyes from the light cutting a sharp path down the center of her brain. "Say that again," she pleaded, and held her breath.

"Are you all right, ma'am?"

It was real. He was real. "I thought I was hearing voices." A deep, rich, masculine chuckle quickly dispelled her fear. The flow of words that would have tumbled from her lips died away when the light was lowered to the ground and she was able to see her rescuer. "You aren't by any chance the man who walked out in front of me, are you?"

"I'm afraid I am."

She wished she could see him better, but the lantern he'd set down afforded only a small amount of yellow light. She had the impression of youth, though, height and strength. Just what she needed. "You wouldn't happen to have a car, would you?"

"No. Like you, my conveyance is axle-deep in a ditch."

As he'd talked he'd squatted in front of her, and she couldn't decide if the pain in her head or the appearance of the man himself was causing the breath to catch in the back of her throat. "Oh...my...." She was staring into the greenest eyes she'd ever seen and couldn't look away no matter how much she told herself that staring was rude.

"Can you stand up, ma'am?"

"What?"

"Stand." He chuckled again. "We need to get to shelter, have a look at your injuries and get you warm."

Warm. He made the word sound like a sexy invitation for something deliciously sinful. Sydney readily accepted by slipping her hand in his, had a fleeting thought of how welcome his dry skin felt against hers when he pulled her to her feet, then succumbed to the spinning darkness once again.

THE FIRST THING Sydney was conscious of was a sense of well-being—coziness. The second thing was a helluva headache. With each heartbeat she felt as if the top of her head were going to come off. The pain was so bad she struggled to time her breaths between each hammering beat. After a few minutes she chanced easing her eyes open, only a fraction, testing the pain against the light in the room. To her surprise she found she was no worse for the experiment and opened her eyes wider. A fuzzy glow surrounded her. For a second she thought she might be dead, then the haziness cleared a little and she found herself staring up at a ceiling made of crisscross split logs aged and blackened by smoke. The light danced and winked above her head, making the logs look as if they were fading in and out. Where was she? One thing she was sure of was that it wasn't in a modern hospital.

Afraid to move her pounding head too much, she shifted her gaze and spied the answer to the spooky light. A fire was burning in a big stone fireplace at the foot of the bed. Strange, she thought. She was in a bed, neatly tucked under the covers.

She braved a more thorough look, turning her head slightly, eyeing the room, trying to take her scrambled thoughts off the fact that she should be scared—if not scared, concerned, or at least curious—but the trouble was, she felt safe. Now *that* was a puzzling thought, she told herself, then let her gaze ramble around the room, picking out an item here and there. A lantern, the brass shining like a mirror, was positioned on a spiny-legged table near the doorway. And through the doorway, she could see another big stone fireplace and the corner of a rocking chair. Mounted over the fireplace were four antique rifles. With a sigh of relief, Sydney realized she was in the man's hunting cabin...but where was he? Very slowly, Sydney moved her head and began to inspect the sparsely furnished bedroom once again. There was an armoire against the far wall and a table within arm's reach. The bed was one of those old fashioned, mammoth four-posters. Other than that there was little else.

Everything looked new yet old. She worried over that discovery a second, couldn't come up with an answer and gave up. Either her imagination was playing tricks on her or the injury to her head and her blurred vision were the culprits. Sydney blinked a few times and was able to see more clearly.

Except for the sound of the rain on the roof, the place was quiet—too quiet. She was about to call out when something caught her attention. Above the fireplace was a portrait of a beautiful young woman. It was one of those really old paintings in a wide, ornate wood frame. Somehow she doubted that the owner of the portrait was the owner of wherever she was. The room was neat, clean, but nothing looked as expensive as the portrait and its elaborate frame.

Sydney studied the painting. She figured by the stiff way the woman was sitting, the high-neck lace collar and the style of dress that this was someone's beloved great- or great-great-grandmother. Blond hair, thick and lustrous, was pulled back from the lovely face. Several thick curls tumbled over her shoulder, just caressing the top of her breast.

Sydney thought a hunting cabin was an odd place for such a portrait. She was just beginning to look away, her gaze already on the move, when a flash of movement jerked her eyes back to the painting. She could have sworn that there was a change in the expression, that just for a second that sweet smile had changed to bitter sadness and the large aquamarine eyes had filled with the glimmer of tears.

Fear clutched at Sydney's throat, paralyzed her muscles. Suddenly, all her aches and pains were forgot-

ten. She was a child again, awakening in the middle of
the night and seeing monsters all around her. Monsters
that had eyes that glistened with cunning. The kind of
monsters that disapeared when she squeezed her eyes
shut, only to reappear when she was about to drop back
into exhausted sleep. The grown-up Sydney had to remind herself that she was no longer that child. But
damn, she could have sworn that just for a second she
saw a shimmering tear roll down that soft, rosy cheek.
She shivered, more relieved than she'd admit that the
painting was back to normal.

"God, you're such a ninny," she whispered, and was
suddenly amused at how her voice squeaked. She
cleared her throat and called out, "Hello. Is anyone
here?"

Silence.

Well, she could try to get up and take a look around.
But as she began to lever herself up on one elbow, the
room spun around and the pain in her head took her
breath away, forcing her to ease back down. When the
dizziness and nausea passed, Sydney lay staring at the
quilt neatly tucked around her, suddenly feeling lost and
helpless, her own tears very close to spilling over. She
didn't like the weakness and self-pity, and as she mentally gave herself a pep talk, she absently plucked at the
tiny knots of the quilt, then realized what she was doing and jerked her hand away. Her mother was an antique dealer, and her passion—no, obsession—for old
quilts must have rubbed off. Sydney knew enough to
realize that she was covered with a masterpiece, one that
belonged on a wall or in a museum. The intricate appliqués of wild animals and colorful flowers were works
of art in themselves. The quilt showed a forest scene
with huge oak trees, their spreading limbs throwing

shadows over the variegated greens of a meadow, and a blue stream meandering between velvet green banks. It was totally enchanting, very old and beyond price.

She was totally absorbed in the quilt when a deep, masculine voice touched with worry said, "You need a doctor."

Sydney screamed, jumped, then moaned as pain shot through her head like a bullet. When she could speak, she said through gritted teeth, "You have the worst habit of popping out of nowhere." Slowly opening her eyes, she scowled. Oh, Lord. He wasn't a figment of her imagination. Now that she had the benefit of light, she saw that he had these rugged good looks of an out-doorsman—tanned from the sun, tall and slim but wide across the shoulders. She figured he was probably older than she'd originally thought, maybe in his late twenties. Sydney looked into his eyes, and the sweetness and worry that she saw there touched her. She wanted to re-assure him that she was really okay now, but the words seemed to dry up like dust in her throat, and all she could do was stare. Suddenly he smiled, one of those heart-stopping smiles that was contagious, and she knew she was grinning like an idiot. There was some-thing about this man that made her feel—she struggled for the right words—good inside. "What's wrong with me?" she asked.

"You need a doctor, ma'am."

"If I remember correctly, you've said that before." She liked the old-fashioned "ma'am" courtesy. "I'm Sydney Tanner, and I haven't figured out yet if I owe you my life or should be furious with you for causing the wreck." She waited until he'd eased down beside her, picked up her hand and was holding it in his be-fore she went on. "You did step out in front of my car, didn't you?'' Funny, but his closeness seemed to ease her pain. ''Who are you?''

''Andrew Joshua Wallace, ma'am. And I am very sorry about what happened back there on the road. After so long . . . your appearance out of the blue was rather a shock.''

Sydney had been giving him the once-over while he talked, taking in the butter-soft leather pants, the rough material of his faded blue shirt, the way his hand felt—rough and hot to the touch. He talked strangely, too. An accent or maybe an inflection she just couldn't place. Certainly there was none of that nasal East Texas twang in his speech.

She noticed how the light from the fireplace seemed to form a golden glow around him, giving him a luminous, almost shimmering quality. Sydney closed her eyes for a moment, more to hide her fanciful and totally absurd thoughts than in pain. Something wasn't right. Maybe she did indeed need a doctor—a shrink. When she opened her eyes she found herself almost nose to nose with Andrew. Lights danced in those green eyes, turning them as bright as emeralds. She could feel his warm breath on her face and smell soap and leather. She was slipping away, floating. Hypnotized.

''Miss Tanner? Sydney!'' He quickly sat back.

''Y-yes.'' She had to mentally shake herself. Warning bells went off in her head, or was it pain?

''We must get you to the doctor—now. Bumps on the head can be very serious. You have two and you fainted when you stood up back on the road. And quite frankly, you don't look very good now, either.''

''How did I get here?''

''I carried you.''

He smiled, and she couldn't help but notice the dimple that winked in and out of his right cheek. "Have I thanked you yet?" Her tongue seemed thick and unyielding, and the room was trying to spin around her again. "How far is it to town?"

"As the crow flies, not far."

She hadn't heard that expression in a long time and managed a grin. "Since we're not crows, how far by the road? Do you have another car?"

Andrew shook his head. "The wagon is axle-deep in the ditch, like yours."

At least he knew firsthand what she'd been through. She could just picture a heavy station wagon in the same fix as her smaller rental car and shuddered at the memory. "Then how are we going to get a doctor?" Instead of answering her, he gazed out the one small window, frowning. Sydney's gaze followed his. It was getting lighter out and the rain seemed to have stopped. His quiet, deep concentration unnerved her a little. "Andrew?" He tensed, and Sydney could have sworn the room wavered and the air tingled with urgency around him. "Andrew?"

He quickly stood, scooped up her purse from the bedside table, stared at it as if it were a foreign object, then handed it to her, "Your pouch." She didn't like the grim set of his mouth or the way a muscle jumped along the side of his jaw. Fear seemed to generate from him like fire from a burner.

"Wait...." But he just slipped the long purse strap over her head. Then without another word, he picked her up, quilt and all, as if she weighed no more than a small child.

"The only way is by horseback," he said.

"Please, Andrew, I don't know how to ride a horse."

SYDNEY THOUGHT she was going to die. Seated cross-wise on Andrew's lap, she was cradled securely in his arms, wrapped snugly in the quilt, but his firm hold on her did nothing to cushion the jarring ride. The lane was a quagmire and the poor horse was having trouble keeping his footing, or hoofing—she had no idea what the correct term was. All she knew was that with each slip or stumble the animal made, it felt as if someone were driving a steel spike through her head. The pain was so excruciating, she couldn't even talk and had to clench her teeth together to keep from moaning out loud. Her vision was distorted again. Everything looked funny, kind of surrealistic. She couldn't put her finger on exactly what it was, but it made her aware of the creepy sensation that kept crawling up and down her spine, making the fine hair on the back of her neck stand on end. They seemed to be shrouded in a dim, gray haze. She figured it must be close to dawn, but even with the sky beginning to lighten, the lane was like a deep, dark tunnel. Water dripped and splashed against her face, and she realized they must be riding under a thick canopy of tree branches. She was suddenly so sleepy she couldn't think....

She must have dozed off because the lack of motion abruptly jarred her awake. They had stopped at the edge of a blacktop road. The road, she assumed, was the same one where she'd had her accident. When was that? Yesterday? Last night? A few hours ago? Time had managed to slip away into nothingness. She wanted to ask Andrew and tried to turn her head so she could see him, but the quilt had been pulled up in such a way that it was like a hood, obscuring her vision. "Why are we stopping?"

"I have to let you down, Sydney Tanner."

"What?" Before she could say anything more, she was sliding to the ground, out of the warm cocoon of the quilt. Suddenly, all her attention was on the muddy earth coming up too fast, the nausea that threatened to make her disgrace herself. She needn't have worried about being dropped; Andrew's hands were firm on her waist, and her feet gently touched the edge of the road. Then his hands were on her shoulders, steadying her as her knees wobbled. When she was a little more secure, she started to turn, but Andrew's grip tightened so she couldn't move.

"Someone will be here soon. Sydney, please tell them I found Mary."

The pressure of his grip lessened, then it was gone. Dazed, confused and without his support, she weaved, caught herself, stiffened her knees and slowly turned around to call out.

The lane was empty.

"Andrew." There was no answer. No sound but the mournful, lonely cooing of a mourning dove. She stared down the tree-lined lane and a lump lodged in her throat. A deep feeling of sadness and loss settled on her shoulders with a tremendous weight. Why had Andrew left her?

It was the sound of a car that broke the spell and caught her attention. Still unsteady on her feet, her head pounding, she turned and faced the morning sun as it edged over the tops of the trees. Sydney raised her hand to shade her eyes, and waited.

A police car pulled to a stop beside her, and a young man jumped out. His uniform was wrinkled and mud splattered. The pant legs were soaked to the knees, and when he took a few steps toward her, his leather shoes squeaked with water. He was tired and uncomfortable,

but his smile was huge. "Ma'am—Miss Tanner—
Thank God. We've had people out looking for you all
night. Are you okay? Damn, you look like hell."

Sydney couldn't have said anything if she'd wanted
to. She let the young man take her arm and lead her to
the car. He reached in through the window, pulled out
a thick blanket and wrapped it around her before he
carefully tried to assist her into the back seat of the
cruiser.

"I think I'd better get you to the hospital, fast. You
look like you're going to drop."

"Wait," she croaked, like a frog with a cold. "Have
to find him." She tried to pull away and turn around at
the same time, and the young man had to catch her.
"Have to find him before...have to know why... The
portrait, something about the lady. Firelight, probably
the firelight." What remained of her sudden spurt of
strength melted away, and she went limp.

"Oh hell, oh hell. Lord, lady, please don't die on
me." He hustled her into the patrol car as gently as he
could. Then gritting his teeth, expecting the worst, he
placed two cold, shaky fingers against the side of her
neck. He closed his eyes and sighed when he felt the
steady beat.

Sydney settled back, pulled the edges of the blanket
closely around her and started to shiver uncontrolla-
bly. She didn't hear the young cop alerting the other
searchers on his radio that she'd been found, nor did she
hear him inform the hospital he was bringing in a
woman suffering from possible head injuries, exhaustion and exposure. Sydney sat with her eyes closed, unaware of the tears leaking out from under her eyelids.
The feeling of loss overwhelmed her.

CHAPTER TWO

"HOW MANY FINGERS am I holding up now?" the doctor asked.

Sydney squinted. "How the hell do I know? I'm still seeing spots from the light you were shining in my eyes."

"Head hurts like the devil, does it?" He waggled his fingers in front of her face. "Come on, how many?"

"Three." Sydney glanced at the plastic name tag above the pocket of the white smock and laughed, then wished she hadn't when a sharp pain stabbed behind her eyes. Dr. Doolittle was a thin wisp of a man with a hairline that had receded to the back of his head and a full walrus mustache. The growth on his upper lip fascinated her. She'd never seen one quite so...so... abundant. It was a couple of shades darker than what hair the good doctor had on his head, and when he talked it bristled and twitched like the whiskers of a rabbit. She briefly wondered why bald men found it necessary to compensate for their lack of hair by growing beards or mustaches. If he'd been taller, bigger, he could have twirled the ends and made a great villain. On second thought, the oversize horn-rimmed glasses that magnified his dark eyes totally ruined that image. Actually, the man was kind of—for a second she thought ugly, then changed her mind—boyish and appealing. In fact, on closer inspection, he was rather cute in an odd sort of way. "Am I in la-la-land, Dr. Doolittle, or is this a nightmare?"

"Depends."

"On what?"

He held his arm farther away. "On how many fingers I'm holding up."

"Two. Now, where am I?"

"Emergency room at Wallace General Hospital. Don't you remember being brought in?"

Sydney caught the quick frown. "Of course. I guess I must have passed out."

"Like a light, Miss Tanner."

She could tell she was going to have to pry every word out of him with a crowbar. "Don't stop this intriguing repartee, Doc. Tell me what's wrong with my head and how you know my name."

"Besides the headache and two rather large lumps on your very hard head, I can't find anything. The X ray shows no fractures, probably a mild concussion. As to your name, Nurse Paulson—" he nodded to a woman standing at the foot of the bed "—has a friend with the local law and also looked in your purse." He snapped the penlight off and slipped it into his breast pocket. "Your vision seems okay now."

"Well, it wasn't earlier." Sydney glanced around the antiseptic white walls of the emergency room and grimaced. "Place smells like a morgue."

Dr. Paul Doolittle chuckled. "Have you ever been in a morgue, Miss Tanner? If not, believe me, the smell is very different." His mustache twitched, and he looked like a mouse sniffing a delectable morsel of cheese. "One more time, how many fingers?"

"Six. And I was on the police beat long enough to know how a morgue smells, and this place brings back old memories."

"Ah, that's right, you're a reporter. Emma said Howard told her about the wreck and the search party."

"Emma?"

"Nurse Paulson."

The monster headache didn't squelch Sydney's natural curiosity, and she glanced at the nurse. Emma Paulson was one of those tiny, slightly overweight women who carried the extra pounds with complete disregard of the fact that with any movement she might split the seams of her clothes. Sydney studied the nurse for a moment and immediately had her pegged. The merry brown eyes, wide smile and the way she listened to every word that was said, the way she studied every gesture and expression—Nurse Emma Paulson was one of those people who made it her business to know everyone else's business. She was young, in her early twenties, obviously bright, and Sydney, being an excellent judge of character, bet Emma was a chatterbox. Oh, she knew Emma's type very well, and knowing the type, she also knew that Emma was a reporter's dream, a deep well of information. "Who's Howard?" she asked the nurse, who was now studying her intently.

"He's the local law."

The doctor snorted.

"Well, actually," Emma said with a laugh, "Howard's the sheriff's son and just joined the force. But he's as proud as a strutting peacock that he found you."

Sydney noticed Emma's red-stained cheeks. "This Howard's a close friend of yours?" She saw the quick glance Emma gave the doctor from under her long lashes before she ducked her head, refusing to answer. Sydney suddenly found herself glancing into innocent-looking brown eyes, and in a blink, so fast she wasn't sure if she saw it or not, she could have sworn that Emma gave her the most wicked of winks.

"If you two ladies are through talking, I'm a busy doctor."

"Bull," Sydney said. "There's not another soul in the emergency room. Now, tell me what's wrong with my eyes."

"Nothing."

"Well, something *was* wrong. More than just a couple of bumps on the head. Everything was kind of funny."

"Can we be a little more specific? You're a big-city reporter—just give me the facts, ma'am."

Sydney couldn't help smiling. "A comedian and a doctor. And how did you know I was a reporter?"

"Emma's a pretty good detective."

"Ah," Sydney said, "my purse again."

"Right. Now, if we may...the vision problem?"

"It's strange and hard to explain. Maybe it wasn't my eyes, but the light from the fireplace or the lantern. Everything had this golden glow to it. Kind of a shimmer all around the edges, if you know what I mean," she said, more musing out loud, lost in thought, than trying to explain to the doctor. "Now that I think about it..." Her words trailed off as she noticed the puzzled expressions on the two faces. "Well, it's hard to put into words, but when we were leaving the cabin, the light got gray and fuzzy. Spooky is the only word that comes to mind. It had to be my eyes."

Dr. Doolittle motioned for the nurse to take Sydney's blood pressure. Then he leaned forward, pulled his penlight from his pocket and began examining her eyes again. "Miss Tanner—"

"Sydney, please."

"Fine. Sydney, what firelight or lantern light are you talking about? You were found wandering on the road. Open your eyes, please. I can't see your pupils with them squeezed shut."

She did as asked, reluctantly. "Damn, that makes my head hurt worse."

"Sorry, but tell me again about the light—the cabin."

"After the wreck I was taken to a cabin, wrapped in a quilt and kept warm till this morning. Then I was dropped off at the edge of the road where the policeman came along and picked me up." Why the hell were they acting as if she'd just admitted to escaping from the crazy farm? She blinked a couple of times to clear the dancing spots away. "Look. I took this shortcut that I shouldn't have. The storm caught me. I couldn't see my hand in front of my face."

"I thought you said the vision problems started after the car wreck?"

Her head was pounding a mile a minute, and she was having trouble thinking straight. "I had this wreck. No, the car was sliding, then suddenly—"

"Don't try to talk anymore," the doctor interrupted. "Emma, I think Miss Tanner ought to stay at least one night. We'll keep a close watch on her."

He was leaving, and Sydney managed to prop herself up on one elbow. "Wait." Her voice echoed through her head like someone beating a bass drum. She groaned and fell back against the pillow.

"Is there anyone you want me to call for you?" Dr. Doolittle asked.

"What? No, not for a couple of bumps on the head."
Before she could say anything more, the doctor made a
quick exit, and Sydney heard the nurse's rubber-soled
shoes squeak across the floor behind him.

"Wait a minute. Why the funny looks when I told
you and the good Dr. Doolittle about the cabin and the
firelight?"

Emma laughed. "I like the sarcastic way you say his
name. Kind of puts him in his place. That's not to say
Dr. Doo—mind you, we only call him that behind his
back—anyway, he's a good doctor. He just has this in-
flated ego. I'll be back in a little while with a gown, then
we'll get you into a room and make you more comfortable."

"You didn't answer my question, Nurse Paulson."

"No, I didn't, did I?"

"Well?"

"Howard said he found you out on Piney Creek
Road. There's nothing around there for miles but tim-
berland."

"No houses? A cabin?"

"No, nothing."

"Poppycock," Sydney moaned, but she was talking
to empty space. She closed her eyes and mumbled,
"Maybe your Howard had the wrong road. I know
what I saw and what happened."

IT WAS THE SOUND of hushed laughter and low voices
that awakened her. Sydney didn't have to see him
through the open curtains of the emergency room to
know who one of those voices belonged to. He was
turned sideways, leaning against the nurses' station,
obviously charming the pants off an old woman judg-
ing by the way she was giggling like a teenager.

There was no doubt in her mind that it was Andrew. The same tall, slim, wide-shouldered build. The same thick hair as black as jet, the same strong-jawed profile. He might have changed into tight-fitting blue jeans and a crisp white shirt with the sleeves rolled up to the elbow, but it was the same man. She remembered his gentleness and concern. Most of all she remembered his touch and the way it made her feel safe, and yes, as strange as it sounded, the way he made her feel special. What she couldn't understand was why he had taken such good care of her only to leave her beside the road. But she was going to find out.

"Andrew," she called. Her voice was shaky, a thready whisper, like some dumbstruck shy kid, so she cleared her throat and tried again. "Andrew." She watched as he glanced around, studied her for a second, said something to the nurse at the desk, then walked over.

"Well, hello there."

Damn, she was going to be a tongue-tied idiot, and because she was never at a loss for words, she became angry at herself. The displeasure showed in her sarcastic tone. "Well, hello to you, too. I appreciate all you did for me, but how about telling me why you just dumped me at the side of the road?"

"I beg your pardon?"

She couldn't gauge his expression. One moment he was smiling, his green eyes sparkling with laughter; the next moment she saw nothing but a blank stare. He was gazing at her as if she belonged in the kind of jacket with buckles down the back. Confused, she snapped, "Okay, game's up."

Andrew studied the earnest, somewhat indignant face, intrigued by the anger in those clear blue eyes, and couldn't help but smile. She was a great-looking woman with pale skin and short, straight chestnut hair. He was fascinated by the way the overhead lighting turned that head of hair into a bright red flame and would have bet his Merlin that an explosive temper lurked very close to the surface. He had the vague feeling that he knew her, or was supposed to know her, and racked his brain for a name to fit the face. She sure as hell wasn't one of his old girlfriends. This was one woman a man wouldn't easily forget.

He glanced over his shoulder at Anne English, the desk nurse. He saw her watching them and gave her a look that shouted "Help," but he got only a shrug in return. He turned his attention back to the lady in the bed. She'd said something about games. "I like games," was all he could think to say. "Let's start this one off by introducing ourselves." He held out his hand. "I'm Andrew Wallace."

"Yes, yes. I know very well who you are. We just spent the night together."

That caught him off guard. "No."

"Oh, yes."

"No. I mean—" he raked his fingers through his hair "—I mean, no, we didn't. Believe me—"

"Sydney Tanner," she snapped, "so don't act like you don't know me."

"Believe me, Sydney Tanner, I'm not senile nor am I absentminded. If I'd spent last night with you, I would have remembered."

For once in her life she was shocked speechless, not from anger but from a sudden stab of pain. Why was he denying that he knew her? A warning bell went off: maybe he was married. She felt sick at the thought, then could have kicked herself for being a fool. She needed time to think without the damn pain in her head clouding her judgment. When Emma Paulson strolled in, she almost welcomed the intrusion. She quickly noticed that Andrew looked relieved.

"Hi, Drew." Emma set down the hospital gown and slippers on the end of the bed, her gaze bouncing between her patient and Andrew. There was something very weird going on. The tension was so thick she could have cut it with a knife. "You two know each other?"

"Yes," Sydney said.

"No," Andrew said at the same time.

Emma shifted her gaze from one to the other, and when neither said anything, she decided to crack the silence. "I think it's a miracle Miss Tanner's alive, don't you, Drew?"

"I didn't know she was in danger of losing her life."

Sydney snarled something under her breath, but what she said was lost as the nurse babbled on.

"Oh, my...surely you knew. Her car went into a ditch on Piney Creek Road. That's all your family property around there, isn't it?"

Sydney gave him a look that said, "Get out of that one," then glared at him.

"Anyway, Howard found her out on the road this morning. Everyone in town knows, Drew."

"I was here all night," he said, but wouldn't look her in the eye.

"Were you?" Emma said, giving him a puzzled look, but decided to let the lie pass. "Mr. Clay had a fall yesterday, didn't he? How's he doing this morning?"

Sydney didn't particularly enjoy being left out, but was like a starved woman for any information about Andrew.

"The old coot's feeling foolish and mad at the same time." Andrew watched every move, every expression of this Sydney Tanner from the corner of his eye. She didn't look too pleased with the turn of conversation, and he figured it was as good a chance as any for him to slip away. He had even taken a couple of steps back when Emma's next words pulled him up short.

"Miss Tanner's a reporter with the *Washington Post*, in D.C."

"I know where it is, Emma," he said.

Sydney immediately noticed the change in him. He'd been smiling, seemingly interested in what Emma was saying—though she hadn't missed the way he'd been edging away—when suddenly he froze. His reaction wasn't new to her; she'd seen it many times before when someone found out she was a reporter, but it usually came from someone with something to hide. And most people, at least, tried to hide behind a cool politeness. She found out very quickly from his expression that Andrew was not a polite man. "You needn't go all prune-mouth at the mention of the word *reporter*," she admonished.

He couldn't help but laugh as he continued out of the room, saying over his shoulder, "I'm not prune-mouthed. I'm disgusted. You wallow with the pigs, Miss Tanner, and no matter how hard you try, you can't come out smelling like a rose."

She'd heard worse and almost sighed with relief, but he was getting away and she wasn't through with him. "Andrew, come back here! We have things to talk about."

"Don't hold your breath."

Sydney stared at the moving curtains, her eyes narrowing slightly. *We'll see,* she thought. *We'll just see about that.*

Emma eyed her curiously. "You two *do* know each other?" She pulled over a wheelchair and helped Sydney up and out of bed. Once her patient was settled and had regained her color, Emma dumped the hospital gown and slippers in her lap and began wheeling her down the hall. "Drew's a wonderful man. Clay took a tumble yesterday—"

"Who's Clay?"

"Drew's grandfather."

"Is he married, Emma?"

"Who, Drew or Clay?"

"Andrew." For some reason she couldn't have explained if her life depended on it, her mouth went dry.

"No, not now. Was, though, until a couple of years ago. But I thought you two knew each other...."

"You're fishing, Emma, and trying to take advantage of my condition."

Emma laughed. "Well, of course. You can't blame a girl for trying. Nothing exciting ever happens in this town. Then out of the blue we have a freak storm, someone finds a car in a ditch and no driver, the rental record shows the car was rented to a Miss Sydney Tanner, a search party is called out, and this morning you're found standing by the side of the road dazed and babbling about a man and firelight." She paused only long enough to take a quick deep breath. "It's obvious you and Drew were trying to hide the fact that you know each other by pretending that you didn't know each other.... At least, that's the impression I got. I ask myself why? What we have here is a mystery."

If you only knew, Sydney thought as she grabbed the arms of the wheelchair. The faster Emma talked, the faster she pushed the chair until they were speeding down the hospital hall. "Emma, please, this isn't a race. You're making me dizzy and sick."

"Sorry. But I love mysteries."

By the time she was changed and settled in bed, Sydney's head was killing her again. She watched through slitted eyelids as Emma fussed with the covers, moved the water pitcher and glass closer. "How long do I have to stay in bed?" When she spoke, Emma jumped.

"Well, Dr. Doo's a very tricky man. When he says twenty-four hours, you can bet he means forty-eight. He's a little concerned about you, you know."

"Why? He said there was nothing physically wrong but a few bumps and bruises." She managed to capture the sudden elusive gaze of the young woman. The wide-eyed, innocent look didn't fool her. "Emma, what did he say?"

"I'm not supposed to talk about a patient's condition, at least not to the patient."

"I see." Sydney sighed and closed her eyes. "Doctor-nurse privileges, huh? I was going to tell you about Andrew, but..."

"Oh, you play dirty." She pulled a chair close to the bed and sat.

Sydney knew she had her, and it amused her to realize how easy this woman was to manipulate. She was immediately ashamed of herself, then wondered why. For some odd reason she liked this Emma Paulson, enough to feel the pangs of shame for what she was doing. First thing a good reporter learned was to manipulate, con and sometimes outright lie to gain people's trust and make them open up. After doing it for so long, manipulation seemed to have become second nature.

Sydney winced. The realization of what she'd just thought hurt more than the pain in her head. Those were her father's words, his doctrine, one she'd sworn she would never adopt. But she refused to think about her father and glanced at Emma, managing a rather sickly smile. "Don't you have other patients?"

"We're not real busy right now. Besides, the doctor asked me to keep a close eye on you."

"Why?"

"He thinks your injuries may have been more serious—said something about observation because of your hallucinations."

That brought Sydney fully alert. "I did not hallucinate."

"Maybe it would help if you talked about your experience. You know, cleared your head."

Sydney was fast changing her opinion of Emma. She was good, just a little too much of the guileless look, the voice just a tad too eager. Resting her head back on the pillow, Sydney closed her eyes and said, "Maybe you've missed your calling. You just might make a good reporter."

"Tit for tat." The nurse's smile turned sly, then they both laughed.

Emma might be a budding detective, but Sydney had the fencing experience. "I want to get out of here. I have to find Andrew and talk to him."

"Oh, he's probably gone by now. He checked out his grandfather earlier. And you've changed the subject."

If all else failed, resort to one of human nature's basic instincts: sympathy. "My head hurts like the devil."

"Lord, I'm sorry." Emma jumped up, straightened her crisp white uniform and glanced at her watch. "The doctor said if you slept I was to wake you every hour. I'll see you soon."

"Emma..." Sydney slowly rolled her head back and forth on the soft pillow, testing to see if the movement made her sick or dizzy. It didn't. "Where's my purse?"

"Locked up in the hospital safe."

"Would you bring it to me when you come back?"

"Only if you promise that when I do, you won't skip out of here without telling me what's going on."

Sydney yawned and agreed. As soon as the nurse had gone, she reached for the telephone, only to find there wasn't one. Disgusted, she realized that until she got her purse, she was a prisoner. The thought of her purse brought back Andrew's earlier words. Strange... If she shut her eyes tight, she could see him clearly. He'd held up the oversize bag and called it a pouch. There were other things about him, odd inconsistencies, things that she couldn't put her finger on but that left her with some nagging feelings. There was also the fact that Andrew refused to admit he'd found her and taken care of her. Maybe he'd been somewhere he wasn't supposed to be, or maybe he was trying to hide something. Emma was a mystery lover; so was she. The only problem was, she usually read the last couple of pages to find out who done it before she started the book. This time she was going to have to play it to the end....

SYDNEY COULD HAVE SWORN she'd only closed her eyes for a few seconds when Emma began gently shaking her awake.

"How many fingers?"

Sydney groaned and squinted at the hand waving in front of her face. "Not you, too."

"How many?"

"Three."

"Good, go back to sleep."

This little game was played four or five times; by the sixth time, Sydney was sitting up, waiting for Emma. "I feel fine and I want out of here."

Emma jammed her fists on her plump hips, eased the door shut with her foot and said, "You better stay right where you are or Sally's going to catch you."

Sydney sighed. Why was it in small towns, where everyone knew each other, they just took it for granted that strangers automatically knew who they were talking about? "Who's Sally?"

"Aren't you here to do a story on Senator Fowler?"

And why, Sydney thought again, did she suddenly feel as if she'd known Emma all her life and was keeping secrets from her bosom buddy? "Who's Sally, Emma?"

"Sally Pearson. She's a reporter with the *Wallace Morning Sun*. Well, she's not really a reporter. She covers the social events here in town, but she likes to think of herself as an ace reporter." The nurse pursed her lips and made a face, clearly telling her captive audience what she thought of Sally's talents. But she could see her antics weren't working, and her patient was rapidly losing patience. "She heard about your wreck and the search party. Weaseled your name and identification from Henry—he's the police chief, and Joyce, that's Sally's daughter, dates him. Anyway, she listened in on Buddy's—that's Buddy Hilton, who owns the paper—telephone conversation with your editor. I don't remember his name."

"Samuel Doughtery," Sydney said. She could tell this was going to take some time and drew her legs up to her chest, wrapped her arms around them and rested her chin on her knees.

"Your editor, in D.C., had called—"

"The police chief?" Sydney asked, a little confused. "Why would Sam call him?"

"He didn't. Henry's the chief of police. Buddy's the owner of the paper. Sally said it was a professional courtesy call."

Sydney grinned as she watched Emma flap her hands impatiently at having to explain all the relationships.

The nurse realized she was being teased and quickly held up two fingers. "How many?"

It was too much for Sydney. She started laughing, and a moment later, so did Emma.

"I like you," Emma said. "It's crazy, but I feel I've known you a long time." Both women fell silent and stared at each other.

The nurse was not her usual type of friend. Then again, she really didn't have any close female friends.

It *was* weird, Sydney thought, but she felt that way and told Emma so. But there was something in Emma that reminded her of her younger sister, Carla. Oh, not in looks, but before their mother had poisoned Carla's life with money, ambition and social standing, Carla had had that same bright-eyed, fun-loving, deceivingly innocent look. Now Carla was as hard as her mother.

"I lost my train of thought," Emma said. "Oh yes, Sally. She's lurking around the halls, trying to find you."

"I don't want to talk about what happened. Not yet." She threw back the covers and scooted to the edge of the bed. Except for the monster headache, one she thought she could now live with, she felt fine. A little stiff and sore, but nothing that warranted another minute in the hospital. "How do I check out of here?"

"You can't, not without Dr. Doo's permission. Besides, where will you go?"

"I've got reservations at some place called the Wallace Inn," she said, and Emma made a disgusted noise in the back of her throat. "Okay, what's the matter now?"

"Patricia's a lousy cook, a worse housekeeper and the biggest gossip in town." She saw the laughter lurking in Sydney's expression and sighed. "Patricia owns the Wallace Inn. You absolutely *cannot* stay there. She'll listen in on every phone call you make, and when you're out she'll go through all your things. Besides, even if you were to leave here, you can't stay by yourself. You need to be watched. Head injuries are tricky devils. You simply can't afford to leave today."

"Emma . . ." she pleaded.

"No. I will not aid and abet an escape, either."

"No, no. Just go talk to that Doolittle fellow of yours."

Emma glanced around. "He's not mine, and he won't agree," she said stubbornly. "Unless . . ."

"What?"

"Well, I'm about to get off duty. Since Mom died, I've been living alone in our big old house. If you're determined to leave—" Sydney nodded "—how would you like to come stay with me?"

"Oh, I couldn't," Sydney said, but not very convincingly. "You realize I'm going to be here three or four days—maybe a week. It depends on how the indepth profile on the senator goes."

"Doesn't matter." They grinned at each other like conspirators, like schoolgirls.

ANDREW WALLACE OPENED the passenger door of the big Cadillac, then held out his hand to the elderly gentleman in the wheelchair only to have it knocked aside like a pesky insect. "Come on, Clay. Don't be so damn hardheaded."

Clayton Wallace glared up at his grandson, his bushy gray eyebrows nearly meeting. His thick white hair was standing up in all directions as if he'd just stuck his finger in a light socket, and the scrubby stubble on his cheeks and chin made him look like a derelict or drunk. He was neither. He was a tall, dignified man, a pillar of the community and founder and owner of Wallace Industries. Being ninety-three hadn't diminished his capacity, intelligence or his Machiavellian ways. His problem—and short stay in the hospital—was caused by a rather brilliant, devious plan that had unfortunately gone a little awry.

Years ago Clayton had developed a strategy to lure his grandson back to his rightful place in the business; it had begun with an elaborate series of phone calls made by his lovely wife. Pleas to Drew for help from a delicate, tearful granny who insisted that her husband's reasoning and health were slipping away with old age had done the trick. It had also been about time those old wounds between father and son were healed, and if it took a grandfather's lies, then so be it. Besides, he'd run Wallace Industries for far too long, and though he wasn't about to give the reins over completely, he admitted he needed a little help. So he'd had it all neatly planned out.

But like a fly in the ointment, he'd been caught in his own trap. The scruffy appearance had worked. The lapses in memory had worked. The cane he'd acquired to shuffle around with had *not* worked. The end of the blasted thing had caught in a crack in the brick patio as he was running to get out of yesterday's rainstorm.

He was now burdened with a cast from his toe to just below his knee, not for a broken bone, thank the good Lord, but to ease the torn muscles and ligaments. A cumbersome contraption that was going to help him get the very thing he'd been playacting to achieve: sympathy, guilt and insurance against the departure of the prodigal grandson. It was a hell of a price to pay, he thought grumpily, for one's own flesh and blood. But it was worth every twitch of pain. Only the good Lord and his Rosa knew how lonely he was and how he hated running the business alone. Not that the company needed running—it seemed to have a heart and brain of its own. Yet one couldn't build a company of that magnitude and walk away; there were other people's lives and livelihoods to consider. Someone had to watch over it, baby it along when it needed it.

Now, like the good actor he'd recently realized he'd become, he knew the show must go on. He swallowed his pride, accepted the offered hand and allowed himself to be lifted, pushed and tucked into the car. "Hell of a storm yesterday. Never in all my long years have I seen anything like it. Weird. Dammit, Drew, watch out for my leg. Next thing I know it *will* be broken."

"Clay, you're a real pain in the butt." Andrew knew very well what his grandfather had been up to all along. He'd managed to ignore the old man's attempts to get him to come home until two years ago. What Clay thought was a well-laid plan, one his grandmother had happily confessed to, had come as no surprise. But time had a way of tempering old memories and softening the edges of harsh words. A bitter divorce and his father's need for help during his struggle for the senate seat had both played a part in weakening his once fierce decision never to return to Wallace.

Andrew slid behind the wheel of his grandfather's Cadillac, started the engine, switched on the air conditioner and let the car cool while he fiddled with the controls. He couldn't figure that reporter out. What game was she playing? He'd have to be careful.

"Hospital was abuzz about the young woman found wandering out on Piney Creek Road."

Andrew pulled away from the curb, hoping that his lack of interest would curtail the old man's chatter.

"Did you hear anything about her?"

He had a sneaking suspicion that his grandfather already knew all about the woman. "I saw her in emergency when I stopped to find out about you." The fierce glare of the sun reflected off the hood and blinded him. Andrew fished around in his pocket for sunglasses, shoved them on and sighed with relief. Lack of sleep and too much alcohol had given him the mother of all headaches.

"What's she look like?"

He wasn't going to get any peace and quiet. "Okay," he said.

"Okay! What kind of word is *okay* for a woman? I heard she was a real looker. Did you happen to get her name?"

Andrew shifted his position, rolled his tired shoulders and sighed. "Sydney Tanner. She's a reporter, Clay."

Clay didn't say anything, and Andrew's hands tightened on the steering wheel.

"So...what does she look like?"

"Jeez, Clay," he groaned. "I didn't pay that much

attention. Pretty. Brown hair. Actually, it was kind of red—chestnut.''

"You mean auburn. I like auburn."

He was trying to concentrate on the winding road ahead. "I guess." Her hair had looked soft, silky. The kind a man would love to bury his face in. He liked the way it was cut—short and straight with wispy bands that made her eyes look huge.

"Is that all? Didn't you notice her eyes? What color? In my day—"

"Blue, Clay. They were blue." He bet those eyes would turn a deep sea blue with passion. "Expressive eyes. Her skin's clear and smooth." Skin that just begged to be stroked. "She has a tiny black mole just above the corner of her mouth." A very kissable mouth it was, too. "There's fire in her. Probably all that red hair." He hadn't realized he'd spoken his last thought out loud until his grandfather corrected him.

"Auburn," Clay said.

"Hmm. Yes."

"Seems you got a pretty good look at her, after all."

Andrew glanced at the old man, found him staring at him with a funny grin and quickly looked away. What was he up to now?

"Heard she knew you," Clay said innocently. "Called you by name."

"Dammit to hell. If you know so much, why'd you ask me in the first place?"

"Where were you, yesterday, Drew, when the storm broke, and all last night?"

It was a question Drew wasn't prepared to answer. Not now, at least.

CHAPTER THREE

THE GREAT HOSPITAL breakout was as disappointing and as uneventful as a stroll down the street. Sydney eased onto the front seat of Emma's car, closed the door and immediately began digging in her purse for her sunglasses. "I don't see anyone running after us." She'd just barely had time to slip the dark glasses on when she was forced to make a fearful grab for the dashboard as the little car vibrated to life like a dog shaking off river water.

Emma goosed the gas pedal, and the engine coughed then kicked into rumbling, bone-shaking life before it decided to settle down with a surprisingly steady purr. "Paul was agreeable to our plan."

Sydney's mind went blank. She'd had too many names thrown at her the past few hours. "Paul?"

"Dr. Doolittle."

"Right." She absently glanced down at her jeans and shirt, realizing for the first time that someone had gone to the trouble to see that her things were cleaned and pressed. Her running shoes puzzled her, though. Once new and white, they were now a dull reddish pink color.

"After I told Dr. Doo you weren't going to stay at the inn alone, that I was taking you home with me, he was willing to release you into my expert care. That is, after he called your boss and fixed everything up. You know, insurance, things like that. He said to tell you to drop by tomorrow or before you leave to sign some papers. But you're to take it easy for a couple of days."

"Thanks, Emma. You're sure it's okay, my staying with you?"

"To be honest, I could use some company. Besides, I want to know how you and Drew Wallace know each other." She sensed Sydney's weariness and decided to wait awhile before wheedling answers to all these questions she had.

Sydney squeezed her eyes shut as Emma pulled out of the parking lot without checking the traffic on the street, then she almost laughed out loud. What traffic? Except for the few cars at the hospital, the town looked deserted.

Wallace wasn't any different from any other small town. She knew what to expect. There would be the middle-class neighborhoods, some homes kept up with pride, some run-down. There'd be the inevitable dog lounging in the shade waiting for his young master to come home, and a bicycle, a red wagon or a skateboard lying half in the yard, half in the driveway, just asking to be run over by the man of the house when he drove up. Oh, she knew these neighborhoods, where the women stayed home while the husbands toiled all day in some office.

Sydney shivered. The memories rubbed too close to the bone.

Then there was the other side of town, the poor side, the wrong side of the tracks, so to speak, where life was harsh, cruel and unforgiving. And of course there was the wealthy section of town, probably only about seven, maybe ten, really wealthy families in the whole area. They'd live in big homes, with rolling green lawns, huge shade trees and riots of flowering bushes. There'd be cool, tiled patios, tall glasses of iced tea, polite dinner conversation, polite, well-brought-up children and even more polite friends.

Sydney grimaced and shook her head. It didn't matter if they were in California, Virginia or Texas; small towns were the same all over. God, how she hated them. Hated the smell, the feel, the way you were looked at if you were an outsider. But then she reminded herself that small towns and big cities were all the same, really. The only difference was that the division of the economic classes was just more visible in small towns.

She stared out the window, taking in Wallace, still wet and dripping from the storm. Main Street was easy enough to spot, with its big square stone courthouse squatting on a big square plot of grass, surrounded by big, perfectly spaced, spreading oak trees. Sydney was about to turn away when she noticed a blot on the perfect setting. One large oak, maybe four or five hundred years old by its size, was lopsided. It looked as if the old tree had been cut in half, all the healthy branches and green leaves weighing heavily on one side, while the other only had one huge limb that stuck straight out then curved upward, its few top branches bushing out like an umbrella. That's what it reminded her of: a long arm holding up an umbrella.

As they traveled on slowly, she shook off her fanciful wanderings and began to do part of the job she had been sent to do: observe. She had to admit the town was in better condition than most small towns in this day and age. The recession and outright poverty seemed to have skipped Wallace. The buildings, with their old brick facades and painted shutters, oversize windows and carved signs proclaiming the proprietor's business, looked renovated, revitalized and prosperous. It was just the right setting for Senator James Darcy Fowler.

With his good looks, charm and money, he claimed to be one of the new generation of politicians and had vowed that his country and the people deserved an honest man to represent them. In his first two years in office, he'd managed to stir up a hornet's nest in Washington. Sydney had heard the rumblings of Washington politicians as their constituents began to rebel against their old ways. Some very powerful men had decided that to keep their own skins intact, the country was in need of another Camelot. There were whispers that those same powerful men were keeping close tabs on James Fowler. When the whispers stopped, Sydney and her editor knew something was up. She had a feeling that Fowler was being secretly groomed for a higher office. She'd been pleased that Sam had thought enough of her assessment of the situation, her hunch, to assign the story to her and not one of his top-echelon staff reporters.

She'd been excited about coming, excited about the prospect of finding out what and who the real James Darcy Fowler was. But now, driving down the idyllic little street with the sun shining and a sudden cool breeze stirring her hair, she wondered what had happened to her enthusiasm. All she could think about was Andrew Wallace. Her reporter's nose told her there was something going on, something out of kilter—undercurrents.

"Hey, Sydney. Sydney," Emma said. "Are you okay?"

"Sure, just thinking."

"About Drew."

Sydney laughed. "How did you know?"

"You've got a funny look on your face."

They pulled into a long driveway. Beyond the trees and the wide expanse of green lawn was a small, two-story white Victorian house, gingerbread and all. "What a darling house, Emma."

"You keep changing the subject, Sydney Tanner. But remember, I've got you in my home night and day for a while." She pulled to a stop at the side of the house. "I'll get it out of you soon."

An hour later Sydney was tucked into a four-poster with a lacy pink canopy. She glanced around the frilly room and wondered what sort of woman Emma's mother had been. She didn't have to stretch her imagination much. There was such a homey, family feeling about the house, such love and warmth, it brought back her own childhood longings. Emma was a lucky young woman who'd obviously been loved and cared for. Sydney realized she was envious. Her own parents had divorced when she was nine, and it hadn't been one of those sophisticated, cold separations, either. The bitterness, friction and jealousy still existed between them today.

"How about some lemonade and a couple of aspirin?"

Sydney watched as Emma walked into the room balancing a big frosty pitcher and glasses on a tray. "Sounds great." The nurse had changed into jeans and a long shirt, and her hair was now falling softly around her head. She looked fifteen. "Emma, you don't have to wait on me like I'm an invalid. The headache only gets worse when I move around too much."

"Good, it's getting better, and I don't mind waiting on you. I'm used to it."

"But this isn't the hospital. It's your home." Emma was frowning, and Sydney grinned. "Okay, I'll shut up." She took a long drink of the lemonade and savored the sweet-tart tang of real lemons. "How old are you?"

Emma laughed, a light, tinkling sound. "Probably older than you think. Thirty."

Her new friend couldn't be older than her! "I don't believe you."

"It's the Paulson curse. Mom said when I'm eighty and look forty, the curse will be a blessing. We'll see. But now that you know I'm old enough to hear all the gory details of your mystery, why don't you tell me everything?"

"You just won't give up, will you?" Sydney popped a couple of aspirin and lay back. "There's really not much to tell. I made a bad decision and took a shortcut on the wrong road. The storm hit. I crashed into a ditch. No, that's not exactly true."

Emma was sitting in a chair by the bed, her elbows propped on her knees, her chin resting on her fists, a rapt expression on her face.

"I could barely see, then all of a sudden a man was standing in the middle of the road."

"Drew? What was he doing out in that storm?"

"Yes . . . and he never said."

"So, what happened next?"

"Emma, do you want a minute-by-minute account of this?"

"No," she said with a laugh. "Second-by-second."

Sydney closed her eyes briefly, seeing in her mind every detail, replaying the accident like an old movie. "I was shocked to see a man standing in front of the car, so I stomped on the brakes, but instead of stopping I slid off the road.''

''And Drew helped you out of the car?''

Sydney bit her lip hard. That wasn't the way it happened, but why? Why hadn't he helped her out of the car? ''No. I hit my head and passed out, and when I came to I crawled through the window, then passed out again. The next thing I knew, he was standing over me.''

''Strange,'' Emma mused. ''Why didn't Drew get you out? What happened next?''

''Nothing exciting. Andrew helped me up, I passed out again, and when I awoke I was in some cabin. A place all nice and cozy with a fire burning in a big stone fireplace.''

''What cabin? Where?''

''How should I know?'' Emma's questions were only adding to her own. Plus, talking about what had happened made her feel rather foolish. It was all sort of like a dream where none of the pieces really fit together. And what was worse, she felt as if she'd been duped, somehow. Used. Andrew Joshua Wallace was going to be very sorry if he thought he could get away with making her look the fool.

''Dammit, Sydney, what did he say to you? Surely you two talked?''

Sydney laughed, a sound somewhere between frustration and hysteria. ''Talked? Not really.''

''Nothing. Not a word. You were together for hours and didn't talk at all?''

''Look, Emma, I know it sounds crazy—hell, it's crazy to me, too—but I just can't explain it. Not much conversation passed between us besides our names and him telling me I needed a doctor. The next thing I knew

I was sitting on his lap and we were trotting down the road on a horse."

Emma paused to refill their glasses. "What horse? Where did the horse come from?"

"Well, that's another thing I'm not too clear on."

Emma absently handed Sydney her glass. "Weird. Howard told me he found you just standing there alone, lost and confused. There wasn't anyone else around, and he certainly didn't mention anything about seeing a horse. What possibly could have happened to Drew and why would he just leave you on the road?"

"Your guess is as good as mine. He let me down off that damnable horse, then just disappeared."

"Not a goodbye, good luck, kiss my... " Emma let her train of thought trail off and blushed.

Andrew's parting words seemed to stick in Sydney's throat. "Well, no." Suddenly she didn't want to talk anymore. She didn't want to tell Emma what he'd said, though she couldn't understand her reluctance.

"There *is* something more. Come on, Sydney don't stop now."

Sydney set the sweating glass on the nightstand, rubbed her face, then stared at Emma a second, trying to overcome the absurd feeling that she would somehow be betraying Andrew if she told. But confusion and her own anger won out. "Just after he let me off that horse, he said, and I quote, 'Tell them I found Mary.'"

"That's it?" Emma whispered. Then loudly, "That's all? What the hell does that mean?"

Sydney hadn't realized she'd been holding her breath, silently praying that Emma could give her the answer. Slowly, she let out her breath in a hiss and closed her eyes. "Do you know anyone around here named Mary that Andrew's involved with?"

Emma was silent, thoughtful, then she said, "No. I'll admit Wallace is a small town and generally we all know who's seeing who, but I can't think of anyone by that name who Drew could be dating. But then Drew... Listen, Sydney, all you have to do is talk to Drew and get him to explain."

"Sure, Emma. I tried that in the hospital and he acted like he'd never seen me before."

Emma sighed. "Now I wonder why he would do that? This gets more and more curious."

"Emma, how well do you know Andrew Wallace?" She watched as the woman sipped her lemonade, wanting to strangle her for taking her time.

"What? Sorry, I was just thinking." Emma gulped some of her drink. "You might as well know, I've had a crush on Drew all my life. No, no, he's never been anything but friendly and I don't really know him that well. Hell, I know his grandfather and grandmother better. No, I was thinking about why Drew acted so strangely in the hospital. At first he may have just been teasing you. Then when I came in and blurted out that you were a reporter... well, he hates reporters."

"Why?"

"Why?"

"Yes, Emma. And don't look at me like I'm crazy. Why?"

"You're the reporter. I'd have thought you'd know because of William."

Sydney's fingers twitched, she wanted to wrap them around Emma's neck so badly. "Who's William, and why should I know him?"

"Was. He died in a car accident two years ago. I thought you would have known because William Wallace, Drew's father, ran against Senator Fowler. It was a pretty close race, too, and right down to the wire when William suddenly pulled out. Anyway, the way I heard it, Drew thought there was something fishy about the whole mess, like maybe the election was rigged—I don't know. Everyone knew Drew and his daddy didn't get along, but Drew knew his father well enough to know the old man wasn't a quitter.

"When Drew's father was killed a few days after the election, Drew and Buddy had a real public shouting match over that. Drew said things to Buddy the rest of us thought but would never have had the nerve to say. And he beat him up, too. Buddy Hilton printed a disgraceful obituary about William in the *Morning Sun*. Then, to make matters worse, the *Sun* came out with a special edition that evening. Buddy really vented his spleen on all the Wallaces. Totally uncalled-for. He made Drew look like a fool and the Wallaces look like a bunch of criminals. So you see, Sydney, that's the reason Drew didn't want to talk to you when he found out you were a reporter." Emma seemed satisfied with her explanation. "You look sick. I'll leave and let you get some sleep."

Sydney did feel sick, but not for the reason Emma thought. Actually, she'd just realized that Emma was probably a better reporter than she was. In all her background research on Senator James Darcy Fowler, she'd never once come across anything that led her to believe there had been a cloud around his election. But she could certainly rectify that problem. It was what she was going to do about Andrew that really bothered her. If she was smart, she'd just leave it alone. But something deep inside her wasn't going to allow her to do that. A man who saves your life then leaves you on a road with nothing but a cryptic remark owes you an explanation. She planned on getting one tomorrow.

MORNING DIDN'T BRING any answers. Sydney sighed as her friend's car hiccuped and almost stalled at the end of the driveway. It had taken all her skills to get the information she needed from Emma and to keep her from coming along. Ever since Sydney had awakened, she'd had a feeling of urgency. When she thought about what had happened, her heart would pound, her hand would shake and her mouth would go dry. She breathed deeply as she recognized the beginning of an obsession. She'd had the same symptoms before when she was hot on a story... and that was supposed to be what she was here for. But these endless questions, theories, the mental list she'd begun making had nothing to do with what she'd been sent to Wallace to do. She was letting her personal life interfere with business, and that was unthinkable. Dammit, she told herself, she should just do her job and let the other go. What did it matter if a man had rescued her but didn't want anyone to know about his good deed? What difference did it make? She was alive, unhurt and no worse for the wear. *Just let it go, Syd,* she thought, but in the next second she knew she had no intention of doing that.

She gingerly touched the three sore spots on her head and grimaced, then glanced down. The grimace turned to a wry smile. Emma had brought her the bad news that her rental car was totaled and had been hauled away by the rental company. All her belongings, which were in the trunk, had been soaked. Some could be cleaned, and some were beyond redemption. All she had for the time being were the clothes she'd been wearing on the day of the storm and the personal items that were in her purse. Right now she was dressed in Emma's mother's clothes and looked like a walking advertisement for Laura Ashley. The long, pastel pink-and-green floral dress with a wide white lace and linen collar was as foreign to her as a tuxedo was to a cowboy. She was used to power dressing—tailored suits and dresses. The only feminine touches she liked were shorter skirts, high heels and accessories. Now she look liked something that had waltzed out of the pages of a Victorian novel.

Except…except for her shoes. Sydney glanced at her left foot, wiggled it a little, then sighed. The leather of the running shoe was that weird shade of pink, and the shoelaces were a darker reddish color. Emma had explained the mystery of the pink shoes: East Texas dirt was red. Mix it with water and it ran like blood, and it was bound to leave stains when you wandered around in it.

That was what she was doing in Emma's car, driving through Wallace, determined to get answers to these questions that had troubled her all night. She picked up her friend's directions to Wallace Industries. Emma had told her Andrew worked there part-time, and they'd decided that it was the most logical place to find him at this time of morning.

Once she had passed the city limits, she slowed the car, counting the side roads until she came to the fifth one, then she turned right. After about twenty minutes, she had the nagging feeling that she was lost again. Her old instincts seemed to have deserted her ever since she'd stopped at that gas station to ask directions, then ended up in a ditch. Now she was back on the same sort of road, with tall trees densely crowding each side and red muddy ditches still deep with water. It wasn't long before the thick stands of trees cleared out to open fields.

Sydney told herself she was only going to go a couple of more miles before she turned back. But after those miles she told herself only one or two more miles; she didn't care if she had to drive all day to find Andrew. When she caught sight of a sign marking the entrance to Wallace Industries, she slowed enough to make the turn, then realized she'd been so engrossed in finding the right road that she hadn't been paying attention to her surroundings.

After parking the car in front of the office entrance, Sydney opened the door and eased out, her gaze fastened on the landscape. She slowly turned full circle, dazed at the sight. Emma had neglected to tell her what Wallace Industries did: logging. Everywhere she looked there were huge stacks of felled trees. The air was pungent with the scent of pine and raw resin. She puzzled over the fact that the stacks of logs were being rained on by towering sprinklers, the spray catching the sun and creating rainbows everywhere.

In the distance she could hear the rumble of trucks and another sound that took her a minute to identify—the buzz of machinery. Saws, she figured, and if she was right, it explained the strong scent of raw wood. Somewhere, not too far away, was a lumber mill.

Sydney took a deep breath, stepped up to the office door, pushed it open and entered the cool reception area. She ignored everything around her and marched up to the woman at the desk. She knew how to project authority, how to intimidate with a look, a lift of the eyebrow. She had reduced politicians to stammering idiots.

Before she could open her mouth, the middle-aged, well-endowed, rather motherly receptionist said, "Mornin', sugar. What can I do for you this lovely mornin'?"

Sydney glanced down at herself, realized she wasn't exactly dressed for power, authority or intimidation and was suddenly confused. She tried for a stern expression and cleared her throat. "Would you tell Mr. Wallace I'm here?"

The woman slowly ran her gaze up and down Sydney. "Which Mr. Wallace?"

"Andrew Wallace," Sydney said with a nod. What the hell was the matter with her? *Pull yourself together, Syd.* It usually took her only a few minutes to get past a vigilant, protective secretary. "Listen—"

"Second door at the end of the hall," the woman said, and began typing, obviously giving Sydney about as much thought as a pesky teenager.

After a moment's hesitation, Sydney spun around and marched down the hall. Maybe the problem was that she was just winging this thing. She hadn't thought out everything she wanted to say and do. She'd jumped when she should have looked first. That wasn't like her at all. She should have taken the time to develop a plan. Too late now, she found herself in front of the second door at the end of the hall. To knock or not to knock? And why the hell was she hesitating? She would have barged into the office of the president of the United States given the chance.

Sydney yanked open the door and barreled into a solid, warm human wall. By the time she could regain her balance and her dignity, she found herself staring into familiar, yet not so familiar, green eyes. Memories suddenly filled her head, and for a fraction of a second she smelled fresh rain, a wood-burning fire and warm leather. But something wasn't right. This man was wearing designer jeans and smelling of expensive after-shave. She heard a deep voice say something but couldn't make out the words, only the urgency in the tone.

She shivered as she stared into Andrew's eyes. Was there a hardness, an intelligent cunning there that she hadn't noticed before? Was his hair shorter than she remembered? Was his frame bigger, his skin paler? Could there be any gentleness in that enigmatic, sharply planed face?

"What do you want?" Drew couldn't believe what he was seeing. Strange, he thought, but somehow she didn't seem like the same person he'd seen at the hospital. That was, until she opened her mouth.

"We have some talking to do, Andrew. You really didn't think I'd let you get away with it, did you?"

Andrew plucked a bright yellow hard hat from the end of a stuffed longhorn head, jammed it on and shouldered his way past Sydney. "Lady, I don't have the foggiest what you're talking about."

His long legs quickly put distance between them, and Sydney set out in what she knew was an undignified trot to catch up. Once at his side, she said, "Listen, is there some quiet place where we can talk uninterrupted?"

"We don't have anything to discuss."

"Wrong."

Drew yanked open the back door and stepped out into the rising morning heat. He turned and almost knocked Sydney over. "Folks say you're here to do an interview with the senator. You go right ahead, but leave me and my family out of it."

"What?"

Drew laughed, "For some reason, playing dumb doesn't quite suit you, lady."

He made the word *lady* sound like an insult. "Sydney," she said. "You know damn well my name is Sydney Tanner. And at this moment I couldn't care less about Senator Fowler or your family. What I want to know is why—"

"You can't follow me without a hard hat."

Sydney reached up and snatched the hard hat off his head, then settled it on her own. "There. Why won't you talk to me, Andrew? Saving someone's life is nothing to be ashamed of. If you'd just—"

"Sydney, if I'd saved your life, I'd have owned up to it. But I didn't." He'd been so absorbed in trying to solve the company's own problem that up until that moment he'd only been half paying attention. He hailed a man who was getting into a truck parked nearby. "Bob, toss me your hat." A bright orange bullet sailed through the air. Andrew caught it, put it on and strolled off, leaving the beautiful nut case behind.

If she really wasn't interested in his connection with the Fowlers, then she truly was a fool, and that was a shame—she was a damn sexy woman. He liked the way her blue eyes sparked with anger and the way the sunlight caught the red in her hair and made it shine like a newly polished copper penny. It wasn't long before she caught up with him. "Look, I don't know you from Eve and I don't like nosy reporters. Now, whatever your game is, it won't work, so I'm going to ask you nicely to leave. If you don't, I'm going to call the sheriff and have you arrested."

She liked it when they played rough and threatened her. It meant she'd hit a nerve, and frayed nerves caused tempers to flare, and when that happened her victims

usually ended up saying something they normally
wouldn't have. "This is all very simple," she said as she
jogged beside him. "You just tell me why, after you
went to the trouble of saving my life, taking me to the
cabin and then bringing me to help, that you deny it
now. I just want to understand."

Drew stopped and swung around. "Look, I don't
know what you're talking about. I've never seen you
before. I didn't save your life!"

They'd reached the mill. Before going inside, Andrew opened a locker and picked up a pair of headphones. He tucked his hat under his arm, placed the
headphones on, returned the hard hat, then stepped inside the mill with a wide smile.

Sydney followed him in but quickly realized she
couldn't hear herself think, much less talk or be heard.
Huge saws with blades as tall as a man sliced through
logs, trimming them, then cutting them to specific sizes.
Other machines stripped bark and sorted the lumber.
The air was full of sawdust and the scent of newly cut
wood. He thought he was so smart. Little did he know
that she'd outslicked the slickest politicians in Washington. A little strategy was needed here, she decided.
He couldn't stay in this den from hell all day. This was
a small town and he wasn't going anywhere. Neither was
she, not for a while.

Sydney watched him go and shrugged. She'd catch up
with him later. After all, Emma had given her directions to his home. She also reminded herself that she'd
come to Wallace to do a story, and she had a senator to
contact. In a town as small as this, he was bound to have
heard about her accident and wondered why she hadn't
contacted him as soon as she'd been released from the

hospital. The problem was, the senator and her story were the furthest things from her mind at the moment.

The door to the lumber mill closed behind her, cutting off most of the noise, and she sagged with relief. The pain in her head had returned. Sydney headed back the way they'd come and was walking across the reception area when a voice stopped her.

"You find Drew, sugar?"

Sydney forced a polite smile. "Yes, thank you." She was about to exit the office when she stopped, turned around and asked, "Why are all those sprinklers wetting the logs?"

"Why, sugar, it's to keep the pine resin down and cool so the logs don't explode in the hot sun. Everybody knows that."

"Of course." Sydney winced, and a moment later she mimicked the woman's last words as she got into Emma's car. Then something tugged at her thoughts, and a shiver went up her spine. She quickly stepped out of the car and stared at it, then shook her head and got back in. She could have sworn the car was an old Ford Mustang, but she was wrong. She was really losing her mind. "Maybe," she joked aloud, "Wallace, Texas, is the twilight zone."

CHAPTER FOUR

THE DAY WAS IDEAL for a drive. Sydney had been carefully following Emma's directions to the senator's house and was surprised to realize they had guided her onto the Piney Creek Road—the scene of her accident.

She felt suddenly hot then cold—a feeling of dread—then her heart started hammering with excitement. Slowly she came to a stop and stared down the long blacktop road. She laughed and screamed at the same time, almost strangling as the sound caught at the back of her throat. Emma hadn't given her directions to Piney Creek Road; she'd found it on her own.

"Oh damn, this is weird," Sydney muttered, and just sat there staring down the long straight road.

After a moment she saw a man on a horse cradling a bundle. She blinked at the sight, then blinked again and the mirage was gone. But the startling vision of a horse and man slipping and sliding on that muddy lane adjacent to the road was so vivid, she had the sudden sensation of swaying and bouncing. She could smell the wet earth all around her and feel the cold raindrops on her face. The vision was almost enough to make her head start aching all over again.

Suddenly she experienced an overwhelming urge to continue on down that muddy lane and find the cabin Andrew had taken her to. She was even pressing on the gas pedal when a flash of common sense and a strong dose of fright pulled her back to reality. She knew it would take a tractor to navigate the lane now, and instinct warned her she wanted nothing to do with what was down there.

Sydney put the car in reverse and backed out onto the highway as quickly as she could. Her hands shook. She felt light-headed, confused and scared—the kind of heart-pounding scared she felt when she woke up from a nightmare—and she didn't understand why. She braked quickly and again felt the strong pull to drive down that road. But, she told herself, she was a realist and didn't believe in mirages, visions or anything she couldn't explain.

Sydney shook off the creepy, unsettling feeling and the confusion, and forced herself to concentrate on what she'd come to Wallace to do. She wiped the clammy dampness from her forehead and reminded herself that she had important work ahead. She had a senator to interview.

A QUICK STOP at the first gas station and a telephone call to the senator's house warned her. The cool reception from the good senator's wife spoke volumes as to how they felt about being kept waiting. She said they'd heard about Sydney's accident and her short stay in hospital and had been anxious to hear from her.

Sydney listened to her own polite excuses and Lauren's equally polite acceptances, then promised she'd be there shortly. As she hung up and climbed back into the car, she knew she was in trouble. She'd met Lauren Alden Fowler many times at Washington parties. Met, she reminded herself. That meant a quick handshake in a reception line or a hurriedly spoken recognition at a party. Her lack of knowledge about the senator's wife had compelled her to cram some last-minute research before she'd left D.C.

Lauren Fowler was a beautiful iceberg: platinum blond, arctic blue eyes, tall and willowy. She was also the perfect new breed of political wife: elegant socialite and envied hostess, loving partner, head of her husband's public relations campaign and a brilliant businesswoman. She was a millionaire in her own right from her Lone Star Beauty Spas in Dallas and Houston, and according to the *Wall Street Journal,* the European introduction of Lauren's personal line of makeup and health products was destined to be a huge success.

Senator Fowler had surrounded himself with an intelligent, young, hardworking staff, headed up by John Laker as his campaign manager. Fowler's staff was so loyal to him that the news media never heard any tremors of juicy gossip from that quarter, and that in itself was miraculous. Washington leaked like a sieve. Every politician had his secrets, and there wasn't a senator's or congressman's office staff that could keep them. Hell, even the president's office dribbled state secrets like a basketball player.

Once again Emma's excellent directions were a godsend. Sydney drove up the long U-shaped brick lane of the Fowlers' home, Rosehill. It was a majestic white plantation-style house, reminiscent of the French homes she'd seen in Louisiana. The huge columns, porches that wrapped around both floors, tall windows and lots of rose bushes completed the picture of old-money wealth. Sydney had traced the Fowler money trail back only as far as the Texas oil boom of the early 1900s. Now, gazing at the old home place, she wondered just how much further back the money could be traced, because it was obvious to her the house had been there a lot longer than the Fowlers had.

She had one of those quick, nightmarish visions of herself struggling to make a ladylike exit from the small car as Lauren watched. Sydney pulled the car to a stop, grabbed her purse, jumped out and sprinted up the wide steps of the veranda. She banged the heavy brass knocker a few times. While she waited, she gazed back toward Emma's car, realizing for the first time that the Corvair—that's what she'd finally decided it was—was a peculiar shade of blue. She was trying to put a name to the color when the door opened and she swung around to come face-to-face with the senator.

James Darcy Fowler was thirty-eight years old, with sandy blond hair and hazel eyes. She would have liked to call him a Yuppie, but that didn't exactly fit. Fowler had the good looks of a mature all-American with an abundance of charisma. Combine that with intelligence, a pinch of a good con artist and a wide, boyish smile, and he could sway even his most hardened opponent over to his way of thinking.

"Miss Tanner. Please, come in."

The senator was sexy as hell.

"I was surely glad to hear you weren't seriously hurt. Lauren called the hospital yesterday, hoping you'd take us up on an invitation to stay at Rosehill, but Dr. Doolittle told us you'd already made other arrangements."

The Southern hospitality just oozed like honey. Sydney bristled like a brush stroked backward. "I'm staying with Emma Paulson. She's a nurse at the hospital. The doctor thought it was a good idea since I'd gotten a couple of good knocks on the head." As she followed him through the house, she took in the antiques, the beautiful wood floors, the expensive knickknacks.

"Emma Paulson." He glanced over his shoulder as the reporter followed, noting the way she surveyed his house and tallied up his wealth. He'd never tried to hide the fact that he was an enormously wealthy man, and he wasn't about to apologize for it now. "She's Alice Paulson's daughter, isn't she? I was sorry to hear about Alice. She was a fine woman."

Rather surprised that he knew Emma's mother, Sydney only nodded.

The senator opened his study door. He and Lauren had never, ever, let the media invade Rosehill, and any knowledge they had of his personal life was carefully orchestrated by his staff. He wondered if he'd made a mistake in letting Lauren and John talk him into this.... He found it fascinating the way Sydney hesitated at the sight of an eighteenth-century Chippendale sideboard. Not many would recognize it for what it was, and he guessed that she was also aware there were only five of those sideboards in existence. Then he remembered who she was and where she was from, and any faint doubts he had about her and the interview drifted away.

First impressions were the most important. Trust your instincts—that was Sydney's policy. And the minute she saw Lauren and John Laker, she knew something was afoot. She could feel the tension in the room and wondered at it. Then as quickly as the greetings and small talk were exchanged, questions about her accident and her health were answered and she was made comfortable with a glass of iced tea, everyone seemed to relax.

Sydney pulled a tape recorder from her purse and turned it on, noticing how an awkward silence chilled the room. She hadn't missed the surprised look at her appearance, nor the quickly masked glance of contempt from Lauren Fowler. It irked her no end that she had to sit there dressed like a Victorian flower wearing running shoes.

She knew how intimidating a tape recorder could be and used it on many occasions for just that reason. She set the machine on the coffee table with an attention-getting thump. "I want to thank you for taking time off during your vacation to give us this interview. Though I must say, Senator, after the fire storm you caused with the public disclosure of how some of your fellow statesman are taking cash favors from lobbyists, I'm surprised you'd want any more reporters hanging around. Why'd you do it right now, when your party is desperately trying to present a united front?"

"Miss Tanner," John Laker interjected, "it was our impression that the purpose of this interview was to get to know the Fowler family and not take potshots at the senator. Your editor implied that you—"

"I doubt if Samuel Doughtery implied anything, John, especially about me." She'd had a few run-ins with John Laker in Washington. She didn't care for him there and doubted her opinion of him was going to change by getting a hometown viewpoint. "And you know me and my work, John, so you know I don't write a society column. I'm not here to tell our readers about the rose gardens."

Shame, shame, she thought, she'd just broken the first rule of Southern hospitality: she'd attacked before she'd gone through all the niceties. Maybe these people had been influenced by Washington and its sham Southern charm and etiquette for far too long, or maybe they had forgotten their roots. They might have expected Southern politeness, but she wasn't a Southerner; she was a Texan, and that said it all.

Senator James Fowler smiled his charming smile and said, "Those fellow politicians are crooks, Sydney, and the American public has a right to know exactly how their elected officials are voting—not for their constituents' interests, but to line their own pockets. That's fraud and theft as far as I'm concerned. If you know anything about me, you know I can't and won't tolerate corruption." He surprised everyone by reaching over and turning off the tape recorder. "Let's get off the record for a while, shall we? I don't think John meant anything. He does know your work very well, Sydney. We all do, and that's why we agreed to let you come here."

Sydney saw John and Lauren exchanged a quick glance. It was a look between conspirators, and she found it puzzling. She refused to look away when they caught her studying them.

The senator went on, "You're here to do a story on me—the Fowlers—and though you don't want to see my rose gardens, I must insist that you do, because this house, the land, and yes, the rose gardens are who I am, what I am and the roots of what I believe." He offered her his hand, and as they stood, he smiled warmly. "You need to get better acquainted with the Fowlers as a family and not as public figures."

God, she thought, scolding herself, she'd been about as subtle as an elephant. She even went so far as to admit that she was not herself. She was being too critical, too bitchy, and could only blame her mood on Andrew. She had to shake loose that nagging feeling or make an ass of herself. She had to be as charming and as cordial as her host. She had to be alert, clever and perceptive if she wanted to learn what was behind the senator's facade, because she didn't believe any politician, no matter how new to the game, could be as honest as Fowler portrayed himself.

Sydney smiled as the others rose. "I'd love to see the house and learn about your family. I must tell you, the earliest I came across the Fowler name was during the early 1900s oil boom in Beaumont."

The senator chuckled. "You made the mistake of following the Fowler money. Fowlers were dirt farmers here in Wallace long before my great-grandfather, Darcy Fowler, made a name for himself. He was a smart lawyer and got in on Spindletop and Petrolia in the early 1900s. Gained quite a reputation as a wheeler-dealer. My father, James Henry, followed in old Darcy's footsteps by being in on the big East Texas strike."

Despite herself, Sydney found she was interested. "Then it was your grandfather that was the senator?"

"That's right, Senator Henry James Fowler."

"You mean, James Henry?" She was confused by the names.

"No, James Henry was my father." He laughed. "If you're going to learn about any family history you'd best be prepared for repeat names both on the male and female sides."

Sydney nodded, then asked, "What about your mother?"

"She passed away when I was in my teens."

"But which one of the Fowlers was known as "Hang 'em High Fowler?"

"Really, Sydney," Lauren gasped. "Don't you think those old nicknames are dreadful? Surely you're not going to drag all that nonsense up?"

"It's all right, Lauren," the senator said with a chuckle. "That fine old gentleman was Judge Jacob Fowler. He was my great-great-grandfather, and as much as Lauren dislikes the name, he was a tough old bird but a just one from all I know about him. You'll have to remember that Texas in 1870, when he was made a judge, was a pretty wild, lawless state.''

"Jacob Fowler," Lauren said as she followed her husband, John and Sydney out of the room, "his relatives and some friends moved to Wallace in about 1850. They were old French Louisiana families who realized early on that their plantations were worn out and the land sucked dry because of poor crop management. And even though they were strongly steeped in their French culture, they quickly adapted to the rough Texans and their ways. Fowlers fought with Texans and for Texas in the Civil War."

Sydney nodded. Texans were very proud of the fact that their ancestors fought and died for Texas and settled this rough and dangerous land. And though no one ever claimed to have tamed it, they certainly bragged that they'd learned to live in respectful harmony. Inwardly she braced herself for more of the inevitable history lesson on Texas and the Fowler family, but surprisingly, Lauren fell silent and let her husband take not only Sydney's arm, but the lead in the conversation.

Rosehill was magnificent and pretty impressive for what he had called the early Fowlers—dirt farmers. The grounds were beautiful, the stable modern and immaculate. She was shown the tennis court, swimming pool and the senator's hobby: his rose gardens. She was a little overwhelmed, not to mention hot, sweaty and ready for the offered glass of iced tea by the time they reached the patio. "Then Rosehill has been in your family since Hang 'em...I mean, Jacob Fowler moved with his relatives from Louisiana."

The senator grinned. "No. The Fowlers inherited Rosehill much later from a relative—the Darcy-Claytons."

They had all stopped at the patio door as if there was an urgency to the explanation, as if it needed to be made before she reentered the house. Sydney was thinking only of the cool interior and a cold drink. She didn't want to know any more right now, but something prodded her until she asked, "Who were the Darcy-Claytons?"

"Really, James," Lauren snapped. "It's hot. Can't we go in?"

But the senator and Sydney ignored her, their eyes locked in some inner struggle neither of them could understand. "The Darcys and the Claytons were the other families that came up from Louisiana. Jean-Luc Darcy built Rosehill, or I should say rebuilt Rosehill. He moved every stone, brick and board from his Louisiana plantation home. When his daughter, Sara Elizabeth Darcy, married Samuel Clayton, he made them a gift of the house. The Claytons had settled next to the Darcys, so the combining of the two properties made an imposing estate."

Sydney stopped dabbing at her damp forehead to concentrate on the family history. "So where do the Fowlers come into it?"

"James," Lauren said, "Sydney's hot. Why don't we continue this conversation in the house."

"In a minute, Lauren." He didn't know why it was so important for Sydney to know the rest. "Old Samuel's wife and sons died in an Indian attack, leaving only his two daughters. The eldest daughter should have inherited everything but was disinherited, and the youngest daughter died before her time from the grippe, so Samuel left Rosehill to his sister-in-law, who had married my great-great-grandfather, Jacob Fowler.''

Her reporter's nose twitched, and Sydney asked, ''Why was the first daughter disinherited?''

''James, Sydney...enough,'' Lauren insisted as she gently shouldered her way between them to the door and opened it. The sudden rush of cold air snapped the line of conversation in two.

Everyone filed in. Sydney welcomed the cool air but felt oddly empty. She quickly attributed her queer feeling to a lack of food and the heat. She wanted to know more and puzzled over her sudden interest in the Fowler family history. Hadn't someone, somewhere, sometime said that to understand the present you must know about the past? She needed to know, she realized now, but her chance disappeared when John told the senator there was a phone call he needed to take.

''Lauren,'' her husband said, ''show Sydney the rest of the house, and I'll catch up with you in a minute.''

Lauren quickly became the perfect hostess and tour guide, though the tension and strain in the air were unexplainable.

As they trotted down the wide spiral staircase after touring the second floor, Lauren said, ''I don't think interior decorating is your *thing.*''

Little did she know, thought Sydney. She'd had antiques crammed down her throat since she was eleven years old. Maybe she'd learned by osmosis, but she hadn't missed the carved nineteenth-century French stool called a *taboret* or what Lauren referred to as knickknacks, like the rare, handpainted Sèvres porcelain *écritoire* or lady's lap desk.

''Why don't we go find James,'' Lauren urged.

Sydney couldn't have agreed more and lengthened her stride. As they passed the living room on the way to the senator's office she took a quick peek, then stopped dead and backtracked. With Lauren at her heels asking what was wrong, Sydney walked directly across the room, halting only when she came up to the fireplace. The portrait over the marble mantel had drawn her the way a hypnotist's crystal draws its subject.

Everything faded: sounds, sight, smell. She saw nothing but the beautiful young woman with the high-neck lace collar. Her thick blond hair was pulled back from rounded, rosy cheeks. Several curls cascaded over one shoulder. Luminous aquamarine eyes stared at her with sadness, and the smile was bittersweet. This was the same woman, the same painting that was in Andrew's cabin. It was Lauren's intrusive voice that jerked Sydney's attention away.

"If I had my way, that woman's face would be the face for my new cosmetic line, but James would never hear of it. A shame," she mused. "Have you ever seen such gorgeous skin? And those eyelashes and hair..."

Lauren saw only beauty and profit. Sydney saw such a poignant mixture of love and sadness in those brilliant blue eyes that a lump clogged her own throat. This was a beautiful woman who loved deeply and knew she was loved in return with equal depth. "Who is she?" she whispered.

"Samuel Clayton's daughter—Mary Clayton."

Sydney's heart suddenly seemed to stop. Without taking her gaze from the portrait, she said slowly, "Mary Clayton," testing the name out loud. "I've seen this portrait before."

"That's impossible. This is the original."

"A print?" Sydney questioned.

"No. This is the only painting of Mary Clayton."

She wanted to tell Lauren that she was wrong, that there was indeed another portrait of Mary Clayton and it was hanging in Andrew Wallace's cabin. But she held this bit of information back. A hot flush touched Sydney's cheeks, and she said more loudly this time, "Mary Clayton."

"No." The senator spoke from the doorway. Both women turned toward the sound of his voice. "Her name was Mary Clayton-*Wallace.*"

Sydney turned back and stared at the portrait as she continued to listen to the senator.

"She was the oldest daughter of Samuel Clayton and Sara Elizabeth Darcy-Clayton. The old man disinherited her for marrying a Wallace."

The shock took the breath from Sydney like a punch in the stomach. She was sure that outwardly she showed no sign that her insides were shaking and her nerves were frazzled. Even the fine hairs on the back of her neck were standing on end. And though she knew something odd was happening to her and she questioned it, she couldn't figure out why.

"Is something wrong, Sydney?" the senator asked.

Why would an old portrait make her so angry? Granted, she'd seen it in Andrew's cabin; granted the woman was Mary Clayton-Wallace. Her thoughts began jumping around in all directions. . . .

She'd been quiet for so long, she knew the senator and his wife were staring at her. She cleared her throat, tried to pull herself together and gather her fractured thoughts. But the only coherent thought she had was that Andrew had lied to her. For whatever reason, he was playing her for a fool, and she damn well was going to find out why.

Suddenly she had to get out of the house and as far away from the portrait as she could get—away from everything—and think. She didn't know how she did it, but somehow she managed to make a graceful exit from the senator and his wife. Back in Emma's car, she stared blindly at the rearing mustang in the center of the steering wheel, then gave the key an angry twist. The engine sputtered to life, threatened to die for a second, then settled down to a purr.

She drove to the nearest gas station and made two calls. One to Andrew's office, where she learned he'd left for the day and also where he could be found. And one was to the hospital to leave a message for her friend that she would be gone longer then she originally thought. Then Sydney she was on the road again with Emma's directions to Andrew's house clutched like a club in her fist.

She was a rational, realistic person who'd always known when to cut her losses. The odd part about this whole mess, she told herself, was that she couldn't back away and look at the situation objectively. There was something about Andrew—she'd felt it the moment she'd first seen him standing over her. "Come on, Syd, you're a realist. You always face the music no matter how hard it is. Admit what you felt was desire—unexplainable, unreasonable and certainly unexpected desire for a stranger. And when you saw him again in the hospital, the feeling was there then, too. Oh, you tried to cover it, deny it even, but it made you angry and you lashed out."

Sydney shook her head. She was now reduced to talking to herself. She glanced at the directions, slowed the car and made a left turn off the highway. The road to Andrew Wallace's home was as rutted and muddy as

that notorious lane, but instead of stopping and turning back, she guided the tires in the deep ruts and
stepped on the gas, gritting her teeth as she maneu-
vered the small car through the mire. Only a truck could
make it through here, she thought. She had a sudden
vision of Andrew in his truck, the country Bubba's
obligatory rack of rifles in the rear window. He probably listened to country-and-western music, dipped a little snuff, drank his beer from long-necked bottles and
was generally a pain in the butt.

Imagination and fantasies did wonders to relieve
tension. By the time she pulled up in front of the three-
story, white clapboard house that was in need of paint
and repair, her mind was clear. Without a second
thought, she got out of the car and stood gazing up at
the house. The time had passed without her noticing
and the sun was now low in the sky, casting the shadow
of the house across her like an umbrella...or maybe a
shroud. She shivered. The place certainly wasn't Rosehill.

Sydney stepped over the water-filled potholes and
cautiously placed one foot on the first warped, weather-
cracked stair. When it took her weight without mishap,
she hurried up the rest of the stairs and sighed when she
reached the partially open front door. For a moment she
stood listening, then she rested her hand on the peeling
white paint and gently pushed. "Hello," she called.
"Andrew? Anyone home?" When no answer came, she
eased into the foyer, keeping her hand on the edge of the
door, pulling it with her as she moved, making damn
sure it was going to be wide open in case she needed to
make a quick getaway.

She had no business entering the way she was. Someone, if they wanted to split hairs, could accuse her of

breaking and entering. Opening her mouth to call out again, she suddenly swallowed her words, paused, cocked her head and strained to listen. Had she heard voices? She eased farther into the darkening house. No, the place was empty, devoid of furniture and human inhabitants. Only dust motes danced their slow-motion waltz around the floor in the diminishing light.

Then a noise came again. A voice? She stopped dead. Goose bumps slithered over her skin. Maybe she should just leave, come back in the brightness of morning when the darkness of evening wasn't threatening to take over the house.

She waited only a few rapid heartbeats before she made her decision and followed the sounds. As she edged along with the wall at her back, what little light there was grew dimmer, until there was just a tunnel of dusty illumination leading to the cracked door at the end of the hall. That was where the voice was coming from—a weird voice, oscillating rapidly up and down, from a low bass sound to a high-pitched wobble. She almost turned tail and ran when a high note was reached, a screeching sound that just as quickly lowered to a more normal tone.

Sydney stood paralyzed with fear, the wall supporting her sagging weight as her knees gave way. Sweat dotted her forehead; her hands were icy cold. This was foolish, she told herself, and dangerous. She could get killed. With that thought, she quickly decided to leave and was about to take the first shaky step when the voice came again. This time she clearly understood what was being said. She froze.

"If you believe that reporter is here just to talk to old Chunky Fowler, then you're a bigger fool than I am, and that's saying a lot considering the fix I'm in. Her nature is to ferret out information. She'll dig and dig until she uncovers what happened."

Sydney forced her protesting limbs to move and crept closer to the partially open door. She couldn't tell whether the speaker was male or female. The closer she got to the voice, the colder the air around her became.

"I know you think she's a knockout," the voice said petulantly, "and you've got the hots for her—bad—but remember your track record. I know, I know, I don't have any room to criticize. Just look at the mess Morgana's gotten me into."

A shiver shook Sydney's body. Whoever it was in there was having a conversation with himself . . . or herself. The next words chilled her to the bone.

"You should do whatever it takes to get rid of her."

Run Sydney. Run fast. Get the hell out of there! Her mind screamed warnings, but the reporter in her wouldn't allow her to turn tail and run. She had to see who it was who wanted to get rid of her. The air was colder now, almost freezing. With a shaking hand, she reached out and touched the door. It swung open an inch wider. A blast of icy air rushed around her, almost stealing her breath and her nerve. She touched the door lightly again, gained another inch and was able to see about a third of a large and apparently empty room. The voice kept talking, babbling, almost singing. She couldn't have moved a muscle if she'd wanted to as a shadow of some weird shape came into view, moving back and forth across the far wall. Her knees went weak, and without thinking she grabbed the door for balance, except the door, at her touch, swung noiselessly all the way open.

Fear struck. Struck hard and cold, freezing bone, muscle, breath, nerves, thoughts and the ability to scream bloody hell. She took in the entire room at once, but her brain would only assimilate bits and pieces at a time. The room was in semidarkenes, but the far end was darker then the rest. It was there that Sydney saw the strange creature: green, scaly, clawfooted and fork-tailed. Her thoughts skidded to a mind-boggling halt. A miniature dragon? And it talked. She saw its fanged mouth move, heard the sounds, watched in horror as it turned and looked directly at her. She blinked, it blinked—blinked with big, golden reptile eyes. Then, ridiculous long, girlish eyelashes fluttered over the golden eyes, and the creature turned around as if it had never seen her.

The eyelashes had done it. As if she'd received an electrical shock, Sydney jerked to life. Her brain quickly put the rest of the bits and pieces of the room together. At the opposite end of the room, Andrew Wallace was moving up and down long tables of electronic equipment, computers and panels of lights and switches. She realized why he hadn't heard her: he was wearing a headset.

Sydney glanced at the dragon, then back to Andrew, then back and forth again a few times before she realized that the voice of the dragon was actually Andrew's voice, electronically distorted. Clever. She watched the creature prance around and marveled at how lifelike it was. She didn't understand how Andrew was projecting the dragon, but it was so real that when it belched fire she almost thought she smelled the scorch of burned wood.

She'd been so enthralled with the dragon that it took a second to realize that the creature had stopped moving and was slowly disintegrating before her eyes. She spun toward Andrew, saw that he'd seen her, saw the shock on his face, then the boiling anger. He took two long strides toward her, then the headset ran out of cord and jerked his head back before the plug snapped out of the wall. The silence was shattered with music. Marvin Gaye's sexy voice sang, "I heard it through the grapevine."

She couldn't help it. With the release of fear and tension, with the old sixties' song wailing in the room so loudly the walls shook, with Andrew coming at her as if he were going to strangle her—Sydney started to laugh.

CHAPTER FIVE

SHE COULDN'T STOP laughing.

The closer Andrew got, the more she laughed until he totally disappeared in a blur of tears.

"Are you quite through?"

"No...sorry."

Drew bit his lip. "Would you mind telling me what the hell you're doing breaking into my home?"

"The door was open," she gasped, struggling hard to get control of herself.

"And you just waltzed in?"

"Well..." she cleared her throat. God, he was as mad as a wet hen. After seeing the dragon, a wet hen was definitely funnier, and she broke up again. A moment later, she managed to get out, "What can I say?"

"You could start with the truth."

"I did call out."

"Sure you did."

"And I heard a voice and just followed it." She started to giggle and tried to hide the sound behind a cough but couldn't, and at the look on his face she started laughing all over again. "I'm sorry, really I am. I don't seem to be able to stop."

"Dammit," Andrew said. He took a firm hold of her hand and guided her behind a long table of equipment, then pushed her down into a chair. He grabbed a bottle of gin that was on the table and poured her a healthy shot, forcing it into to her hand. "Drink it."

It wasn't until after she'd taken a large swallow that she realized it wasn't water in the glass. A ball of fire exploded in her stomach. Her eyes poured water like a faucet, and if Andrew hadn't thumped her on the back, she seriously doubted she'd ever have been able to catch her breath. There were a thousand things she would have loved to say to him, all of them insults, and she just barely stopped herself when she remembered he did have a legitimate gripe. A change in tactics was called for.

"What was the dragon thing?" she asked. For the first time since she'd entered the room, she got a good look at Andrew. He was too close, too attentive, and it made her nervous. Staring at him, she felt herself sliding slowly down that silken tunnel of desire and marveled at the well of warmth that rushed over her like a hot flush. The music stopped, then started again with Gladys Knight and the Pips singing, "If I Were Your Woman."

Drew smiled. "You feel it, too, don't you?"

"What," she whispered, "are you talking about?"

He grasped the arms of her chair and leaned closer until he could smell the faint fragrance of her perfume. "Go ahead and deny it, but it's there between us, has been since the first time we saw each other. Strange," he said as he stared into her wide, startled eyes, "but I've never felt quite this way before."

"Strange is right," she snapped, and jerked her head away, breaking the spell he seemed to be weaving around her. "Would you *please* turn that music off." Then it struck her what he'd said. While his back was turned as he fiddled with the stereo, she decided to do what she did best. She plastered a sexy smile on her face and said, "You say you felt... whatever it is, when we met on the road that day."

Andrew glanced over his shoulder. "No. I said that the desire was there between us from the first time we met. I didn't say *where* we'd first met."

She knew her cheeks had turned bright red. She could have kicked herself for the stupid trap she'd tried to set and wondered how long it had been since she'd actually blushed. And why would the word *desire* coming from this man make her blush? "Come on, Andrew. It's just you and me here. You can tell me why you won't confess to helping me."

He turned around, propped his hip against the edge of the table and folded his arms across his chest. "Drew," he said. "No one's called me Andrew since the first grade, and I corrected that teacher."

"I just bet you did," she mumbled under her breath. She recognized a stalling tactic when she heard one. "But you did find me on the road and take me to that cabin."

He was shaking his head at her tenacity. Whatever she was up to, he wasn't going to find it out this way. "How's your story on Chunky going?"

"Who?"

He chuckled. "The illustrious senator was known all through junior high and high school as Chunky Fowler... for obvious reasons. It wasn't until he went off to college that he slimmed down."

She couldn't help it; she laughed. "I'm sure he wouldn't want that to come up in the interview."

"Hell, he probably wouldn't care, but Lauren and John would have simultaneous heart attacks."

"Did you have a nickname?"

"Yeah, sure. The nerd."

"No."

"I swear. I was the school nerd—thin, pimply face, brainy, scared of my own shadow and equally scared of girls."

Few men would ever admit what he just had, much less laugh about it. But she guessed by the way he'd turned out that he'd gone through some changes, too. She also had a feeling he'd made up for the lost high school years and lack of girls. "What happened to you?" She wasn't just wasting time with trivial questions; as her eyes roamed the room, she took in everything.

"I went to college, too." He hadn't missed the way she was eagle-eyeing his equipment, trying to figure out what everything was. He watched her gaze move along the table, and he physically moved with it to block her view.

She would have loved to stand up and get a closer look, but she reasoned that if she tried to he'd stop her. As her gaze and his body got to the end of the table, she shrugged and smiled. "You know, you could get rid of me once and for all if you would just tell me why you won't admit to helping me. And if you don't want anyone to know, I promise I won't tell a soul. It will be just between you and me. What do you say?"

Drew pushed away from the table and took a few steps until he was directly in front of Sydney and she was gazing up at him. He grasped the arms of her chair again and leaned forward, forcing her to lean back. "I'll tell you what...."

He was entirely too close. She blinked, tried to stiffen her Jell-O spine and said, "What?"

"You tell me why you're so damn determined to find out about *me* when you're here supposedly doing a story on Chunky Fowler, and then maybe I'll tell you my life story."

"Wait a minute." Sydney struggled to sit up straight, but it only brought her closer to him. "Would you please get out of my face? I can't think." He gave her a puzzled look and pulled back. "First of all, I don't know you from Adam, and I don't want to. Second, I am here to do a story on Chunky—Senator Fowler. Third, the *only* reason I'm interested in you is that you refuse to take credit for saving my life. I think if our positions were reversed, you'd be damn curious, too."

"I see. When I denied plucking you from death's door, you thought I might have something to hide. Being a reporter, it piqued your interest so you harassed me at work and broke into my house."

"Yes. No." She tried to get up, but he gently shoved her back down. "Let me tell you something, Andrew Joshua Wallace. I might be a lot of things—"

"What did you call me?" Drew interrupted her.

"You know damn well what I called you, the nicest of a few names I'd like to call you."

"Yes, yes, but say it again. I want to hear it."

Well, if he wanted to play games, so be it. Sydney figured she owed him that much since technically he was right: she had harassed him at work and broken into his home. While he was staring at her with a rather pensive expression, she ducked under his arm and stood up. "Andrew Joshua Wallace."

"And you say he looked like me?"

"The spitting image."

"My name's not Andrew Joshua."

"Dammit, Andrew—Drew." He was spooking her the way he was staring at her. "I'm going to leave now, okay? If you change your mind..." He started to chuckle, then erupted in a belly laugh. She should have run for it but was mesmerized by his reaction. "What's so funny?" she demanded.

"Either you've skipped your daily medication or the person who pulled your bacon out of the fire was my great-grandfather—he's the only Andrew Joshua in the family. I'm Andrew *Travis* Wallace."

Sydney stared at him. "How old is your great-grandfather?"

"Old."

Sydney stared at him. "Well, I admit I did get banged around—a couple of knocks on the head. My eyes were giving me fits. Maybe he just looks younger then he is."

Drew's lips twitched. "You'd have had to be real fuzzy-headed," he murmured. "Andrew Joshua Wallace was born in 1876."

Her brain computed the date twice, but the significance of the figure wouldn't sink in. Sydney gave an unladylike, long, low whistle. "That's old."

"It is, indeed. There's something else you should know."

She was almost afraid to ask. "What?"

"Old Great-Grandfather Andrew died in 1900."

Sydney managed another whistle from between dust-dry lips. "Ninety-three years ago."

"Exactly... in two days."

Her knees went weak. "Are you telling me I... that Andrew Joshua is a... a...?"

"Ghost?" Drew added helpfully.

Sydney snorted. "Listen, I'm a realist. I don't believe in politicians' promises, the check's in the mail, all babies are beautiful, love at first sight, ghosts, goblins or things that go bump in the night.'' Drew shrugged. She seemed a little shaky on her feet, whether she admitted it or not. He gently grasped her arm and guided her back into the chair. ''Besides,'' she went on, totally unaware that she was sitting down, ''a so-called ghost doesn't, can't, physically carry someone miles in a storm, build a fire and worry about that person's health to the point where he saddles a horse and takes her to get help.''

''You've met ghosts before?''

''No!'' she barked. ''And stop making fun of me. I know what happened to me, what I saw.''

''Why don't you tell me everything about that day, before and after you drove your car into a ditch.''

She had to suppress the sudden urge to scream that the accident wasn't her fault, then decided she was being uncharacteristically childish. She took a deep breath and began to talk. At first the story came out haltingly as she waited for him to make fun of everything she said. When she saw that he was genuinely interested, she became more animated. Once she'd finished, she waited for Drew to say something, anything, but when she got only silence and a strange look, she said, ''Oh, I forgot. The portrait at the cabin—it's the very same one that's hanging over Senator James Darcy Fowler's mantel. Now, what do you think about that?'' Inwardly she was cringing as she anticipated his laughter and waited to be ridiculed. What man would, or could, believe a crazy story like that, anyway? Hell, she didn't believe it herself now that she'd learned that Andrew was not Drew.

Or was he? She was well acquainted with the computer concept of virtual reality, had even played the game, but from what she'd seen in this room, Drew had come up with something far more interesting.... "Would you like to tell me about the dragon and how you did that?"

"What dragon?" Drew snapped. "And what does one have to do with the other?"

"Ah, but I think you *do* see the connection I'm making. You somehow projected an animated object in almost lifelike proportions. It was damn realistic, too. Could you have projected a facsimile of yourself?" She was more than a little unnerved by the way he seemed to freeze, his expression hardening, his green eyes as bright as emeralds.

Drew took a slow, deep breath and said in a voice as soft and seductive as velvet, "Lady, I'm going to give you *one* chance. But let me tell you something, Sydney Tanner. If I find out that you're some corporate spy, or worse, sent by my ex-wife, there won't be any place, not the tiniest hole or crack in this whole world, that you'll be able to hide from me. I've lost enough. I won't lose this, too. No, before you open your mouth to make a smart comment or lie, think about what I said."

This man was paranoid about something, but she didn't think it had anything to do with what had happened to her. "I understand, and I have my own little threat. If I find out this whole thing is some joke, or maybe an invention of yours that you're trying to keep secret by perpetrating some hoax on me—" like him, she took a slow, deep breath; unlike him, her voice wasn't softly controlled, but shaking with emotion "—I promise, I'll find out what you're doing and expose it to anyone who will listen." She paused. "I take it we understand each other?"

"Completely." Drew showed a lot of white teeth in a fine imitation of a friendly smile.

Sydney mimicked it to perfection. "Good. Now, what I need you to do is swear to me that it wasn't you who saved me and that it wasn't something to do with whatever you're doing here."

"It wasn't me or my invention."

"Swear it."

"I swear."

"God, then who was it?"

"Old long-dead Andrew Joshua, I guess." He tried to stifle a laugh.

"That's not funny, and you can't possibly believe it."

"Why not?"

"Because, because..."

"Sydney, life is full of surprises, and nothing it dishes out surprises me anymore. This area has marshes, Indian caves, forests so thick a man can get totally lost if he gets two feet off a trail. There are Indian burial grounds all around here. All those things make this prime storytelling country for both tall tales and the truth about the past."

"And you believe all these stories? My God, you're a grown man."

He threw back his head and laughed. "Yes, and cursed with being an incurable romantic to boot. It's hell."

"You actually believe it was your great-grandfather who rescued me? You really believe that?"

"I wouldn't discount it completely."

"Have you ever seen Andrew before?"

"No, but that doesn't mean I wouldn't want to."

"You're crazy." He was pulling her leg—he had to be. There was no way she was going to believe that she had looked into the eyes of a ghost and felt that love and warmth. "Okay, say it's so. Answer me this—why would this relative of yours appear to me?"

"That I can't tell you. But I bet Clay or Rosa might be able to shed some light on this situation."

He was confusing her. "Who are they?"

"Rosa is my grandmother. Clayton Darcy Wallace is my grandfather and, by the way, Andrew Joshua's son."

"This is ridiculous. You sit there talking as calmly about this as if you were talking about a neighbor."

Drew chuckled. "You don't know much about small towns, do you? We remember and talk about the dead as if they were alive. That, city girl, is part of living in a small town. Your life isn't just about who you are, it's also about where you came from. Go hang out in front of the local diner, icehouse or the newspaper office. The old-timers sitting around will be happy to tell you stories, tales their fathers told them, tales those fathers had handed down from their own fathers. The stories are all told in the present tense. The people in those stories are as alive as the storytellers. We are who we were. Didn't anyone ever tell you that?"

It was all too much for her. Sydney stood up and brushed down her long floral skirt. "I don't believe you're taking me or this situation seriously. There has to be another explanation."

"Maybe." Drew watched her walk away, and just as she reached the door, he said. "By the way, did I tell you that Andrew Joshua was hanged ninety-three years ago?"

A cold, fierce shiver slithered over her. "Hanged?" She didn't want to know why; something in her screamed not to ask. She'd even taken a few more steps, but the word slipped out involuntarily. "Why?"

"He murdered his wife, Mary Clayton-Wallace."

That did it, Sydney thought. She ran out of the house.

As she reached Emma's car, she was shocked that it wasn't pitch-black outside. It seemed she'd been in that house for hours, when in reality it had been less than thirty minutes. She glanced around quickly trying to get her bearings, some explanation for what she'd been told. She'd made her escape but had to stop and decide what her next move was going to be.

The sun, now an overripe red, was just beginning to set, making the sky look as if the evening breezes had blown streamers of dark blue ribbons across it. She rubbed the Mercedes hood ornament like a talisman as she rounded the front of the car. Ghost! she thought. What a joke. There had to be another explanation. Of course there was another explanation.

Sydney cranked up the engine, drumming her fingers on the steering wheel as the car shimmied to life like an overendowed, over-the-hill stripteaser. Once the shaking had settled down, she turned all the air-conditioning vents toward her hot face and drove away, absolutely refusing to look back at the house, afraid she would see Drew in the doorway laughing his head off.

She was a prize fool and had probably fallen for the oldest trick in the book: make the city girl look like an idiot. Dragons and ghosts—what a load of manure. The best thing she could do right now was not think at all, especially about what Drew had told her.

When she reached Emma's driveway and saw the house ablaze with lights, she felt a comforting rush of relief. Her foot suddenly became as heavy as a lead weight on the gas pedal. She squealed to a stop inside the garage and was just climbing out of the car when two things happened that froze every muscle in her body and sent her heart pounding. She heard a hissing sound and saw an eerie blue flickering light in the far corner of the garage.

She was a realist, she reminded herself, and these things just didn't happen to realists. As quickly as the strange noise and light appeared, they disappeared. It was Emma's voice that jolted her to life again. Sydney sagged against the open car door, fighting to catch her breath. When Emma called out again, she realized that her voice was coming from where the noise and light had been. And now that she was merely frightened and not scared out of her wits, she could see the stairs that led to the floor above the garage.

"Syd, come on up!"

She slammed the door, more out of self-disgust than anger, and climbed the narrow stairs. When she stepped into the room, her first thought was to turn around and run. But after a second, she scolded herself for being a ninny. The weird thing standing in front of her was not a being from outer space. It was her friend wearing a long, heavy leather apron, scarred and burned from use, and a welder's helmet with the protective face cover flipped up over her head.

Sydney looked around and was drawn to the work in progress. She wondered if anyone in this town was what they seemed to be. "You're a sculptor."

Emma, suddenly nervous with Sydney eyeing her work, slipped off the welder's helmet and ran her fingers through her damp hair. She flinched and looked a little sick when Sydney began to laugh.

Sydney saw the hurt she'd caused and told herself

that Emma obviously wasn't any different from any other artist: she was very sensitive about her work. She threw an arm around Emma's shoulders. "Your work is wonderful! I was laughing about your car. I just realized what was so puzzling. You put it together from a lot of different models. What did it start out as?"

"A 1966 Mustang." Emma smiled. "Everyone in town knows the car now, so I guess I've become rather blasé about it. I was dying for you to figure it out." She pulled the heavy leather apron over her head. "Actually, I thought you'd have caught on sooner."

"I've been a little distracted. But I'm impressed as hell with what you're doing," Sydney said absently as she glanced around the room, awed by the talent she saw. "How long have you had the car? And how long have you been doing this?" She gestured with her hand, indicating the array of sculptures.

"I've been sculpting since I was eleven but working with metal for only about six years. I finished the car about five years ago. It's what got me into working with metal, actually. A crash almost totaled my Mustang, and the repairs were going to cost me an arm and a leg. So I scavenged around in the junkyard and came up with different car parts, and I just made them work." Emma was babbling but couldn't seem to stop as she followed Sydney around the room.

Sydney stopped in front of a frame of steel: a six-foot female nude. There was a crudeness about the work— the raw look of the skeletal frame, the open lines—yet there was something delicate and fragile in the highly polished metal, the line of the breast, the turn of the wrist and cocked head. This was a symbol of the modern woman: strong, capable, yet soft and feminine.

"This is first-rate, Emma. Have you ever shown your work before? Sold anything?"

Emma ran a loving hand over the sculpture. "Never had a showing, never wanted one, really. This is sold, though." She turned her head and smiled at Sydney. "Lauren Fowler commissioned me for something for her spa lobby. Actually, I think she was just cultivating the locals when she asked me. I wouldn't be surprised if the senator told her to do that." She jammed her hands into the big pockets of her overalls. "She dropped by the other day to see how I was coming along with the job." Emma was suddenly grinning like a possum eating persimmons.

"She was impressed, wasn't she?" Sydney asked.

"Knocked the snooty bitch's socks off."

"As well it should. It's magnificent." It was good to hear someone else voice her own opinion about Lauren Fowler. Sydney wiped her damp forehead with the back of her hand and glanced around again. "What's that going to be?"

For the first time Emma looked closely at Sydney, saw the thin line of perspiration and how pale and shaky she looked. She ignored the question and said, "Come on. I'm used to the heat in here, but you're about to keel over. Did you eat anything today?"

"Eat?" Sydney shook her head. "I don't think so. No."

The kitchen was cool and welcoming. Sydney collapsed into the nearest chair, worked her shoes off, sighed, then leaned her head back and closed her eyes. When her fingers were wrapped around something wet and chilly, she lifted it to her mouth and drank deeply. The beer was icy cold and hurt all the way down. "This is going to go directly to my head." She cracked open one eyelid and watched in amusement and gratitude as Emma worked a monstrous hunk of cheese into bite-size slices. She took another drink of beer, and when she opened her eyes again, cheese, apple slices and some grapes lay temptingly on a plate before her.

Emma waited until Sydney had eaten, then asked, "So how did your day go?" She nibbled around the edges of a piece of cheese like an alert mouse. "I take it you found Drew's old house?"

Sydney watched Emma and smiled. "After the use of your car and the beer you deserve an answer—actually, you deserve the full story."

"*All right*. About time, too." She stuffed a couple of dark green grapes in her mouth and said, "But before you tell me, I've something for you. I went over to the newspaper office this afternoon and asked for a copy of the article Buddy wrote about Drew's family—the special edition I told you about. They said they didn't have a copy because three years' worth of back issues had been destroyed from a roof leak."

"Oh, come on. Don't tell me that the paper isn't on computer."

"Syd, Buddy Hilton is the biggest skin-flint in the county. Only the Lord knows what he does with his money. Besides, the *Wallace Morning Sun*'s been in a decline for the past two years. Computers? Not likely. It wouldn't surprise me if he was still hand-setting the type every night himself. Anyway, Sally Pearson told me to check at the library. Well, the wildest thing happened . . ."

"The library didn't have a copy, either," Sydney said.

"Bingo. They had every issue but that one. Funny, but no one could understand what had happened to it. They're always so careful, they said. Someone must have stolen it, they said. A shame, they said. What's going on, Sydney?''

"Either someone's trying very hard to cover up something or it's a red herring, a way to throw me off what's really going on. Why? I don't know, but I'm going to find out."

"Ah, the red-herring trick. But what's really going on?" Emma asked. "You know, we're not actually a hotbed of intrigue in this town."

"Oh, I wouldn't say that, not after the day I've had." She decided it was time to tell Emma everything—everything except what Drew was working on in his house. He obviously wanted that kept secret.

About thirty minutes later, Emma was staring at her, her mouth gaping, her eyes wide with astonishment. Suddenly she began to laugh. "Oh, Sydney. A ghost! I love it."

"This is not funny, Emma."

"No. It's serious. I'm... of course, Drew's putting one over on you, Syd."

Sydney took a deep drink of her beer. She was a little light-headed and immediately ate some more cheese and apple. "Does he have a twin brother...a crazy twin brother, maybe?"

"No."

"Of course not, that would be too easy."

"I take it from that question that you believe him when he says he didn't rescue you."

Sydney thought her answer for a minute. "Yes, and I think deep down I must have sensed it the moment I saw him at the hospital. Then, when I went to the lumber mill and saw him in the light of day, the doubts persisted. I guess that's why I didn't press the issue much. He's the same man, yet he's not. There were odd little differences—general build, a loving sadness in Andrew's eyes that Drew doesn't have." Or maybe, she thought, she didn't want to believe that Drew had lied. "But ghosts, Emma... I don't believe in ghosts."

"Or won't?" Emma cackled out loud like a witch, then began laughing. She lowered her voice to a whisper. "You know, the story about Andrew Joshua Wallace is one of those well-known hush-hush stories around here."

Sydney perked up. "What do you mean, hush-hush? And stop trying to scare me. That's already been done enough today."

"It's part of our town history, and I wish I'd paid more attention. It's just most of the time when the story comes up, the old-timers talk about it in low tones, as if there's something to be ashamed of. Andrew was hanged in the town square. The town has been divided on the issue for as long as I can remember. There're a lot of people around here who believe his trial wasn't legal or fair because the judge was Jacob Fowler and the prosecuting attorney was Darcy Fowler, who was supposed to be crazy in love with Andrew's wife, Mary Wallace. But you know how stories get blown out of proportion and embellished."

Sydney felt the chill again, the slither of eeriness that crept over her skin. She shivered. She hadn't told anyone except Emma of Andrew's parting words. But since Emma knew, why hadn't she told her about Mary Wallace then? Was everyone in this town hiding something. "Emma, when I told you what Andrew said when he finally left me on the road, why didn't you tell me about Mary then?"

Emma's cheeks turned bright red. "I swear I wasn't trying to keep anything from you, Syd. I was just so busy trying to figure out your and Drew's mystery relationship that it never occurred to me that that Mary was Mary Wallace—a ghost! Mysteries are right up my alley. Ghosts are another thing altogether.''

''Well, I don't believe in ghosts. So that means that someone who looks like Andrew or is making himself look like Andrew is out there.''

''For what reason? Saving damsels in distress on Piney Creek Road? I don't think so.'' Emma stared off in thoughtful silence, absently popping grapes into her mouth. ''Did you ask Drew where he was at the time of your wreck?''

''No. Boy, I'm some investigative reporter, aren't I?'' Sydney gripped the nearest chair and pulled it closer, then propped her feet on the cushion. ''Have you ever been out to that old house? What the hell is he doing out there, anyway?''

''The Chinquapin House.''

''What?''

''The place is called the Chinquapin House because there're only chinquapin trees surrounding it, a perfect circle of them, actually. That's a strange phenomenon in these parts, with all the pine and oak trees.''

Sydney tried not to shiver. The whole town was becoming a horror story. ''Then you've been out there?''

''Yeah, a couple of weeks ago. I was browsing around the hardware store when Drew called Jim and wanted him to deliver some special paint he'd ordered. Jim was busy, and since I was free—and dying of curiosity to see what he was doing with the old house—I offered to make the delivery.'' Emma paused as she got another beer. ''You know he's remodeling that old place, and he's doing a damn fine job from what I managed to see.''

"You must be kidding," Sydney scoffed. "It's kind of dark and spooky."

Emma chuckled. "Yeah, I can see why you'd think that. Most of it's still empty and a mess. He's only remodeled and air-conditioned one bedroom and the kitchen, as far as I know."

"Emma, what does Drew do for a living?"

"You know, I really don't know. He hasn't always lived in Wallace. After college he took off to California. Later, I heard he married, moved to Houston, then Dallas, then back to California. The next thing I knew, William Wallace, his father, was running against James for the senate, and Drew came home to help with the campaign. Back then he was newly divorced and as friendly as a porcupine. He moved in with Clay and Rosa and started helping Clay with Wallace Industries, too. After his father was killed in that car crash, Drew surprised everyone by staying. I guess old Mr. Clay talked him into it." The telephone rang and she said over her shoulder as she went to answer it, "A few months ago, Clay gave him the old Chinquapin House. That run-down place was where Clay was raised by his relatives."

Sydney closed her eyes. If she had the energy, she told herself, she'd get up, drag herself up the stairs, turn on her laptop computer and write down everything that had happened to her in the past few days.

"Don't go to sleep, Syd." Emma said as she walked toward her. "You have a dinner date with Drew, and he'll be by to pick you up in thirty minutes."

She should have been angry with Emma. Hell, she should have been furious with Drew for even asking after the way he'd treated her. Instead, she jumped up and like a schoolgirl said, "I don't have a thing to wear. Literally nothing, Emma."

"Sure you do. Mother's things fit you to a tee."

That's what she was afraid of. "But shoes, Emma. I've only got these wretched tennis shoes...."

SYDNEY GAVE ONE last look in the full-length mirror, suppressed a shudder and forced a smile. "It's a different me, Emma."

"You look beautiful, soft and feminine."

Sydney flinched. It was a damn good thing that her boss and co-workers couldn't see her; actually, they'd never recognize her. Emma had attacked her short hair with a curling iron. Now, instead of her usual straight style, she was sporting a fluffy do that softened the strong lines of her cheekbones and jaw. And the pale orange lipstick seemed to give her a dewy look.

Sydney backed away from the mirror, cocked her head to one side, studied the dress and stifled a sigh. Another Laura Ashley ensemble, this one of midnight blue, with a wide, old-fashioned lace collar, long sleeves with lace cuffs and a loose, dropped waistline. Emma was so proud of her work that Sydney didn't have the heart to tell her that she hated it.

She glanced down at the navy blue flats—a half size too small—and this time she shook her head. "Emma, these shoes are not going to do. They're already pinching my toes."

"Well, it's those or your own shoes. I don't think you really want to wear them. Besides," she said with a laugh, "the pinkish red laces will clash horribly with what you're wearing. Come on, a few hours of pain won't kill you. Think of the millions of women who deliberately buy their shoes a size or half size too small.

You've just joined some secret sisterhood of pain. And if they get to hurting too badly you can always discreetly slip them off under the table."

Sydney gave up. Little, rather mousy Emma had proved to have a will as strong as the steel she worked with. The word *no* was not in her vocabulary either. If her feet were going to hurt her, she sure wasn't going to add her heavy purse to the problem. She quickly stuffed her driver's license for identification, and some mad money in the pocket of her dress. Sydney glanced at the bedside clock, then at her computer sitting on the Queen Anne desk. "I have about ten minutes until he's supposed to pick me up. I'd like to get some work done."

"Sure, I need to go get dressed myself. The good doctor is taking me out to dinner, too." She held up her hand at the discerning expression that crossed Sydney's face. "I wouldn't even think of suggesting a double date—that's pushing things just a tad too far."

Sydney laughed as she sat down at the desk. She hadn't double-dated since... God, now that she thought about it, she'd never double-dated. She'd never had or gone to a slumber party, either. She'd never even allowed herself to get close enough to another female to share secrets and deep feelings.

Sydney absently began typing, putting down all that had happened since she'd arrived in Wallace, Texas, in chronological order. Maybe she'd missed something by being a loner. But then her family life hadn't been conducive to bringing friends home....

She was so lost in typing and searching her memory for some childhood happiness that it took Emma's touch on her shoulder to bring her out of her thoughts.

"Drew's here," Emma's grin was wide and full of mischief. "For some reason you obviously impressed the man. He's actually wearing a suit."

On the way down the stairs, she had time to wonder what Drew usually wore, and her imagination went wild. Jeans and boots? A hat? A fringed leather jacket. A pair of six-guns hung low on his hips? A Winchester rifle slung over his shoulder? She stopped. The picture somehow didn't fit Drew, but it did fit the man she knew as Andrew. As she started down the stairs again, she was a little startled to realize that she had made a final disconnection between Drew and Andrew.

CHAPTER SIX

DREW MET SYDNEY at the bottom of the stairs, and though he thought she was the most beautiful woman he'd ever seen, he reminded himself that until he was sure of what she was really after in Wallace, he was going to keep his distance. He'd learned the hard way that treachery came in all sorts of pretty packages.

"I hope you like Mexican food?"

"Love it," Sydney said. Why the hell was she suddenly nervous? Granted, he did look quite handsome in the dark gray linen suit, pearl gray shirt and multicolored tie. She was genuinely impressed.

Her bubble of inner happiness was soon pricked when she saw his car. "Lord, what a monster—a gas-guzzling, environmental polluter." It was meant as a joke, something to crack the silence, but she should have known better.

"Have you ever ridden in one?" Drew asked a little stiffly.

"No."

"Ever driven one?"

"Well, no."

Drew let the tips of his fingers lightly caress the high-gloss, candy-apple-red paint job as he walked Sydney around the back of the car to the passenger side. "Let me tell you something. A 1957 Chevy convertible is one of the finest American-made cars to roll off an assembly line. So whether you like it or not, you're in for the treat of your life.''

She should have realized that the slur against his car was like a stab at his manhood with a sharp object. Though once she'd slid onto the big leather bench seat and leaned back, she had to admit that nothing she'd sat on in years had the feel this car had. These were the tanks of the fifties and sixties—big, roomy and made for comfort.

Drew watched in amused silence from the corner of his eye as she rubbed the leather, testing its softness. ''Nice, huh?''

''Nice. I must say I didn't know that the seats in these things were quite so big.''

Drew started the car and pulled away from the curb. ''Why do you think every young guy back then would have died for one? They were, still are, the greatest cars in the world for necking in.''

Sydney laughed. ''Times were pretty idyllic and simple then, and that's about all teenagers had to think about.''

''Listen, I'm sorry about the last-minute dinner date, but I need to talk to you.'' He was quiet for a long moment. There were so many disquieting thoughts going around in his head about Sydney. Did he like her? Could he trust her? Did he even want to trust her? He knew full well that he wanted her. Damn, he thought, he was even a little nervous around her, like a teenager again—sweaty palmed, pounding heart. The feeling wasn't totally unpleasant, either. ''Are you still sticking to your story about Andrew Joshua and what you think happened?''

She'd been feeling positively generous until he ruined it with that question. "What I *think* happened? It *did* happen."

"Then you won't be upset if I tell you I've told your story to my grandparents."

"Oh, Lord. They must think I'm a real nut case. I guess you told them all about the man passing himself off as Andrew Joshua and just how hilarious it would be to make me believe he was a ghost."

"Look, you don't understand. I told you, Clay is Andrew Joshua's son."

"And that makes it better? Do you have any idea what a tale like this would do to my reputation if it goes around? Wait a minute." She just realized what he'd said. "Does your grandfather know who is impersonating Andrew."

"Not . . . not exactly."

She was relieved. Someone was finally going to clear up this whole mess, she thought as they pulled into a crowded parking lot.

The Mexican restaurant so aptly named, The Mexican Restaurant, was the best place in town to eat. Drew swore that the "fancy" name didn't diminish the quality or quantity of the food. It had, he assured her, the best Tex-Mex food this side of Mexico.

She knew the finest advertisement for an establishment was a full house. This one was brimming. There was a line outside the door, and the noise from the foyer was almost enough to make her turn away. But Drew caught her hand, and with good-natured gibes from some townspeople, he pulled her through the crowd to the front of the line.

"Alex," Drew called out, catching the attention of a harassed man who was lending half an ear to an old woman while the other ear appeared to be attuned to the milling crowd. Drew got a wave, and the man excused himself.

"Hello, Drew." A welcoming nod and smile was given to Sydney. "Your table's ready."

"Looks like it's getting out of hand," Drew said, then introduced Sydney. "This is Alex Chang, Sydney."

Alex Chang smiled and said, "The reporter who had the accident out on old Piney Creek Road? You were very lucky, ma'am."

Sydney nodded and faked a sincere thank-you. Did everyone in town know what had happened to her? Then she remembered where she was and her question was answered.

"What's the big draw tonight, Alex?" Drew asked as they followed their host, winding their way through tables and people.

"I tried to tell Mama that having a free margarita night until ten o'clock was a bad idea. The bar is packed, but the crowd won't spill over to the dining room until much later. Here's your table and the menus. Enjoy, enjoy."

Sydney watched Alex hurry away. She shouldn't have been surprised that an Oriental owned a Mexican restaurant. After all, nothing in this town was what she'd expected.

Drew caught the waitress's attention and asked Sydney, "Beer?"

She had a feeling she was going to need all her wits about her tonight and declined, ordering iced tea with her meal, instead. Neither of them spoke until after the waitress brought their drinks and a complimentary bowl of warm chips and salsa, yet the silence was not an awkward or uncomfortable one. Actually, it was rather relaxing, she thought. She was experiencing so many conflicting emotions about Drew that, without realizing it, she started to frown.

"It's not really that bad," Drew chuckled.

"What?"

"Liking me."

"What?"

"It sort of shocked me, too, realizing how I felt about you."

"I don't have the foggiest idea what you're talking about."

"Go on, lie to yourself," he said with a smile. "For a while you'll even believe it. I did the same thing."

Sydney dipped a chip in the salsa and popped it into her mouth. She didn't know whether he was serious or teasing. The hot sauce burned her tongue and ate the enamel off her teeth, but she refused to show any sign of weakness. She went on chewing and swallowing, then waited until she couldn't stand it any longer before she took a sip of her iced tea.

Drew watched her, his elbows propped on the table, his chin resting on his folded hands, an amused twinkle in his bright green eyes. "You must have a stomach of steel. I wouldn't touch that stuff on a bet."

The string of curses that formed in her mind wasn't at all satisfying. She glared at the grinning man across from her. How was it, she wondered, that in the game of one-upmanship, Drew always seemed to get the upper hand so effortlessly?

As she waited, silent, mouth still on fire, for the food to arrive, she had a chance to look around the restaurant and was surprised to see the senator, his wife and John Laker at a corner table across the room. They were all staring at her and Drew. More than that, they were all showing their displeasure by various facial expressions.

Drew waited until the waitress finished placing their dinners on the table and left before he said, "Looks like you've made your usual impression on people. You must tell me how, after only a few hours in Wallace, you've managed to make so many enemies."

Sydney turned to look at him, a caustic remark just barely bitten off as what he said sank in. "What enemies?"

Drew nodded toward the senator's table. "There's three. Of course, I'll have to take part of the blame. They distrust anyone who associates with a Wallace. But from the depth of those frowns, I'd say you've managed to earn points on your own. Then there's Buddy Hilton—owner, editor, publisher, reporter of the *Wallace Morning Sun*. I heard from Al—he's an unemployed gentleman who likes to sit outside the newspaper office—and Al said that Emma's visit upset Buddy mightily. Then there's Miss Wanda at the library. She's a close friend of my grandmother. Anyway, she called me this afternoon and happened to mention that Emma was there today looking for a particular article." Drew took a bite of his enchilada, dabbed at his mouth with the napkin, shook his head and said, "Everyone in this town knows who you are, why you're here and who you're staying with."

"I'm not trying to hide anything."

"No, but I'm sure it's become obvious to you that *they* are, for whatever their reasons."

Now, Sydney thought she was about to find something out. "And what would those reasons be?"

Drew stared at her for a long time before he answered. "Some don't want you to find out certain things. Others are trying to protect some people they care for.''

This wasn't going to be a cake bake, she thought, and suddenly realized that Drew Wallace was a man who liked to play games. She did, too, to a degree. "Who are these people trying to protect?"

"Me. My grandparents. The Wallace name."

She hadn't expected his answer, and her expression must have said so more than any words could have. "Why?"

He'd thought long and hard about what he was going to do. But to head off a potential disaster, he decided to be only as honest as he needed to be. "Are you always a reporter?"

"No, on my days off I'm a rocket scientist."

Drew chuckled. "It's nice to see you have a sense of humor." He dropped his gaze and for a while pushed his food around on his plate.

"And you," she said. "Are you a lumberman or a wizard who conjures up dragons?"

"Like you, I'm multitalented. Tell me something . . . Are you one of those reporters who can be trusted with some off-the-record conversations?"

"Yes," she said sincerely. As she patiently waited, she enjoyed her taco's spicy meat, grated cheese and the freshness of the chopped, vine-ripened tomato. Then she savored the tangy flavors of the bean chalupa, all the while keeping silent.

She recognized the hedging. This was not the time for her to make any more smart-mouth comments that might turn Drew off. It was obvious he had something important on his mind and was wrestling with the problem of how to make his presentation without giving away all the secrets or important facts. She took a generous sip of iced tea and studied him carefully over the rim of the glass, her gaze deliberately bland, hopefully showing only a mild interest.

"I knew," Drew said, "that the missing newspaper article you'd heard about would only intrigue you, make you determined to dig deeper. Buddy wasn't protecting me or my family when he told Emma that particular issue had been destroyed, but Wanda at the library was."

"Who was Buddy protecting?"

Drew sighed, neatly set his fork across the top of his plate and leaned back. "The senator."

A good reporter always took a chance when she listened to anything off the record. Morally, ethically, she was bound to keep what she'd learned to herself and out of her story. Of course, it didn't mean that she couldn't dig up the same information from a different source: she simply needed to let it be known who the second source was.

"What everyone, for whatever their own good intentions, seems determined to keep from you is an article about my father, my family and myself. Dad ran against James for the senate seat. Toward the end of the campaign things got pretty dirty...on my father's part."

"The senator didn't retaliate in kind?"

"James knew where my father's anger was coming from, accepted it and gracefully refused to respond to the accusations."

"What were the accusations?"

"Listen, they're not important now," Drew said, but Sydney's eyebrows shot up. "Okay. It had to do with old history, family history." He should have known she wasn't going to let him get off that easy, but it was crucial that she believe him, that he satisfy her investigative instincts so she wouldn't dig any deeper. "A large portion of James's campaign was based on the Fowlers' and his own honesty, integrity and family values. The Fowler family, their past, is a rather illustrious one, full of philanthropists, lawyers, judges. In other words, a bunch of do-gooders who managed to stay in the public eye."

Sydney was fascinated. So far he wasn't telling her anything new. But he was building a story, deliberately reeling her in; he was playing a game with her. A dangerous game if he wasn't careful. For a brief flicker, she switched her gaze to the senator's table and saw that they all seemed to be very interested in her and Drew. "So, what were your father's revelations?"

"That the Fowlers were an unscrupulous lot of thieves and crooks, that they used their power to corrupt and to further their political careers and their wealth."

"And was he right?" Sydney asked.

"No."

The answer wasn't what she expected. She set her fork across her plate, no longer pretending only a half interest. He had her full attention now. "You're saying your father was lying?"

Drew grimaced. "About James being dishonest and corrupt, absolutely. About the Fowler ancestors...? We all have some skeletons in our closets. But James Fowler is one of the most genuinely honest and caring men I know. He's a great senator and maybe someday he'll be a great president, if the power brokers in Washington don't ruin or destroy him first."

"Were your father's accusations just campaign strategy?" Her surprise had worn off, or she'd thought it had. It told her a lot about how much this man, possibly the whole town, kept tabs on their homeboy.

Drew shook his head. "Maybe it would have been acceptable if that was all there was to it. You have to understand that my family isn't really a fan of the Fowlers. For as long as I can remember, there have always been hard feelings, misunderstandings and outright hatred between us and them. Dad had been in the Texas House of Representatives for more years than I can remember. That position allowed him some power over the Fowlers. Then when James decided to run for Senate, my father decided to run against him.

"He never expected to lose, not with the years he'd put into the political machine and with all his cronies working for him. But toward the end, the polls told a different story. Texans didn't want what my father represented—the old regime, good-old-boy politics. They wanted youth, honesty and someone with charisma. Dad saw the handwriting on the wall and got down and dirty. It only made things worse. A week or so before the election, rather than face the humiliation of a sweeping defeat, he pulled out of the race."

"Is that what the elusive newspaper article was about?"

"Partly. You have to understand that Buddy Hilton and the *Wallace Morning Sun* supported James in his bid for the senate. Also, Buddy had never been a fan of my father, the Wallace family and especially not me. We're the same age, went to school together and have always harbored a mutual dislike for each other. Anyway, a few days after the election was over, my dad faced Buddy out in front of the newspaper office. They had a real public row. You have to understand, my father was a heavy drinker and he was a little drunk at the time, had been since he'd withdrawn. Anyway, later that evening Dad ran his car off the road and was killed. A couple of days later—actually, the day of my father's funeral—Buddy did his style of an obituary. It was a scathing account of my dad's political career. He raked the old man over the coals with veiled slurs and innuendos. Nothing you could prove, you understand, but just enough truth mixed with lies to give the story sensationalism. He all but said that Wallace and the state were better off without Dad.''

Drew tried to smile but failed miserably. Guilt did funny things to his insides. For as long as he could remember, he hadn't gotten along with his father. For whatever reasons, they had always been at each other's throats. Maybe, he thought, if his mother had lived, things would have been different. But like James, he'd lost his mother, lost her when he was ten and needed her most. Drew sighed. Because of his father, he'd left Wallace at an early age, only to return, at his grandparents' insistence, to help with the family company and the campaign. ''Anyway, that obituary was a piece of fluff compared to what Buddy printed next.''

''Is this the article everyone has tried to hide from me...and why?''

Drew's smile was grim. ''Hey, you're from Washington, from a big-city newspaper. I think some did it out of respect for Clay and Rosa. Others may have done it just to keep the senator's name out of it, and some may have been ashamed of their local newspaper's yellow journalism.

''Buddy had the right to write anything he wanted, but he should have had the decency to wait. He hurt Clay and Rosa terribly. I lost it. Stormed down to the newspaper office, dragged Buddy out from behind his desk and beat the hell out of him in the street for everyone to see. That evening, and for the first time in the *Morning Sun*'s history, an evening edition came out, a special editorial edition dedicated to crimes past and present of the Wallace family.''

Will wonders never cease, she thought. He had surprised her again, this time pleasantly so, with his honesty and integrity. He hadn't spared himself or his family. ''Sounds to me like you had stirred up a hornet's nest.''

''No. It stopped. Not another word was said or written. But then, I think Clay may have had something to do with that. My grandfather may be ninety-three years old, but when he's angry he can scare the hell out of you. Mind, he's never said how he stopped Buddy, but I have a feeling he may have visited Buddy late one evening. Buddy's a bully and a coward, and the threat of a painful death may have shut him up. You know, it still amazes me how much damage one man can do with the power of the press at his disposal. Most newspapers have to answer to several people—the owners, corporations, boards of directors, even lawyers. But one man's sole ownership, one man's opinion...'' He shook his head.

There was no way for him to know, she thought, but what he'd said hit so close to the bone it made her wince. The shocker was, she wanted to tell him she knew exactly what he was talking about. In fact, she realized they'd been talking almost nonstop ever since they'd been seated. The thought made her smile.

She was just about to explain her amusement when she happened to catch a movement from the corner of her eye. The senator, Lauren and John Laker were making their way toward them. *This should be inter-*

esting, Sydney thought. She relaxed back in her chair and waited. Drew immediately stood, smiled openly and admiringly at Lauren, shook James Fowler's hand firmly, then gave John Laker a rather reserved nod.

"Well Drew," James said, "looks like you're going to take all the credit for saving Sydney's life."

Drew let the pause that followed the senator's statement stretch. "Actually, Chunky, I had nothing to do with it."

James Fowler didn't seem to mind the childhood nickname, but Sydney was sure from the way John frowned and Lauren's smile faded to a stone mask that neither were too pleased. Especially since Drew had said it loud enough for a few others to hear. It was then, as Sydney glanced around, that she realized two things: the noise level in the restaurant had dropped to a pitch where all ears could easily be attuned to what was being said, and Emma and the doctor were seated at a table not too far away. Emma winked and waggled her fingers, then screwed her face up in an expression of horror when she looked at Lauren Fowler.

"Really Drew," Lauren said with a soft, musical laugh, "why on earth would you deny saving Sydney's life? That's silly. Buddy doesn't know whether to write you up as a hero or..." She let the statement hang in the air like a sword.

The suddenly icy atmosphere couldn't have been cracked with a chain saw.

"Actually, Lauren . . ." Drew began.

If only the woman hadn't opened her mouth, Sydney thought. She knew what Drew was about to say. He wasn't even going to think about it, just blurt it out. Panic-stricken, Sydney kicked Drew under the table and simultaneously swept her hand out as if to express what *she* was about to say. Her fingers caught the rim of her iced tea glass and sent the contents flying right across Lauren's peach silk skirt. Lauren froze and stared down at her ruined clothes.

"Oh God, I'm so sorry," Sydney whispered.

"Actually, Lauren." Drew continued, his voice shaking with laughter, "Andrew Joshua saved Sydney's life."

Sydney was sure that every person in the restaurant had heard. There was a startled silence at their table, then everyone started laughing. Relieved, Sydney laughed a little more loudly than the rest.

"Drew, the joker," Lauren said as she wiped at her spotted skirt. She gave one last glance at her soiled clothes and shrugged. "Come on, James, we promised your father we'd drop by tonight."

The senator was still chuckling as they walked away, but Sydney saw the curiosity in the parting glance he threw at her. When they were out of earshot, Sydney kicked Drew again.

"Ouch! What was that for?"

"You big loudmouth," she fumed. "You know damn well what it was for. How could you? They must think I'm the biggest nut case around. And you may have just totally destroyed my credibility. I have... Wait a minute. You did it on purpose, didn't you?" A thousand questions were racing through her head, a thousand questions but only a few answers. She had that eerie feeling that she was being set up. Used.

Drew motioned for the check, quickly peeled off some bills, threw them onto the table and said, "Let's get out of here. I need to talk to you without half the town for an audience."

She didn't move. "Not until you tell me why you did that."

"Sydney, I swear to you, I didn't mean to say a thing. It just . . . slipped out before I could stop." He rose, circled the table and gently pulled back her chair. She was about to blow a fuse. He bent and whispered in her ear, "You'll make things worse if you cause a scene." When she didn't move, he clasped her elbow and urged her to her feet.

They were barely out the door of the restaurant when she said, "Where were you the evening of my accident? Where were you, Drew?"

"I was home." She jerked her arm from his grasp, spun around and stared at him. He held up his right hand. "I swear to you, Sydney, I was home working, or I was till the storm cut the electricity." He could see her next question coming and headed it off. "Alone. And the lane to the house was so flooded I couldn't have gotten out that evening if I had wanted to."

"You lied to me, to everyone, didn't you? Why?"

"Ah, hell. I learned from the school of hard knocks not to tell anyone my business. Besides, I ended up doing something I'm not very proud of—I started feeling sorry for myself and got stinking drunk." He led her to his car, opened the passenger door, made sure she was tucked in, then slammed the door shut. After he slid behind the wheel, he turned toward her. "Would you mind if I put the top down?"

"No." If she hadn't been a grown, intelligent woman, she probably would have sulked. Instead, she just kept her mouth shut as they pulled away from the restaurant. She breathed in the cool, clean night air and felt herself begin to relax for the first time that day.

"Do you feel like a ride? I'd like to show you something special."

"Sure." It was so peaceful with the top down. The cool wind gently stirring her hair, the rumble of the big engine all around her, the incredible comfort of the wide seat, the endless legroom and her full stomach only added to her sense of well-being. She eased off her borrowed shoes and wiggled her cramped toes. She had no idea where they were going, didn't really know Drew very well, but surprisingly, she trusted him. Her eyelids became heavy and she leaned her head back against the seat, telling herself she'd only rest a few minutes.

It was the absolute quiet that awakened her. She opened her eyes and stared up at the sky. A sky so thick with stars that for a second she blinked, not sure if she were still on earth or floating in a dream on a pillow of clouds.

"Beautiful, isn't it?" Drew whispered.

"Where are we?" she asked, too relaxed to move anything but her head. From what she could see, they seemed to be parked in a flat, open area surrounded by tall pine trees, yet the trees were far enough away that they didn't encroach on them or block out the circle of open sky.

He'd been watching Sydney sleep, studying the line of her jaw, the turn of her nose, her wide forehead, the swell of her breast and her lips. He was crazy about her mouth, all pouty and inviting. He'd been tempted, had almost bent over and kissed her, but after a second's hesitation, he'd thought better of it.

"I call this my enchanted place. When I was a little boy, Clay brought me out here. Seems that they'd clear-cut the area, stripped it clean as they used to do, then moved on. But Clay isn't your usual lumberman—never was. He came back here, planted seedlings, then forgot about this place. It wasn't until years later that he found it again. The trees had grown, but for some reason a huge circle was left bare. The ground is higher here than anywhere in the county, so he says this is his direct route to the stars.''

Drew fiddled with the radio, found the station he wanted, then turned the volume to a low murmur and sighed as he relaxed against the seat. ''There's nothing like the music of the fifties and sixties.''

Sydney listened for a while, then turned her head to look at Drew. ''What is it?''

He shook his head and clucked his tongue. ''It looks like I'm going to have to give you a crash course on romance of the sixties.'' He slipped his arm under her head, eased her toward him and kissed her long and sweetly. With his lips still touching hers, he said, ''That song is the 'Sea of Love.' Many a teenage couple, parked in their cars, necked and swore their undying love for each other to that song.''

''What's so wonderful or special about this music?'' She had trouble getting the question out. Her whole body seemed to have gone limp. She didn't really want to talk or move. She didn't want anything to spoil this moment.

''You see, when you're listening to this music in the arms of someone very special, the words will say everything you're either too shy to say or just don't know how to say. These songs make love to lovers. And it's not just the slow tunes that get in your blood and heat it up. Listen. That's Jimmy Reed's, 'Baby, What You Want Me to Do.' Close your eyes.'' He kissed them shut. ''Let yourself go.''

She snuggled up against his chest, inhaling the scent of his freshly laundered shirt and his after-shave. "Talk to me, Drew. Tell me about yourself." The rumble of his chuckle echoed against her ear. She hadn't the foggiest idea what had come over her. She felt secure, wanted, and as strange as it seemed to her, she felt loved.

"And just what do you want to know?"

"Oh, all the normal things two people find curious about each other when they meet."

"And find they're enormously attracted to each other?" he added.

"Yes." Her quick answer amazed her. The honesty of it downright floored her. "What do you do for a living?"

Six hours ago he would never have told her the truth. But now, for some unknown reason, he wanted her to know every triumph and disappointment in his life.

Sydney raised her head and looked at him. "Do you work for the government?"

"No." He laughed, then ran his fingers through her hair and pressed her cheek back against his chest. "I used to design and develop computer software— games."

If he had told her he was a serial killer, she couldn't have been more surprised. "You mean like Nintendo games?"

"Yes, but in a more realistic form for adults, more action-oriented."

"You said you *used* to. Why don't you do it anymore, and what do you do now? Does it have anything to do with the dragon I saw at your house?" She could hear the sudden increase in his heartbeat. Without knowing how or why, she'd managed to touch a nerve.

Sydney wanted to lift her head and study his expression, see if she could read his thoughts, but instinctively she knew not to distract him. He had to make up his own mind if he was going to trust her or not.

"My ex-wife and I made a lot of money in the business. California was a software designer's paradise. That was, until I got tired of creating mindless games where all you did was destroy dodging objects. I had something else I wanted to do, but Ellen didn't want to take the chance, so she walked out with my last concept for the adult market. When she sold it as her own creation, it severed all my emotional and professional ties with her."

Sydney held her breath as Drew stopped, reached out and turned the radio up.

"Listen to that, Sydney. There's no one in the world who can sing 'When a Man Loves a Woman' like Percy Sledge, except maybe the Righteous Brothers."

"Yes, yes, it's wonderful, but what happened to your work?"

"Oh, I ditched it. Walked away from everything—marriage, money, possessions—and came back home to try to develop something I've been wanting to do for years."

"What?" She had to restrain herself to keep from screaming the question.

"Computer games for children—educational, fun games."

"Oh dear," she murmured, and buried her face deeper into his chest. She couldn't disguise her laughter with the fake coughing fit. She couldn't stop her shoulders from shaking. And when he grasped her arms and held her at arm's length, she couldn't stop the laughter from erupting.

"You find that funny, do you?"

"No." She gulped and struggled to sober up. "It's not you, really, or what you do. It's me." She started laughing all over again.

"Explain," he said. Her laughter was as addictive as chocolate and just as pleasing. He found himself laughing with her.

"This town, Drew. It's this town. Nobody is who they seem or what they appear to be. It's crazy. I'm a good judge of character. I can usually figure people out. But not here. What is it about this place? Lord, just look at me. Even I'm not myself here."

"Ah, maybe that's what's bothering you—you are yourself here."

"Bull." The thought made her shiver.

"Well, turnabout's fair play. Now, you tell me about yourself, Sydney. Who are you?"

CHAPTER SEVEN

SYDNEY TOLD HERSELF she would have liked to lie, and would have if he hadn't started kissing her again. When his hand covered her breast, she didn't try to move it. Instead, she sighed, lost in warmth and sensations she hadn't felt in a long time.

"Where are you from, Sydney? Where were you born?" Drew nibbled the hollow at the base of her neck. He knew who she was, where she was born. After she'd left his house, he'd made a couple of productive phone calls to some influential friends. He probably knew a lot more about her than she would want a stranger to know. But he had to find out what kind of person she was. Could he trust her? He was curious to see if what he knew would match what she told him.

"I was born in Arlington, a small town outside of Dallas," she said as she arched her neck, allowing his searching mouth to explore a little lower. When he worked back up to her ear, she shivered. "But Mother, my sister and I moved to Dallas when I was about eleven."

"And your father?"

Mentioning her father was like dousing her with ice water. She pulled away, straightened in her seat and stared at him. "My father and mother divorced when I was nine."

So far she'd told him the truth, but he didn't think she was going to elaborate any further. He was going to have to trust her, maybe on blind faith. "Sydney, can I trust you?"

She tried to make light of his question and laughed. "Depends on what you're going to trust me with. Wait a minute.... Why do I suddenly get the feeling that this—" she gestured around her "—is all some sort of setup? You planned it, didn't you? The dinner, the drive, the seduction . . . and now what? What are you after, Drew Wallace?"

He'd been told she'd be a hard nut to crack. Before he tried, he had to make her understand something. "You're right, this whole evening was planned. But not the seduction, and not what I'm feeling for you." Aretha Franklin started belting out the song "Think," and Drew quickly turned the radio off.

Sydney reached for the door handle. "Feeling?" The pain in her chest, the sense of betrayal she felt was unbearable. The door handle was unyielding. She grabbed it with both hands and shook it frantically, then it dawned on her that she didn't have to use the door at all. She started to stand up, but Drew pulled her back down.

Dammit, he had never been very good with subterfuge, intrigue or lying. It was a trait his father had always ridiculed him for, taunting him that he'd never make a good politician. Of course, he'd never planned to follow in his father's footsteps.

"Listen to me, Sydney." He held her by the shoulders. "I admit I haven't been totally honest, but neither have you. You're here to do a story on James. Fine. But I had to try to find out if you were going to do a hatchet job on him, and if you were going to dig deep enough so that you'd drag in the Wallaces, too.''

She went limp with bewilderment. ''What are you talking about—hatchet job? I'm here to do a story on an up-and-coming senator who probably has a good chance of becoming president of the United States one day. Besides, I don't do hatchet jobs on anyone.''

''Sure. What about Congressman Lancer? After your article he retired. You also broke Rubbergate, the House banking scandal. It was your list of all the bad check writers that caused the biggest uproar ever in Congress. There were dozens of representatives resigning, not to mention those who were beaten in their state reelections because of what you did. You deliberately kept all the offenders' names in the media long after the story had died.''

''Yes, that way no one would forget that those men abused their elected positions. If they couldn't control their own bank accounts, how the hell were they going to balance the government's? And as far as Congressman Lancer was concerned, he was taking an enormous amount of money from lobbyists to pass favorable bills for special interest groups.''

''What about Admiral Howard-Lang? My friend told me you did a story on him, then he was forced by the White House to resign his position.''

''Listen, the next time you want to find out about me, ask me. Don't rely on secondhand gossip. For your information, the admiral wasn't the only one forced to resign because of me, and I'm damn proud of it. They mishandled then tried to cover up their involvement in a military investigation into the sexual harassment of female military personnel.''

She was as mad as hell but as cool as the evening breeze that blew across her hot cheeks. "You better tell me what this is all about, Drew. I seem to have stumbled onto something, and as you probably know, I don't and won't let go until I have an answer." When he reached out to dislodge a strand of hair that was caught in the corner of her mouth, she flinched away from him.

"I'm sorry, Sydney. I've gone about this all wrong. But you must understand, I have good reason not to trust reporters."

She didn't say anything, just looked at him, but she had a dozen questions to ask and very few of them had to do with the job she'd been sent to do. "How and when did you find all this out about me…and what else did you discover?"

"I made a few phone calls after you left my house today."

"To whom?"

He shook his head and smiled, trying to interject a little pleasantness into the taut atmosphere. It didn't work. "It doesn't matter who. They had nothing but good things to say, other than professionally you are one tough lady and that if I was smart, I wouldn't cross you."

"They gave you sound advice. Maybe you should have taken it. You've crossed me, lied to me, used me and for all I know set me up on the Andrew Joshua thing to make me look foolish in this town's and the senator's eyes. I ask you again, Drew, why? And what's going on?"

Talk about a mess. He didn't think he could have dug himself in deeper if he'd tried. How had things gotten so twisted? "I swear," he said, "nothing I've done was meant to hurt you. And I haven't lied to you or used you to make you appear less credible. I was trying to protect my grandparents, especially my grandfather—and yes, myself—from any more pain."

Totally frustrated, she wiggled out of his hold and pushed him away. "What is it with everybody in this town? No one gives straight answers."

Drew opened his mouth, then closed it. Like the idiot he'd just accused himself of being, he was about to tell her that what he was going to say was off the record. He itched to warn her that if she used what he said, he would deny all of it. He had to struggle for the trust he wanted so desperately to believe in. "After Miss Wanda called me today and told me Emma was asking at the library about the newspaper article, I knew you were interested. And I thought if your interest was stirred, you'd find the article, read between the lines and maybe dig a little deeper into some of Buddy's innuendos about Dad's campaign. When Wanda said she thought the article might be misfiled, I was relieved."

Sydney's stony expression hadn't changed, and he went on. "What only a few people knew and what I had hoped I'd destroyed was proof that my father was hedging his bets to win. But I'm not sure if I destroyed everything, if I left some tidbit around for a smart reporter to pick up on. Buddy's article would have been like waving a red flag in your face. Dad might have been a wily devil, but there at the last I'm not sure he was rational. He'd set up an impressive list of graveyard campaign contributors. But even that wasn't quite enough for him. It wasn't until after his death that I found out how far he was willing to go to beat James. He'd been in the process of taking his plan one fatal step further and bestowing on those free-spending dearly departed the right to vote. If he hadn't withdrawn, it might have been enough to have won him the race.''

Sydney remembered reading history books telling about the graveyard votes Lyndon B. Johnson received during his Texas political career before he became vice president. ''Is that why your father withdrew, because you found out about the graveyard campaign contributions? And is that the reason for the case of the disappearing newspaper?''

''Dad withdrew because James found out about the contributors scam and sent John Laker to force his hand. And I think Buddy Hilton knew, too. My bet is that's what he and Dad were fighting about the day he died. Anyway, what I've been trying to find out was just how much you knew about the campaign and if you were going to use it in your article about James.'' Drew leaned his head back against the seat and stared up at the stars. He knew he was going to have to tell her everything now.

''Dad, in his obsession to beat James, had almost sucked the family business dry. My grandparents were already upset over the nasty turn of Dad's campaign, and then they found out that he was siphoning company money into his campaign fund, but they never dreamed it was part of a graveyard contributor scam. It almost killed Clay just to realize that his son was a cheat, taking money from the business he had worked at all his life. He was furious with Dad, but James's shadow, John, beat Clay to the punch, so to speak. Still, my grandfather was never one to mince words with anyone. God, did he and Dad have a shouting match. Anyway, Dad withdrew from the race and stayed drunk. Then, when it looked like James was going to make sure Clay found out about the graveyard campaign scam...''

Drew sat up and grasped the wheel. "Let's just say that was the day Dad ran his car off the road and killed himself."

"Suicide?" she asked.

"I don't know. We'll never know." He turned sideways on the seat. "You see, Sydney, don't you? I had to find out how much you knew, how far you were willing to go to get a good story. Clay's ninety-three years old. My grandmother's ninety. They've been through enough."

"Tell me something, Drew. Why would you think I would use this information? I have no reason to hurt your grandparents."

"You're a reporter."

"I see," she said. "And we're all cut from the same cloth, right?"

"Well, from my experience, yes."

"Your experience!" she shouted. "What is your experience? A hick-town newspaper owner who's obviously no fan of the Wallaces?" She threw up her hands in disgust. "Deliver me from fools and idiots."

"Listen, my ex-wife was the graphics end of our creative team. I came up with the ideas, the concepts, and I did the programming. When she left me, she took my last idea and claimed it was all hers. When I tried to fight her in court, she went to a couple of newspapers. A juicy fight in California between millionaires is grist for the mill. Needless to say, I was ground up in the whole process."

Reporters were supposed to be impartial, unbiased and coolheaded. That had always been Sydney's rule. But she felt sorry for him. She didn't want to, but dammit, she did. Through the years she'd seen the change in her colleagues. Anything and anyone was fair game.

She knew all too well the piranha mentality of some of her fellow journalists. "So that gives you the right to have an aversion to reporters?"

"Yep, 'fraid so." He grasped her hand and was heartened when she didn't pull away. "You see, I went through all this maneuvering and making an ass of myself for a reason."

His hand was warm and calloused. Not the hand, she thought, of a man who was afraid of hard manual work. She stared at him, wondering if she wanted to be pulled in any deeper. She could, after all, cut and run, right here and now. Or she could let his explanation stand and accept it. But there was something else here in this town keeping her anchored. "What reason?" she asked.

"When I told Clay and Nana about your adventure, about Andrew, Clay said he'd like to meet you."

Something made her insides quiver. She couldn't figure it out: the nervousness, the excitement, the sudden sick stomach. She wasn't a coward, either. "Sure, I'd love to meet your grandfather. When? Tomorrow?"

"How about now?" He didn't give her time to say anything, especially no. He just started the car and quickly backed out onto the road.

Sydney watched the headlights pick out the dark, straight shapes of the tall pine trees that hugged the side of the road. She stared into the blackness, catching the refulgent eyes of the night animals. She fidgeted and twitched. Sydney, the woman with nerves of steel, she thought. Hah! She was as shaky as a teenager meeting her boyfriend's parents for the first time. She got that old sinking feeling in the pit of her stomach as she wondered if they were going to like her or hate her on sight.

Drew sensed her nervousness and wanted to laugh. It was a good sign, he thought.

"Drew, you never did tell me exactly what the newspaper article Hilton wrote was about."

"My family. And the Fowlers."

"Yes, yes," she said irritably. "You've told me that much. But what about your family?"

"Would you wait and let Clay tell you?"

"I guess I'll have to, won't I?"

"Yes."

They rode on, lost in their own thoughts. Sydney knew there were so many holes in Drew's story that she could have fallen through it. Still, she decided not to question him further, preferring to wait and see what happened next.

They were almost back in town when Drew slowed and turned into a long straight driveway lined on both sides with dogwood trees and colorful flower beds. Her nervousness was back. Maybe she was finally going to find out what the hell was really going on and just who the man was who had saved her life.

The exterior of the house was lit up like the White House on an attack alert. She had expected one of the old-fashioned Victorian or plantation-style houses that seemed to be common in Wallace. Instead, she found herself staring at a modern one. There were soaring pale walls, lots of wide, arched windows and a red tile roof. It was an eye-pleasing combination of straight and curved lines, of freshness and light. She had a feeling she wasn't going to be disappointed with the interior, either.

Sydney's feet were a little swollen, and as she tried to stuff them back into her shoes, Drew was opening her door and urging her to hurry up. A voice from behind him made them both turn around.

"Thank heavens you're here. Your grandfather's been like a sore-footed bear in a cage for the past two hours." A tinkling laugh followed the woman's statement. "But then I guess that's just exactly what he is now."

Sydney watched Drew and his grandmother exchange glances and caught the love, mutual conspiracy and amusement that passed between them. She hesitated, feeling like an intruder, then Drew grasped her hand tightly and led her up the porch stairs.

"Nana, I'd like you to meet Sydney Tanner. Sydney, this is Rosa."

Bright hazel eyes quickly inspected her from head to toe. Sydney felt herself inwardly cringe. What a hell of an impression she must be making in her hand-me-down clothes. She had to remind herself that she'd faced down generals, FBI agents and had even incurred the president's wrath. She straightened her spine and stared back, then found herself smiling as hugely as the older woman. If she lived to be ninety, she hoped she looked as young and vital as Rosa Wallace. The woman was stylishly dressed in brown slacks and a silk blouse. Around her neck was an Indian necklace of silver and turquoise. Her hair was thick and pulled up into a bun on top of her head.

As they drew closer, Sydney realized her ramrod posture made Rosa and herself the same height. Their gazes level with each other, the older woman winked.

"I know you're probably a little miffed at Drew for not filling you in on everything. But you see, Clay is the one to talk to about that frightful experience on Piney

Creek Road.'' She threaded her arm through Sydney's and led her through the open double doors.

Sydney was so thrilled that someone had openly mentioned a possible answer to her experience that she was speechless. She simply walked along, her eyes busy taking in everything. What a house, she thought as she tried not to gawk. Once again her preconceived notions were wrong. She got quick impressions of soaring cathedral ceilings with crisscross massive beams, tile floors, furniture made for comfort. There were skylights everywhere. Then suddenly they entered a room that totally took her breath away. The word ''conservatory'' came to mind, even though it was a word she associated with old-fashioned homes and not this modern delight of clean lines and light. But ''sunroom'' was too insignificant a term. This room had a glass roof and three glass walls to let the outdoors in. There was greenery everywhere—pots of flowers, vines hanging from ceiling-high baskets. In the center of the room was an inviting seating arrangement of sofa, love seat, a couple of overstuffed chairs and a few tables. And seated on the sofa was an elderly man in a knee-to-toe cast impatiently tapping the end of his cane on one of the tabletops.

A chill slid over Sydney's skin as the old man fixed his gaze on her, his green eyes so like Drew's . . . and Andrew's.

''Sit,'' Clay ordered, and pointed his cane at the chair to his left.

''Clay Wallace,'' Rosa said in a scolding tone, ''don't you dare start your bullying. Besides, I don't think it's going to do much good with Sydney.''

Clay pursed his lips, and his bushy eyebrows jerked together as he stared at Sydney. She stared back. ''Are you going to tell me who the man was who rescued me?''

Those thick white eyebrows shot up like alert caterpillars. "What's going on here?" he demanded of Drew. "I thought you told me—"

"She's got some notion in her head that we know someone who might have impersonated Andrew," Drew said.

"Wait a minute." Sydney pointed a finger at Drew. "You told me that your grandfather *knew* who the man was."

"No, you assumed he did, and I just didn't clarify your misconception."

Sydney paused, taking her time as she stared at each person in the room. "Okay," she said, dropping into the chair next to Clay. "What's going on, Drew?"

Clay smiled, reached out and grasped Sydney's hand. "Would you do a crippled old man a favor and hold off asking your questions until you've told me everything that happened the day of the storm?" Her gaze reflected her distrust, and his expression melted into a mask of sadness. "I promise I'll answer anything you want."

Sydney could see the old man's pulse beating wildly at the side of his neck, noticed the way he was trying to control his rapid breathing and felt the dampness of his palm. Clay Wallace, she thought, was overexcited. But why? Was it just dread? As Rosa and Drew both sat down, Sydney began telling her story of how the storm had forced her off the road, only to be interrupted.

"No, no, no. Start at the beginning, before your accident. What brought you to Wallace? Please take your time, and don't leave out anything."

From anyone else she would have resented the command, but she heard the plea in the undertone and realized that Clay was a desperate man. She quickly glanced around and saw the same anxious expressions on Drew and Rosa. She was intrigued and a little excited herself. There was something she knew, something she'd seen that had these people on pins and needles.

Sydney began her story again, starting with her job at the Washington newspaper and her assignment. "Your grandson seems to have a problem with the fact that I'm a reporter. He's been dancing around answers to my questions. If I tell you what happened, are you going to do the same?"

Clay chuckled. "I'm too old to worry about what you write or don't write, or if you write about me or my family."

Sydney examined the stern old man's expression, saw the twinkle in his eyes and grinned. She started recounting her unscheduled stop at the gas station and the shortcut she took.

Clay must have sensed her bewilderment, because he leaned forward. "Why are you so puzzled that you stopped and asked for directions?"

"Mr. Wallace—"

"Clay."

"Clay. I have an overdeveloped sense of direction. I never lose my way, and I had detailed directions how to get to Wallace. But all of a sudden I saw one of those local, country gas station/grocery stores and stopped. I know better than to take shortcuts."

"But you did, anyway?"

"Yes."

She glanced down, found a cup of coffee in her hand and stared at it for a moment, lost in thought. Why *had* she taken that shorter route?

"What happened next?" Drew asked. He received a fierce frown from his grandfather and scowled back.

"That damnable storm. It seemed that I had no sooner turned onto Piney Creek Road than it came out of nowhere and closed around me."

"How did you feel?" Rosa asked.

"Storms don't usually bother me. But this one . . . It was weird. I don't mind telling you, I was scared." Her listeners were leaning a little closer, sitting on the edge of their seats, intensely alert. Sydney continued and became lost in the telling, reliving every minute detail. When she came to the part about Andrew Joshua, she expected Clay or Drew to interrupt with all sorts of questions, even scorn or laughter. But everyone was strangely quiet.

Several minutes later her story was finished. Sydney was surprised at how much detail she remembered and was able to relate. She'd told them everything—everything except Andrew Joshua's parting words. She tried to figure out why it seemed so important that she keep that last bit to herself.

Sydney sat back, relaxed and sighed. She ached and realized that every muscle in her body had been tensed. No one spoke. Drew's head was bent as he stared at the floor, so she couldn't read his expression. Rosa was looking at Clay, her eyes filled with worry. And Clay... She found him staring at her, pale and shaking a little, but there was wonder and happiness in his gaze. The silence dragged on. She felt a painful stab of disappointment and hurt. After all Drew had said or led her to believe, it seemed they were going to play games. She started to stand up, then stopped when Clay opened the drawer of an end table and pulled out a small, framed picture.

"Is this the man who rescued you?" He held out the picture.

Sydney reached for it, then hesitated, her fingers just inches from the frame. Her mouth was suddenly dry and her head was pounding. She wanted desperately to look, yet somehow she knew that if she did, everything in her life was going to change.... Curiosity and an inner need to know the truth won out. She grasped the wood frame, turned it around and gazed at her rescuer. The old sepia-tone photograph was faded and creased beneath the glass of the frame. But even the poor quality didn't take away from the man sitting stiffly in a chair, his hands resting awkwardly on his knees. Sydney felt a familiar chill.

There was no denying the man's identity: the strong jaw, the longish, dark curly hair, the broad shoulders, the dimple in his cheek. Even with the stiff pose and sternness of that period's photographs, the camera couldn't mask the sweet turn of his lip as he tried to hide his smile. Sydney glanced at Drew sitting on the arm of her chair, then back at the photograph. They could have been the same man, they looked so much alike. Clay would say it was Andrew Joshua, but it could just as easily have been Drew in a period costume.

Clay must have seen her doubt, her uncertainty, and held out another photograph. "This was taken the same day."

Something deep inside, perhaps a primitive instinct of self-preservation, screamed at her not to look, to get up and run. She took the framed photograph, set it on her lap beside the other, then looked down. This one also showed Andrew Joshua sitting, but just behind him and a little to the side stood an incredibly beautiful woman, her hand resting on his shoulder. "That's the woman in the portrait at the cabin and the same one hanging over Senator James Fowler's mantel."

Clay's bushy eyebrows rose slowly up his forehead. "That's my mother, Mary Clayton-Wallace. The man, Sydney, is my father, Andrew Joshua Wallace."

"I hope," she said, her voice a shaky whisper, "that you're not trying to tell me that *your* Andrew Joshua is the same Andrew Joshua who rescued me?" She had asked Clay but was staring up at Drew.

"I'm afraid that's what he's telling you, Sydney."

"And you believe this story, Drew?"

"Sure. Why not? Stranger things have happened in this world. Stranger things have happened here in this county over the years. You learn to roll with it."

"You—" Her voice deserted her for a moment. "You're stark raving mad, Drew. You're telling me that I was rescued by a...."

"Ghost. 'Fraid so."

Sydney turned to Clay. "You believe this, too?"

Clay nodded at Rosa, and Sydney watched as the older woman left the room only to return with two large boxes. "There are only a few things that Clay has left of his family." As she spoke she opened one of the boxes, folded back mounds of tissue, then gently pulled out a faded blue satin dress with a high-neck lace collar.

Sydney couldn't have dragged her gaze from that dress if she'd wanted to. She was frozen, as still as a block of ice and just as cold, seeing the dress in her mind as she'd seen it the first time. The color, a rich dark blue, would have made Mary's aquamarine eyes even brighter, her pale blond hair more luminous. She watched as Rosa laid the dress aside and opened the other box with the same loving care.

Sydney thought surely her heart had stopped beating; she'd ceased to breathe. She squeezed her eyes shut, then opened them again. Rosa was bringing it to her, holding it out, and as if in a dream, she reached for it, folding the heavy quilt in her arms. She buried her face in the sweet-smelling material, seeing through a blur of tears the appliqués, the wild animals and the flowers whose brilliant colors had dulled with time. "He wrapped me in this to keep me warm while we rode for help. He was so scared that I was seriously hurt and that he couldn't take care of me." She stared down at the photographs, then at the quilt, and whispered, "He wrapped me up to keep me warm and safe."

"That quilt was the first thing my mother made for her hope chest when she decided to marry Andrew Joshua."

Sydney reminded herself she was a realist. She didn't believe in ghosts, especially ghosts that rescued humans from disaster. Yet...yet she couldn't discount how strongly these people felt, either. But she didn't want to know anything else. Didn't want to hear another word about ghosts or Andrew Joshua. "He couldn't have killed her, you know."

Clay smiled for the first time that evening. "No. He loved her. You feel it too, don't you? Drew and Rosa have always agreed with me, but I think they believed it just because I did. But you, you saw him, you know."

"Now wait a minute. I'm not agreeing that what happened...that who I saw was Andrew's ghost." Her mouth was open, more denials on the tip of her tongue, when she remembered something.

Clay read her startled look and leaned forward. "There's more, isn't there?"

Why was she holding Drew's hand? She pried her fingers free and scowled at him as if her sudden revelation was all his fault.

"Please tell Clay what you've remembered," he said.

These were the most single-minded, determined, hardheaded people she'd ever met. "When Andrew left me on the road that morning ... after he let me off the horse, he said, 'Tell them I found Mary.'"

She wasn't prepared for the old man's reaction. All the color drained from his face, his eyes closed and he slumped back against the couch, then was still. In the shocked silence that followed, Drew and Rosa flew to the couch, but Sydney was the first to reach him. His skin was hot to the touch as she worked to unbutton his shirt. But then those green eyes were open, bright and brimming with laughter. "Rosa will eat you alive, young lady, if you lay another hand on me."

"Clayton Darcy Wallace," Rosa chided. "If you ever do that to me again, I swear I'll leave you."

"Now, Rosebud," Clay said in a placating tone, then glanced at Drew. "I guess you've something to say, too."

"I just want to remind you that your tricks have a way of backfiring on you, you old fool." Drew stared pointedly at the cast on his grandfather's leg. He was pleased to see the red stain of guilt on those wrinkled cheeks.

"But you heard—you all heard. Andrew Joshua's found Mary."

Sydney sagged to the floor with relief. "Would someone please tell me what is going on." Clay extended his hand and helped her up. When she would have returned to her chair, he patted the cushion beside him. Drew immediately sat down on her other side, and Clay leaned forward enough to glare at his grandson.

Sydney had a feeling these two were always at each other's throat.

Rosa made herself comfortable in the chair Sydney had vacated. "Start at the beginning, dear, so she'll know the whole story."

Clay nodded. "You're right, Rosa, she has to know it all." He picked up Sydney's hand and patted it. "When Rosebud says start at the beginning, she doesn't just mean with Andrew Joshua and Mary, but to the time when the Wallaces first came here to Texas. That's where the story begins."

"It was back in twenty-nine," Rosa started.

Clay nodded again. "Eighteen twenty-nine, girl. That's when my family packed up everything they owned in Virginia on the word of Stephen F. Austin's offer of free land and moved to Texas. There were my grandparents, their seven brothers, four sisters and their families. Each man got a league of land, and they all settled around each other. Times were hard but good. They made a little money and reaped the rewards of their labor on the land. But times were changing. A Mexican general was trying to reclaim the land. Then after the brutal slaughter of Texans at the Alamo, Texans took up the fight and defeated the Mexican Army at San Jacinto in 1836. The Wallace men returned to their wives and families, and they established the town of Wallace. They were fiercely loyal to Texas and—"

"Sydney wants to hear about Andrew Joshua, dear. Tell her about Andrew's mother," Rosa coached, knowing her husband's long-winded recounting of his family's proud history.

Clay chuckled. "I guess you could say Andrew was a late-in-life baby. Old Benjamin Travis Wallace—that was Andrew's father—was about seventy-six. He'd been a widower for years when he took a shine to a half-breed Comanche girl that the local preacher's family had raised from an infant. They married, and Andrew was born soon afterward. So Andrew had half brothers and half sisters all a lot older than him, but he had aunts, uncles and cousins he could play with. Back then, settlers had strong, bitter feelings about Indians, but no one dared to make a slur against Andrew's parentage. And for all that was said, Benjamin Travis and his wife, Sally Ann, had a blissful marriage till the old man kicked the bucket in about 1880."

"You're getting ahead of yourself, dear," Rosa gently prodded. "Tell her when the Claytons and Darcys arrived."

"Eighteen fifties or thereabouts. Both families were pretty close kin, could trace their ancestry back to French royalty, or so they said. They all moved from New Orleans when cotton had drained their land dry. Same thing with the Fowlers. Old Jacob Fowler was a prestigious lawyer in Louisiana and quickly pledged himself to Texas and the government. It wasn't long before he was made a judge. His son, Darcy Fowler, followed in his father's footsteps as a lawyer and later headed for state politics. I tell you those damn Fowlers—"

"Clay, keep to the story," Drew said impatiently.

Clay scowled at everyone, then went on. "I guess you can tell there were never any deep friendships between the Wallaces, Fowlers and Claytons. Anyway, there was

Samuel Clayton and Sara Elizabeth Darcy-Clayton, Mary's parents. The Claytons and Darcys were rich plantation owners in Louisiana—the real aristocrats of the bunch. Old money and lots of it. In my mind the Fowlers were just shirttail kin, hangers-on. Jacob Fowler had married Sara Darcy-Clayton's rather plain sister, Elizabeth.''

''Clay...'' Rosa warned.

''Well, hell and damnation, Rosebud. Sydney has to know the relationships to understand. She has to see that the Claytons and Fowlers hated the Wallaces. Damn carpetbaggers tried to make claims on Wallace land. That caused an uproar.''

Drew shifted, making his impatience known by the way he moved.

''Okay, okay. I'll get on with it. Mary Clayton and Darcy Fowler were cousins.'' He glared at Sydney. ''You got that straight in your head?''

''I'm with you.''

''Smart girl. Knew you were the minute I laid eyes on you. Well, it was around 1898 and you have these three young people who have known each other all their lives—Andrew, Mary and Darcy. Their families aren't bosom buddies, but they're all on speaking terms. That is, until the strong-willed Mary Clayton ups and tells her pa she's going to marry Andrew Joshua. You have to understand that by then the Wallace family was pretty much wiped out from the wars with the Comanches. Just Andrew Joshua and a few cousins were left. Texas had been and still was a wild place. Samuel Clayton lost his three sons, his wife and two grandchildren. The Fowlers didn't lose many—they stayed pretty much at the capitol making speeches.''

''For heaven's sake, Clay.'' Drew said.

"If you don't like the way I'm telling it," he barked, "suppose you do it."

"No, thanks."

"Then kindly keep your mouth closed."

"Yes, sir."

Clay winked at Sydney. "Mary's pa hit the ceiling. He might never have said a word in public about Andrew's heritage, but people didn't forget mixed blood back then, especially when your daughter was about to become kin to the pack that slaughtered your family members." He saw the impatience in Rosa's and Drew's faces but ignored them. He was getting to the real meat of the story and didn't intend to leave anything out.

"Now, you have to know that Darcy Fowler was crazy in love with Mary. He and Andrew hated each other as rivals do. One of the last big blowups they had was at a county fair. Darcy challenged Andrew to a marksmanship rifle-shooting contest. Darcy won. Then Darcy challenged him with pistols. Darcy won that one, too. He put his bullet through the center of a gold coin and gloated over his victory by threading it on a leather string and wearing it to taunt Andrew."

"Clay, please," Rosa said softly, "we don't have all night."

"Oh hell, you and Drew aren't going to let me tell this my way, are you?"

"No, dear heart. If I did, we'd be sitting here three days from now. Tell Sydney what happened after the marriage."

"Samuel Clayton disinherited Mary, but Mary didn't care. She had escaped her father's bullying, overbearing ways, and she didn't come to the marriage empty-handed, either. She had a full hope chest and her dowry—land her mother left her." Clay stopped to take one of the cups of coffee Rosa was passing around. He stared into the cup, stirring slowly as he gathered his thoughts.

Sydney, like the others, sipped her coffee. It was the last thing she needed—she was already wired. Up until now she'd been getting background; now Clay was about to tell her about Andrew Joshua and Mary.

"Andrew built Mary a house on the most beautiful piece of land in the county, a log cabin just off old Piney Creek Road. That piece of land, by the way, was left to Mary by her mother. It wasn't what she was used to, but Andrew wasn't a man for fancy trappings. From all I've heard, she was happy and loved Andrew to distraction. But Darcy wasn't about to give up. He hated the way she was living, and every time Andrew and Mary came to town, he tried to corner Mary and talk to her. There were fistfights between the two men. Andrew was jealous and had threatened Darcy in front of the townspeople. He'd even argued with Mary in front of others. But they were still happy, and when I was born, everything seemed to calm down. Darcy stopped chasing after Mary. Andrew wasn't jealous anymore.

"Everything changed when I was ten months old. Andrew had taken the wagon and gone over to Taylorville for a couple of days to buy stock. The day he was riding back, a violent thunderstorm hit Wallace. Andrew's wagon broke down on the Piney Creek Road and was almost washed away by the flooding."

Sydney's heart was racing, her breathing shallow. She couldn't believe what she was hearing, yet in her mind's eye she could see it all.

"He had to walk to the cabin, and when he got there Darcy and the sheriff were waiting for him. There was a pool of blood near the fireplace and my cradle. I hadn't been fed or changed in hours. Mary had disappeared. She was never seen again.''

A strange feeling came over Sydney. She felt hot then cold inside. ''Andrew was charged with her murder, wasn't he?''

''Oh, yes. Charged, convicted and hanged all in the span of two days. Darcy Fowler was the prosecuting attorney, and Jacob Fowler was the circuit judge. They railroaded a helpless man, worked the townspeople into a frenzy with their half truths.''

''What did Andrew say?'' Sydney asked.

''He was a broken man. You see, he knew Mary was dead—something in his Indian blood told him she was gone from him forever. He had no one left and gave up. Oh, the court assigned a lawyer, a drunken fool who was probably paid for by Samuel Clayton.''

''He had you, Mr. Wallace,'' she said. ''Didn't he think of you?''

The old man quietly shook his head. The story never failed to move him, and it took a few seconds for him to regain his composure. ''The day the guilty verdict came in, Darcy gave a victory party. That evening a drunken crowd of men went to the jail, busted Andrew Joshua out, hauled him to the town square and hanged him from an oak tree.''

Sydney winced. ''How in heaven's name could that have happened? Where was the law?''

''Texas was still pretty wild then. Besides, the Fowlers were the law, or at least Fowler cousins were. Frank Harper was the sheriff then, and he was Fowler kin. People say he saw the crowd coming, left the cell keys on his desk and went home.''

Sydney was suddenly bitterly angry for the injustice of what had happened. It *was* an injustice. She knew in her heart that there was no way Andrew Joshua could have killed Mary. Then she realized that her out-of-control feelings were for something that had happened years ago. Whatever she felt wouldn't do Andrew or anyone else any good. "It's a sad story, but if—and I'm not saying I believe in ghosts but if the Andrew Joshua that saved me is your Andrew, why would he show himself to me?"

Clay smiled as if she were the most wonderful person on earth, reached for her hand and squeezed it. "I've thought a lot about that. You're an investigative reporter and a damn good one, from what my grandson's told me. I think, because of everything that happened to you on Piney Creek Road, that you're here to clear Andrew's name."

CHAPTER EIGHT

"THAT'S THE MOST ridiculous thing I've ever heard. I'm here to do an article about Senator Fowler, not chase ghost stories." Her nerves were shot. She couldn't sit still any longer and stood up. "I think it's time to leave."

Clay stood, too. "I'm sorry. I didn't mean to blurt it out like that. Please sit down and listen to what I have to say. Just for a few more minutes."

She bet this man didn't say please to many people. "Mr. Wallace, I don't have time—"

"Just a few more minutes."

Sydney glanced at Drew. He shrugged as if to say, "It's up to you." She sat down, deciding to go along with them. But there were some disturbing questions running around in her head. She turned to Clay. "Tell me something. Have you seen Andrew Joshua before or has anyone else?"

"No," Clay said.

"Then tell me something else. Why would Andrew help me? Why am I the *only* one ever to see and talk to him?"

"I wish I knew," Clay said, and there was a wishful longing in his voice. "Sydney, I was born in that cabin and only ten months old when my mother was murdered. I was there when it happened. I probably saw who did it. The place still makes me sad. And, I know one thing as sure as my name is Clayton Darcy Wallace—my father did not kill my mother. You've met Andrew Joshua and you know it, too. You also know something no one else does. You know that Andrew's found Mary, and if he's found her, I think her body, which no one's ever found, has to be somewhere close. That's what makes me believe you really did see Andrew."

He reached down beside the couch and picked up a box tied with string and placed it on her lap. "There are copies of all the trial records in here." He patted the box. "There are also some personal interviews I did years ago with some of the older folks around here who would have been alive then, or who remembered things their parents told them. Just take a look at everything and see if you can get a fresh perspective."

"I'm no lawyer, Mr. Wallace," Sydney said, but she could see that any objections she might have were going to be overlooked.

"You're a fine reporter."

"Yes, but don't you see that the only thing these records can possibly tell me is something I'm sure you already know—Andrew didn't get a fair trial. And nothing can be done about it now." She hadn't realized how hard a grip she had on the box until Drew started to take it away. She wouldn't relinquish her hold, and a little tug-of-war ensued until Drew gave up. She was mesmerized by the pain in Clay Wallace's eyes.

"For years I've gone out to the cabin trying to find answers. I've never seen or heard anything, but there's an aura about the place...a feeling of loneliness. It bothered me so much that I had to stop going. Please, just look at the papers. We're all too close and I'm sure there's something there we're missing. Maybe Andrew Joshua will show you what it is.''

Two days ago, if someone had told her that she would be secretly longing for a ghost to reappear, she would have thought the person crazy. But the idea of seeing Andrew Joshua again sent a warmth through her.

Suddenly Drew had her arm. She remembered saying goodbye to the Wallaces, remembered getting into Drew's car, but it wasn't until the wind cooled her hot cheeks that she snapped back to life.

''Did you or your family know I was coming to Wallace before I got here?''

''Yes. Patricia told Steve and he called Clay.''

''Patricia? Steve?''

''Patricia at the Wallace Inn. You had reservations.''

''And you didn't know, just Clay.''

''I swear.''

''Who's Steve?''

''The mailman. Now, you want to tell me what's going on in that suspicious head of yours?''

Sydney touched the box on her lap. ''If I find out the Fowlers railroaded your great-grandfather and were a party to his murder, it could hurt the senator.''

''Dammit, do you never give up being suspicious? Do you distrust everyone?'' He gunned the big engine and made a quick right-hand turn. He turned up the volume on the radio, and they were blasted with the Righteous Brothers singing ''You've Lost That Lovin' Feelin'.''

Sydney raised her voice to be heard over the music. ''I won't be a pawn in the Wallace family revenge. So let me tell you something.'' She slapped the top of the box. ''Whatever I find in here, I won't use in my profile on the senator.''

GET A FREE TEDDY BEAR . . .

You'll love this plush, cuddly Teddy Bear, an adorable accessory for your dressing table, bookcase or desk. Measuring 5½" tall, he's soft and brown and has a bright red ribbon around his neck—he's completely captivating! And he's yours *absolutely free,* when you accept this no-risk offer!

AND FOUR FREE BOOKS!

Here's a chance to get **four free Harlequin Superromance® novels** from the Harlequin Reader Service®—so you can see for yourself that we're like **no ordinary book club!**

We'll send you four free books...but you never have to buy anything or remain a member any longer than you choose. You could even accept the free books and cancel immediately. In that case, you'll owe nothing and be under **no obligation!**

Find out for yourself why thousands of readers enjoy receiving books by mail from the Harlequin Reader Service. They like the **convenience of home delivery**...they like getting the best new novels before they're available in bookstores...and they love our **discount prices!**

Try us and see! Return this card promptly. We'll send your free books and a free Teddy Bear, under the terms explained on the back. We hope you'll want to remain with the Reader Service— but the choice is always yours!

334 CIH AK9P (C-H-SR-11/93)

NAME		
ADDRESS		APT.
CITY	PROVINCE	POSTAL CODE

Offer not valid to current Harlequin Superromance® subscribers. All orders subject to approval.

© 1993 HARLEQUIN ENTERPRISES LIMITED

Printed in U.S.A.

NO OBLIGATION TO BUY!

If offer card is missing, write to: Harlequin Reader Service, P.O. Box 609, Fort Erie, Ontario L2A 5X3

0195619199-L2A5X3-BR01

HARLEQUIN READER SERVICE
PO BOX 609
FORT ERIE ON L2A 9Z9

MAIL▶POSTE

Canada Post Corporation / Société canadienne des postes

Postage paid Port payé
If mailed in Canada si posté au Canada

Business Reply Réponse d'affaires

0195619199 01

Drew switched off the radio and guided the car to a stop in front of his house.

"What are we doing here?"

He twisted sideways so he could face Sydney. "First of all, whatever you discover about the past couldn't possibly hurt James now. Oh, it might embarrass him a little because he's used his family's illustrious history and strong values in all his campaigns. Second, we're here because you're a distrustful witch—" he smiled to take the sting out of his name-calling "—and the only way I can make you believe that none of the Wallaces are setting you up, using you or out to get the Fowlers is to make you trust me."

Oh, he was good and angry, she thought, and hesitated when he opened her door. After all, what did she really know about this man? Then she glanced up into those green eyes, and even though they were bright with anger, she was lost. Now she recognized what it had been about Clay that had stopped her from refusing his plea outright. She doubted any woman could resist that strange hypnotic quality in the Wallace men's eyes.

"Don't just sit there, Sydney." He turned and stomped up the porch steps.

She quickly followed him, dogging his steps, trying to explain. "Listen, Drew. Whatever you're going to do isn't necessary. I'm sorry. Really, I am. It's just that this whole thing has thrown me." She tugged at his elbow, but he shook her off and managed to get the key in the lock. She trailed him into the empty house, bumped into his back when he stopped and took a firm grip on his coattail. The house smelled old and musty, and the total darkness only served to remind her of her earlier fear of the place.

"Come on, Drew." She wadded the material of his coat in her fist. He wasn't about to leave her alone. "You have to admit the idea of a ghost, of Andrew Joshua, is pretty wild. I mean, ghosts don't have bone and muscle. They don't—" Her voice squeaked a little as he abruptly started off down the hall. She stayed glued to him like a limpet. "I've never even heard one story where a . . . a ghost saves a human being."

"If the word 'ghost' bothers you, why don't you call him a spirit?"

"A restless spirit? Maybe, but still . . ." Her eyes had adjusted to the darkness. She knew where she was and almost panicked when the air around her turned icy. "Why is it so damn cold in here?" She shivered and watched in surprise as Drew patted along the wall. There was a clicking sound, then a small lighted panel sprang open. Drew punched a series of buttons. When a bell echoed loudly throughout the house, she jumped, reinforced her grip on his coattail and whispered, "What was that?"

"Part of the security alarm." He pressed another button and a door swung open.

The blast of frigid air made her teeth chatter. "Is this part of the security system, too? You freeze your intruder to death?"

"Let go of my coat," Drew said as they walked through the door.

"Hell, no."

Drew laughed. "I'm just going to turn on some lights."

"Fine, I'll just come with you."

"Sydney. . . ."

"Okay, okay. But if the lights aren't on in ten seconds, I'm going to start screaming my head off." She reluctantly released his coattail. The material slipped through her fingers, and she had to make a fist to keep from snatching it back.

Drew laughed again. "I would never have thought that you were afraid of the dark."

"So sue me. I don't like it, okay?"

"I bet when you were little you slept with a night-light on."

"No. My father wouldn't let me. Said I was being a baby. Of course, that's what I was. But I sleep with one on now. The lights, Drew!"

He had learned a lot from that rather sad statement and quickly found the bank of switches. Bright light flooded the workroom. He watched her visibly relax and regretted his meanness in deliberately dragging out her agony. "Couldn't your mother have insisted on a night-light?"

Sydney hugged herself in an attempt to keep warm. She tucked her hands under her arms and began to look around. "Mom didn't or couldn't do anything without my father's permission." The beautiful hardwood floor shone in the light, but there was little else to recommend the room. Except for the tables of computers and other equipment, the room was bare. She shivered again. "Why is it so damn cold?"

Drew slipped off his coat and wrapped it around her shoulders. "When everything's turned up and running, it generates a tremendous amount of heat."

"Look, Drew, I'm tired. Whatever you want to tell or show me can wait until tomorrow."

"No." He finished turning on all the computers and equipment. "You know I don't trust reporters, don't you?"

"Yes." She didn't know where this was all leading but had the feeling she was going to come out on the short end of the stick once again.

"And you know my trust of women is at an all-time low?"

"Yes."

"And you don't trust me or my family, right?"

"I didn't say that, exactly." Sydney watched as he walked over to a closet door. When he opened it, she took a step forward, her lips parted in surprise. Inside was another set of doors, those of a walk-in safe. Obviously, whatever he was working on was either worth hiding or worth a lot of money. As he fiddled with the combination, she thought the answer was possibly both.

Drew pulled open the doors to the safe, walked in and rolled out a table. On it was something like a small movie projector, except it had other equipment wired to its sides. If she'd had her wits about her, she would have told him to stop or simply walked out of the house. This was a ploy, one she'd been subjected to many times during interviews. Drew was about to take her into his confidence to make her trust him. It had never worked before and it wasn't going to work now. But curiosity kept her silent as she watched him work.

Drew quickly made a few adjustments and lowered the lights at the far end of the room. "My life, not to mention just about every penny I have, is tied up in this. But I trust you, Sydney."

Fascinated and puzzled, her gaze followed his every move as he slipped a portable microphone over his head, clipped the small battery pack to his waistband and adjusted the mike close to his mouth. Then he attached small pieces of white tape over each eyebrow and at the corners of his mouth. Each patch had a wire running from it to another battery pack, which he clipped to the other side of his waistband, along with a remote control. A little amused at the way he looked, Sydney wondered what he was going to do next, when he turned on the projector.

Movement at the opposite end of the room snagged her attention away from Drew. She turned, then stared openmouthed. In the middle of the floor, no more than a few feet high and wide, was a mountain range, complete with trees, moss-covered rocks, a shimmering pond and the entrance to a large cave. "Oh my, what is it, Drew?" she asked, never taking her eyes off the apparition. The scene was so realistic she could almost smell the dampness, the rich earth and the ironlike scent of rock. She heard a noise, cocked her head and listened, realizing that it sounded like bare feet heavily slapping against a wood floor. Suddenly, the leaves on the trees trembled and the glassy surface of the pond began to lap at its edge.

Before Sydney could once again ask what was happening, a puff of smoke billowed out of the cave entrance followed by a small gush of bright fire, then someone—or something—had a coughing fit. She couldn't believe her eyes. There was the dragon again, and on closer inspection she was stunned at just how real it looked. It was only about twelve inches high, but there was incredible detail in the luminous scales, the forked tail, the long, sharp claws. This was no computer-enhanced projection, no cartoonist's animation: this was live action and very lifelike. The creature would have been intimidating, even a little frightening, if it hadn't been for the long, girlish eyelashes and rather pitiful expression in its yellow eyes. Sydney also realized that unlike most reptiles, the dragon's eyes weren't slitted but were large and round, giving him a human expression. Those eyes were staring at her now, and the eyelashes fluttered.

She was captivated, then enchanted as the creature began to move, and when the forked tail swung around and slammed into a rock outcropping, she began to laugh. The dragon hopped around, holding its tail and mumbling under its breath.

"Think it's funny, do you?" he said.

Sydney looked at the creature, then over her shoulder at Drew. He had moved up right behind her. "Did you say that or the dragon?"

"Merlin," Drew said, "can speak for himself. Watch." He placed his hands on her shoulders and turned her around.

Sydney laughed as she watched Merlin pace back and forth outside his cave. "What's the matter with him? He seems angry."

"Angry?" Merlin said. "Angry! My dear young lady, I could spit dragon's teeth." He slapped his clawed paw over his mouth at the gaffe.

"Merlin, tell Sydney who you are and why you're here."

Merlin focused his rather silly gaze on Sydney and tried to look fierce. "I am Merlin the Great. Merlin, adviser to King Arthur and the Knights of the Round Table. Merlin the Magician."

"Merlin…" Sydney mused, and was amazed at how natural it seemed to talk to and interact with him. "And why are you a lowly dragon, Master Magician?"

Merlin glanced down at one foot and held it out, inspecting the long claws in disgust. "I made the fatal mistake of miscalculating the talents of a mere witch by the name of Morgana. That witch stole my secret to the dragon's breath and used its magic against me to find the Holy Grail." He hung his head and shook it, then looked up. "If I don't find her, she'll destroy the world with her evilness."

"You're a magician," Sydney said. "That should be easy for you."

"You think so, do you? Look at me." A thin stream of smoke drifted from his nostrils. "I'm a dragon and I'll stay this way until I take back the dragon's breath, and then get my hands on the Holy Grail." He spun around too fast, and his forked tail struck the mountain wall. Merlin yelped as small rocks tumbled down, forcing him to dodge them. He straightened his horny shoulders and lifted his head with as much dignity as he could muster. "One other small detail I've neglected to tell you... The Holy Grail is enchanted, the most powerful of any magic that ever existed. It will allow Morgana to travel through time."

The live action stopped, everything froze, and like a child whose new toy has been snatched away, Sydney wanted to stomp her foot and demand that Merlin come back. "This is your children's game, isn't it? You're going to use Merlin and his quest to find the Holy Grail for your games?"

"Yes and no." He was delighted with Sydney's reaction. For the first time since he'd met her, she had let down that wall she'd built around herself. The urge to wrap his arms around her and hug her close was so strong that he was actually reaching for her when she moved away and sat down on the floor beside Merlin and his kingdom. Drew grinned and thought that Merlin just might turn out to be his adversary instead of his ally. "I'm going to use Merlin and the evil Morgana to teach children history... and, I hope, some important values,'' Drew said as she crawled around the circumference of the scene, studying the details from every angle. He wondered if she'd even heard him.

Sydney couldn't believe how lifelike everything looked, even up close. Merlin's scales shimmered like lustrous pearls. She reached out to touch him, knowing the scene was only a projection but expecting to feel a solid form. The disappointment brought genuine pain when her fingers slipped through and the image was projected on the back of her hand. A thousand questions raced through her head, questions she doubted Drew would answer. She did have one answer, though: Drew Wallace was a genius. "What do you call this?" She made an all-encompassing gesture.

"TPLAI, or Tabletop Projected Live Action Imaging."

Ever the realist, she said, "But it's on the floor."

Drew laughed. "It's scaled to its maximum now so I can refine the details, work out the bugs, so to speak. But when it's finished it will be able to be projected onto a tabletop."

"Why a tabletop? Can't it free-float in the air?"

"No. It's meant as a game—kids will sit around it, in front of it with their controls."

He went on to explain and immediately lost her in technical terms, so she tucked her dress carefully around her, crossed her legs, placed her elbows on her knees, propped her chin on her entwined hands and stared at Merlin and the cave as if it were a roaring fire, something to gaze into and lose her thoughts in.

Drew went over to one of his computer tables, reached below and opened a small refrigerator. He pulled out a bottle of wine and a couple of glasses, then walked back to Sydney, sat down and handed her a glass of wine. Like Sydney, he stared at his creation, still a little in awe. "You like Merlin, do you?"

"Oh, Drew. He's wonderful."

"He's a good listener, too."

Merlin nodded, winked and cocked his head, as if he were indeed ready to listen.

Sydney laughed. "You never stop, do you? What do you want to know?"

"All about you. So far you've artfully dodged every question I've had."

She sipped her drink and marveled at just how relaxed and comfortable she was with Drew.

"I know you were born in a small town, so you know what they're like. But how did you get so far from that small town?"

"You mean how did I get out?" She took another drink of wine, set the glass down and stared at Merlin. "When I was a child I thought the place where I lived and my family were the center of the universe. My dad had a good job. Mom was a housewife and member of all the right local clubs. We were upper middle class, lived in a nice home in the right part of town. I was popular in school, made good grades and my parents were happy, or so I thought." Sydney fell silent, staring at Merlin but not seeing him as the memories flowed back with painful clarity.

Drew could almost feel her misery but didn't dare say anything. He adjusted the microphone next to his mouth and eased the remote control from his waistband.

Merlin sighed, fluttered his eyelashes, then rested his head on a boulder and stared at Sydney. A puff of smoke escaped his mouth. "What happened?" he asked, his voice soft with sympathy.

"Everything started to change. Dad didn't come home at nights. Mom cried all the time. And, of course, small towns being small towns, it didn't take long for everyone to find out that Dad was having an affair with the boss's daughter."

Merlin's head came up and a sizzle of fire scorched the moss on the boulder. "Your friends at school found out."

"Everyone else, too. My mother was told by her best friend. That's when things got really bad. Mom isn't one to suffer in silence. She made scenes, public ones." Sydney realized that she'd never talked about those childhood traumas, that she'd always held her feelings in, kept the pain to herself. That long-ago pain had taught her a hard lesson she'd never forgotten: she couldn't trust anyone. Sydney stared into Merlin's eyes and saw all the understanding and sympathy she'd never received or allowed herself to accept from anyone before.

"Dad wanted a divorce to marry his new love. At first the town took sides, but you have to know that Dad's mistress's family was very powerful and wealthy, and not just in our small community. They not only owned the local newspaper but several others in Houston, Dallas and San Antonio, so they contributed greatly to those cities' economies. Mom and her public scenes soon became an embarrassment and a liability."

Merlin cocked his head and drummed his long claws on the rock. "And through it all, what did your father have to say to you?"

"That I was still his daughter and his love for me wouldn't change."

"But it did?" Merlin asked, and laid his head back down on the boulder.

"Yes," Sydney said, and let her thoughts drift back further over those years. No matter what she told Merlin—Drew—he would never see or understand the embarrassment, anguish and grief she'd gone through. But as she'd talked, she'd relived in her mind every detail, every hurtful word. What surprised her now, though, was that she'd expected the agony to grow. Instead, the knot that had always been in her chest seemed to loosen.

Drew thought it was time she faced reality. He pushed a few buttons on his remote, then slipped off his microphone. "It must have been devastating for your mother, and I take it she must have married your father when she was young, so she was left pretty helpless."

The thought of her mother helpless made Sydney laugh. "Right after the divorce and settlement, Mother enrolled in college. In three years she had a degree in business and started her own antique shop."

"And if she'd stayed married to your father, do you think she would have accomplished as much?"

"No. She would have stayed a housewife and made every one of us suffer for it."

"What was your father's occupation?" he asked.

Why did she hesitate over his question? she wondered. Then she knew. "Dad was editor of the local newspaper. After he married Eloise, her father made Dad editor of their Dallas newspaper." She was talking so fast she was almost babbling. It was like a hole in a dam that had grown bigger and bigger. She needed to talk, to let it out. "When Eloise's father died, I guess everyone was shocked that he left the publishing business to Dad. And Dad never lied about his loving Eloise—they're very close."

Drew picked up her wineglass and handed it to Sydney. "Your father was a journalist?"

Sydney took a sip, then looked at Merlin, realized he was frozen again and glanced at Drew. "He won a Pulitzer for a series of stories on Vietnam veterans—Thomas Shannon."

"I read those stories," Drew said, and was impressed. "But the name?"

"For professional reasons I decided to use Tanner—my mother's maiden name." She wasn't ready yet to open up that particular can of worms. She didn't want any more questions, she told herself, and leaned toward Drew. It didn't matter a damn to her that those green eyes were full of warm compassion. Hell, she'd been attracted to men before. *But not like this,* a little voice whispered in her head. What could it possibly matter if she just moved a little closer, gave him the option to make a move? She inched toward him, got a whiff of his after-shave, put down her wineglass and kissed him. Just, she told herself, to shut him up. It was only meant to be a friendly peck on the lips, but when his warm mouth covered hers, her arms slipped around his neck and she pressed against him. Drew pulled her closer and their combined weight forced them off balance. They slid over sideways to the floor, entwined in each other's arms.

Drew was the magician, and she'd done the unthinkable and fallen under his spell. She wasn't herself, hadn't been since she'd come to Wallace. Actually, that wasn't quite right. Nothing had gone as she'd expected since she'd come face-to-face with Andrew Joshua.

She must be losing her mind, she thought, or her willpower, but it never entered her head to stop Drew. They rolled around on the floor, frantic to get each other's clothes off, pulling, tugging, laughing as buttons popped and zippers ground loudly.

"This is crazy, Drew," she managed in a gasp as her bra loosened and his hands caressed her breasts.

His lips traveled over her shoulder and up her neck. "I know." Half of his shirt had caught on his shoulder, and he tried shrugging off, but it stuck to his damp skin like a sheet of wet tissue.

"We shouldn't." Her dress was bunched around her waist, and with his help, she managed to wiggle out of it.

"I know."

"I'll be gone in a couple of days," she said, then his hand slipped between her legs, and she relaxed and closed her eyes.

"Maybe."

"We'll never see each other again."

"Stranger things have happened, Sydney."

"Like?"

"You just might decide to stay."

"I . . ."

"Why don't you stop questioning everything and just enjoy."

She chuckled, a broken sound of amusement and desire. She'd never been so hungry before or wanted someone as much as she wanted Drew. Now she knew what her friends had meant when they talked about being carried away, of losing control. She was riding her own roller coaster of emotions. The ache was a driving need, alien and welcome. Her world was spinning out of control, and the only word she could manage to utter was "protection." Drew's chuckle and nod of reassurance were comforting.

A few minutes later, they lay panting, the icy air in the room cooling their damp flesh. Sydney had never realized just how hard a floor could be. She wiggled under Drew's weight, trying to find a more comfortable position. When he raised his head and stared at her, his eyes bright with laughter, she didn't know how to take the amusement. Then she smiled. "I feel like a teenager groping on the floor."

"Groping?" Drew said. "I'm crushed. That, my girl, was my finest hour." He ducked his head, burying his face in the crook of her neck, and mumbled, "Well, maybe my finest few minutes."

She couldn't help the giggle that escaped and quickly wondered when, if ever, she'd laughed with someone after making love. "If this had happened in that monster car of yours . . ." Her voice trailed off as the words turned into a rather erotic picture in her mind.

"Ah, now you see why those kids loved that car," Drew said. "Think about the top being down, parked under a sky full of stars and a big full moon." He sat up, handed Sydney her dress and helped her slip it over her head and zip it up.

"Drew, do you see my underwear anywhere?" She heard a rumble, a cough, then his laughter erupted like a bass drum. She followed his gaze and smiled. Somehow her panties had landed in the center of Merlin's setting, and it looked like he was standing on them, his long claws curled around the lace edges.

"My sentiments exactly, Merlin," Drew said. "Keep her underwear and we might just keep her here for the night." Suddenly he felt a chill set in, and it had nothing to do with the temperature of the room. "Stop thinking, Sydney, of all the reasons you and I shouldn't have made love."

It was scary the way he was reading her mind. "I have to go, really I do. Emma—"

"Emma knows you're with me." He tucked his shirt into his slacks. "But come on, I can tell you're not going to be happy until you're away from me awhile so you can think."

"I'm sorry, Drew. This was wonderful, really it was. It's just that I can't stop thinking about... everything. All this business with Andrew Joshua has unnerved me completely. I'm not used to being rescued by a ghost."

He locked the workroom door behind them, double-checking his security, then led her out of the dark house. "So you finally believe you saw him, that no one was trying to trick or use you?"

She laughed. "If I say yes, I've committed myself and I'm going against everything I believe in."

As they climbed into the car, he said, "Oh, you mean you might have to believe that all babies are beautiful?" he teased.

"The check *is* in the mail," she said over the roar of the engine.

"Politicians tell the truth?"

"That's one I might have to draw the line on," she said, then started laughing again. "But, maybe there are ghosts, goblins and things that go bump in the night."

"And what about love at first sight?" he asked.

Sydney sobered. "I'd have to think seriously about it."

"Maybe that's your problem—you think too much."

For a while they traveled in silence, a comfortable, companionable quiet.

"Tell me something, Sydney. Why are you working in Washington if your father owns three newspapers?"

"Dad and I don't see eye to eye on journalism or politics, never have and never will. He's like Buddy Hilton, Drew. He totally controls his empire and he's from the old school of politics—favors, power and money buy votes and men." Any conversation about her father depressed her. They had been at loggerheads from the time he divorced her mother and married Eloise. When she obtained her degree in journalism, he offered her a job on any of his newspapers and she'd had the joy of turning him down.

She stared into the night, letting the wind blow through her hair. The town square came into view as Drew stopped at a light. Her gaze was drawn to the old tree, the one that was half-dead. She said rather absently, "That's where the townspeople hanged Andrew Joshua, isn't it?"

"Yes," Drew said. "That's not an earthshaking revelation though, Sydney. Small towns usually did their hangings on the town square. Most of them had oak trees."

"I understand, but tell me, when did half of that tree die?"

He stared at the huge oak. "You know, I believe hearing that it started to die the day after Andrew Joshua was hanged." The light turned green, and as Drew drove through the intersection, he said, "But Andrew wasn't hanged on the dead side, Sydney. He was hanged on the side that's still living."

Sydney shivered. She should have known; nothing in Wallace and nothing about Andrew Joshua was predictable.

CHAPTER NINE

LIKE THE WARNING BEACON of a lighthouse, every window in Emma's two-story home seemed to be shining. It wasn't until Drew had turned into the driveway that they both noticed the police car parked out front.

"Something's wrong," Sydney said, and was out of the car before Drew had brought it to a halt. She ran up the porch steps with Drew right behind her. "Emma," she called. "Emma!"

"We're in here," Emma yelled from the kitchen.

Sydney skidded to a stop in the doorway when she saw Dr. Doolittle and a young man in uniform she vaguely recognized. She just knew she was right; something *was* wrong. Emma looked pale and strained.

"What happened?" Sydney watched her friend struggle to keep her tears in check and was immediately at her side, her arm wrapped reassuringly around the woman's shoulders.

"I've lived here all my life, Sydney. We never lock our doors." She choked up and shook her head.

"Tell me what happened." She glanced at Paul Doolittle. With his walrus-mustached mouth turned down at the corners and his eyes wide with distress, he reminded her of a Saint Bernard.

"Someone broke into the house tonight. They did a pretty good job of ransacking it."

Sydney led Emma over to the table and gently pushed her into a chair, then she pulled up one for herself.

"What did they take, Emma?" Drew asked.

"That's what we've been trying to figure out," the young policeman said. "As far as Emma can make out, nothing's has been taken."

Drew squatted down beside the distraught woman and took her hand in his. "Come on, Emma. It'll be okay."

She glanced around at everyone. "I'm all right, really I am. It's just that whoever did this is more than likely someone I know. Why would they do this and not take anything?"

Sydney was watching the local cop's nervous actions. "You're the one who picked me up on Piney Creek Road?"

"Yes, ma'am."

"Howard, isn't it?"

"Yes'm." He straightened his long, thin body and stuck out his chest. "I'm glad to see you're better."

"I haven't thanked you for taking care of me that day." She knew everyone was listening and went on to break the tension in the room. "And Emma told me you're the one who retrieved my rather soggy luggage."

"Yes'm."

"Thank you."

"Welcome." His cheeks had turned bright red. He cleared his throat, then looked at this watch. "Well . . . well, if you'll just check your things to see if anything's missing, I'll get back to the station and make my report."

"My things?" Sydney asked, and immediately stood up.

Emma grabbed her arm. "Your purse—everything was emptied out and gone through. I didn't know what or if anything was missing."

Sydney marched up the stairs, taking in the evidence of the criminal's presence. A drawer here and there had been pulled open. A closet door was open, its contents on the floor. She'd been on the police beat long enough, raced to the scene of enough burglaries, to know there was something wrong here. Everything was so neatly messed up that it increased her curiosity. When she stopped to look in Emma's room, her suspicions grew as she noted the same neat mess: a couple of opened drawers, a mussed bedspread, an open closet door.

When she got to her bedroom, though, she pulled up short. This was different. Her room had been thoroughly searched. All the dresser drawers had been emptied onto the floor, the closet was completely bare and she had to step over the pile of clothes in the middle of the floor. Sydney reached down and picked up a wrinkled, turquoise linen blouse, one of hers that Emma must have gotten back from the laundry that evening. Something or someone seemed determined to keep her from wearing her own clothes, she thought as she looked around in disgust.

She found the contents of her purse spread out on the bare mattress, and she checked through them. She counted her credit cards, cash—nothing was missing. For a frantic moment she peered around, then sighed when she found her laptop computer on the desk exactly where she'd left it. She was about to turn away when she noticed the tiny green light. Someone had turned on her computer. She kicked sheets, clothes and covers out of the way, pulled the chair out, sat down and pressed the shift key. The small screen was blank.

She quickly browsed through the files. Nothing seemed to be missing.

Drew gave a long, low whistle from the doorway. "Your room seems to be the worst."

"Doesn't it. Drew, can you tell if someone has been going through my files?"

An eyebrow went up and his lips tightened. "Sure." He made his way over to her. "That's a marvelous little gadget. Did you know that every time you log on, it registers a time on the hard disk?" He touched her shoulder, and she got out of the chair. "Let me see what I can figure out."

"Even though my room got the worst of it, nothing's missing, Drew."

"Doesn't make sense."

"Not unless someone got exactly what they wanted and then tried to cover up what they were after." She blinked at the screen. It was filled with gobbledygook, but he was nodding in total understanding.

His fingers flew over the keys. "You think someone was after what you had in here?"

"Yes."

"And just what *do* you have in here, Sydney?"

"Other than some other stories I've been working on, there's my notes on the senator's story...."

"What else?"

"This is silly. Who would want that?"

Drew leaned close to the screen, studying each symbol. "What?"

"I entered everything that's happened to me since I arrived in Wallace—in detail, even about Andrew Joshua."

Drew hummed a response, then chuckled. "Here we go. Other than your entry a couple of minutes ago, the last time was at 10:36 this evening.'' He glanced at his watch. ''It's one o'clock now.''

''Someone knew that Emma and I were out for the evening?''

''Could be. Or it could be a local teenager looking for some drug money.''

''Drew, get real,'' she groaned and picked up her wallet. ''I have three hundred dollars in cash and another couple of hundred in traveler's checks.''

He ignored her. ''Do you have any blank disks? Do you back up?''

''Of course.'' She snatched up the small plastic box next to the computer and flipped it open. She was about to hand him one when her hand froze. ''Drew, there are two diskettes missing.''

''Thought so. Someone helped himself to your hard disk.''

''They copied some files.''

''They weren't picky, Sydney. Probably didn't have time. No, they copied everything.''

''Damn. Oh no... Emma. What am I going to tell Emma? This is all my fault.''

Drew switched off her computer and stood. He took her in his arms and held her for a minute. ''What do you care about Emma? You've only just met her.''

''How could you say that! Of course I care about Emma. We've... she's my friend.''

''In just a couple of days? I guess I assumed by all you've said that you didn't trust people easily or quickly.''

''What does that have to do with this?'' She angrily pulled away, stepped over the mess on the floor and left the room.

The three people in the kitchen looked up when Sydney and Drew entered. "Nothing's missing, Emma. I'm sorry."

"Sorry? For what?" Emma asked.

"I think—"

"Howard," Drew interrupted, "why don't I walk you out and explain a few things. Besides, there's something I left on the front seat of my car."

Sydney sat down at the kitchen table with Emma and Paul, took hold of Emma's hand and did some explaining herself. After she was through, she said, "I'll go check into the inn tomorrow, Emma. I'm so sorry this happened because of me."

Emma reached over and took Paul's hand. "See, I told you she was my friend," she said, then turned back to Sydney. "Paul thinks you've been using me. I keep trying to tell him that you're letting me help you solve a mystery, but he doesn't believe me."

"What she's doing is getting you in trouble. You could be in danger."

"Oh hell, Paul. From what? A computer thief?"

"You know, he just may be right, Emma. There's more to all this than I've told you. Actually, it's become even stranger." Sydney took a deep breath and told Emma and Paul everything she'd learned that evening. It was a lengthy explanation, and when she was finished, Emma's dark eyes were overbright with excitement. Paul was frowning.

"Surely you don't believe this ghost business? No person in his right mind would."

"Are you sure, Paul, beyond any reasonable doubt?" Drew asked as he walked back into the kitchen. "Howard's going to keep a watch on the house for the next couple of nights." He turned back to Paul and said,

"What about near-death experiences? Surely as a doctor you've come across patients who've had them. Can you explain them?"

Paul shook his head, his mustache twitching at one corner.

Sydney shot Drew a crooked grin, then noticed the box he was holding and went hot and cold all over.

"Oh, are those the Wallace papers?" Emma asked, and everyone turned to stare at her.

"How did you know about these?" Drew asked. He set the box down in front of Sydney.

"Paul and I ran into John at Ropers this evening." She caught Sydney's disgusted expression and smiled. "Ropers is a local night spot everyone goes to, and John is John Marsh, president of Wallace State Bank. John was real ticked off at Clay and was making his displeasure known to anyone who would listen. Apparently that 'old fart,' Clay Wallace, had called him at home this evening and demanded he open the bank so he could get the Wallace papers from his safe-deposit box."

"Did anyone hear him?" Drew asked.

Paul grimaced. "You know John, Drew. He's in his element when he has an audience. Everyone at Ropers heard him. Why?"

Drew glanced at the box. "I wonder if someone thought that the box might be here?"

"That's crazy," Emma said. "Isn't it?" She glanced around. "I mean, how would they know Clay would give it to Sydney?"

"Clay has nothing to hide. Besides, he's always enjoyed rubbing this town's nose in the fact that they hanged an innocent man," Drew reminded her. "I'd bet my life Clay told John he was giving the papers to Sydney tonight, and John let that slip, too."

Emma threw back her head and laughed. "Lord, Sydney, things have really been hopping since you came here. Talk about shaking up the little folks."

"What do you mean?" Sydney asked.

"Well, first there's your grand entrance into Wallace, then the little scene at dinner tonight with the Queen Bee and the senator. And if you think word hasn't spread that you're claiming Andrew Joshua saved your life, then you're dead—no pun intended—wrong. Even Buddy Hilton's called here a few times wanting information about the break-in, but what he really wanted was an interview with you."

"Oh, no." Sydney could visualize the headlines, and cringed.

"By the way, Drew," Emma said, "I thought you might like to know that Sally Pearson let it slip to Howard—they're second cousins—that Buddy's put the paper up for sale. He can't carry it on his own any longer, and he's not about to take on a partner."

"Serves him right," Drew said, and everyone smiled at the venom in his voice. "Maybe there is some justice in the world, after all."

While Drew was talking, Sydney caught Emma's rather glazed expression as her friend stared at the box. She had to bite her lip as one of Emma's fingers lightly ran along a rough edge. When Emma realized all conversation had stopped and everyone was watching her, she yanked her hand back as if the box's seam was as sharp as a knife's blade.

"I was just thinking—"

"Oh, God." Paul moaned, and the corners of his mustache drooped even more.

Emma ignored Paul's interruption. "Maybe I could help go through these papers." She caressed the top of the box the way a lover would caress a soft cheek.

Sydney refused to look at Drew, knowing if she did she'd crack up completely. "Of course you can. I wouldn't think of opening it without you. As a matter of fact, why don't we all take a look at them? Maybe one of us will find what Clay missed." She glanced at Drew a little uncertainly, then said, "You don't think Clay would mind, do you?"

Drew grinned. "I think he'd do just about anything you asked."

"Now listen, everyone—" Paul raised his voice "—I'm a man of science, a doctor. I don't believe in ghosts."

Emma sighed "We're just going to look at some old papers, Paul, not have a séance. Besides, I don't believe in ghosts, either." Emma turned to Sydney. "Do you?"

"Not me," Sydney replied. Then in unison they all turned to look at Drew.

He shrugged and grinned. "What can I say? I believe in love at first sight, that the check's in the mail, that all newborn babies are beautiful and in ghosts, goblins, things that go bump in the night, magic and dragons."

Sydney knew she was blushing like a stupid adolescent. She also knew that Emma's keen gaze was bouncing between her and Drew like a rubber ball. It was time to steer her friend's overactive imagination elsewhere. "Emma, why don't we straighten up first before we start reading?"

"Are you out of your mind?" Emma's outraged expression made everyone laugh. Paul started to get up, and Emma growled, "Sit."

Sydney groaned after she opened the box and saw the stack of yellowing papers. On top were the court trial records, all handwritten in an elaborate script. "This isn't going to be easy," she said. But they were all eagerly waiting, and she started dealing out the papers like a deck of cards. When everyone had a stack and was eagerly starting through them, she looked down at the ones she'd decided to take: the trial records of Andrew Joshua Wallace.

After an hour of absolute quiet and a couple of cups of coffee, her strained eyes and brain just couldn't assimilate the words any longer. Sydney set down her stack, finished, but still not sure what she'd read. "He let them convict him. Andrew Joshua never said a word in his defense, not even on the witness stand. He never answered a question. Why?"

Drew, his own eyes red with fatigue, glanced up. He took a sip of cold coffee and grimaced. "These—" he waved some papers in his hand "—are interviews Clay and Rosa did years ago with some townsfolk who were around in 1900. One woman, Mary Clayton's best friend, believed Andrew was innocent. She swears he knew somehow that Mary was dead and was brokenhearted with grief. He just didn't care what happened to him."

"That's rather selfish, isn't it?" Emma piped up, never lifting her head from what she was reading. "I mean, he had a son, an infant who needed him."

"Maybe there's something none of you realizes or understands. Andrew Joshua was passionately, deeply, in love with Mary. Though they never found her body,

I think he knew in his heart she wasn't alive. No, he didn't think of his child, his and Mary's, but I think he was in shock or overwhelmed with despair and grief."

Paul was the first one to break the silence. He set his stack of papers down and stared off into space for a moment. "I've lived here twenty years. I heard all the stories about the Wallaces and the Fowlers, but this... " He tapped the papers, stroked one corner of his mustache, then the other. "The night the vigilante group hanged Andrew ... it's so predictable, like seeing an old movie."

"You mean planned?" Drew asked.

"Yes. The sheriff usually went home between eight and nine. That night he didn't leave until ten o'clock. The vigilantes came shortly after. He always took the cell keys with him, but that night he put them on top of his desk and left the jail-house front door unlocked. During the investigation after the hanging, he said he'd been sick and was running a fever. His wife corroborated his story."

"Neat," Emma growled. "And listen to this. Darcy threw a victory party at the local saloon. It says here that he was buying drinks all evening. This—" she held up a frayed paper "—is an account from the bartender. He stated he didn't know who started talking about hanging, but by that time Darcy had left, so he had an alibi. Neater and neater."

Sydney rubbed her eyes. "I don't know what your grandfather wanted me to find, Drew. Did Andrew kill Mary in a jealous fit? Did someone else kill her? But I do know this—the trial was a travesty of justice. First of all, the judge should have stepped down because of a conflict of interest. After all, he was a Fowler, Darcy's father, and just a little too close to the whole affair. In the second place, Darcy Fowler should never have been the prosecuting attorney. He was personally involved—he loved Mary and had an obsessive hatred for Andrew." She rolled her head around to loosen up her tight neck muscles. "But justice was pretty loose back then, and Texas politics were worse than rotten, so I'm not surprised."

Drew handed his papers back to Sydney, as they all did. "I've read some of these before and never found any answers. But Clay refuses to believe that Andrew Joshua, his father, killed Mary then hid the body so no one could find it. I think Clay was hoping you'd prove him right. After all, you're the only one who's seen and talked to Andrew Joshua. He told you he'd found Mary, and I think Clay hopes Andrew will come back and tell you where her body is."

Sydney shivered hard.

Emma retrieved the papers from Sydney's limp hold and neatly straightened them. "Has anyone ever wondered why Andrew Joshua would appear to Sydney? I mean, why not Clay or you, Drew? You're family, blood. Why Sydney, an outsider?"

Paul groaned and stood up. "I don't believe in ghosts. Sydney was knocked on the head and she hallucinated."

"But," Emma said, "if she was hallucinating, how the hell did she know about Andrew Joshua, Mary and the cabin?"

Paul threw up his hands and shook his head. "I don't know and I don't want to know. I'm going home." He turned to leave, and Emma jumped up and followed him.

"And tell me this, Paul Doolittle, Mr. M.D., man of science and nonbeliever. How could she have described the cabin? Wait a minute!'' she shouted. ''What about the painting of Mary Clayton?''

The front door slammed, and Sydney and Drew looked at each other. Sydney was the first to speak. ''I don't have any answers to those questions, and it's damn frightening.''

''Maybe you were in the right place at the right time.''

''You mean the wrong place and wrong time, Drew.''

''No, I don't. Think about this. The day Mary was killed and disappeared, there was, and I quote from other sources, 'a monster storm.' We know that Andrew Joshua was driving his wagon back from Taylorville that day when the storm hit. They found his wagon on Piney Creek Road the next day. Now picture this and see if the scenario sounds familiar. He was caught on the road in the lightning, thunder and unrelenting rain. There was no stopping, no going back, and suddenly the horses went wild. He was probably knocked out, and when he came to, he had to walk all that way to the cabin.''

The scenario, as Drew called it, was all too familiar, Sydney thought. ''And when he finally got back to the cabin, it was to find Darcy and the sheriff there with the baby—Clay—a pool of blood on the stones by the fireplace and Mary gone. The men knew, everyone knew, Mary would never have gone off and left her baby alone. Something terrible happened in that cabin.'' She ruffled the papers in front of her, then started searching through them. She found what she wanted, read for a moment, then set them aside. ''Damn. I thought I'd overlooked something.''

Drew picked up the coffee cups and took them over to the sink. ''What?''

"It's nothing. Just that I wondered why, when Andrew Joshua got to the cabin, Darcy and the sheriff were already there."

"I thought that was funny, too. How did Darcy know something was wrong, wrong enough to bring the sheriff with him?"

"Because he'd been there earlier, that's why. But I'll tell you this, Drew, his own testimony is fishy. He said he knew Andrew Joshua was in Taylorville, had been for two days. He was worried about Mary and rode out to the cabin to check on her." Sydney shook her finger at Drew. "He went to check on her, when only three days before, knowing how jealous Andrew Joshua was of Darcy, Mary had been forced to hurt and embarrass Darcy publicly by telling him he was not to hang around her any longer!" She frowned. "He said in his testimony that when he got to the cabin, Mary was gone, and he saw the blood and panicked. This is where it gets sticky. He rode off, leaving the baby! He says he didn't see or even think about Clay, he was so worried about Mary. Could he really have been so obsessed with Mary that he'd forget a helpless little baby? Especially when that baby's cradle was next to the pool of blood? He said he just headed back to town, and when he was almost there, he got caught in the storm, and that's why it took him so long to get to the sheriff."

Drew yawned. "As Emma says, neat."

"Emma said what?" Emma asked as she bounced back into the kitchen. She had the look of a woman who'd been thoroughly kissed.

"Nothing." Drew slowly stretched, then reached for Sydney's hand. "I'm dead on my feet." He gave her hand a gentle tug. "Walk me to my car. I want to talk to you."

On the way out, Sydney glanced at the kitchen clock and almost staggered from the shock. It was four o'clock in the morning. No wonder she was weaving along behind him; she was as tired as he was. Outside, she stopped and took a deep breath of the cool night air. "Wait a minute," she said, and started to turn around. "You forgot Clay's papers."

"Keep them for a while."

She groaned and followed him to the car. "You just want me to read them again, don't you?"

Drew chuckled, then said, "Maybe." He leaned against the door of the car, placed his hands on her shoulders and pulled her unresisting body to his. Tiredly, she laid her head against his chest, and he rested his chin on top of her head. "You're not sorry about tonight, are you?"

She didn't need to be hit between the eyes with a two-by-four to know what he was talking about. "I'm surprised, even a little shocked at myself." She looked at him and managed a small smile. "I don't usually jump into bed . . . or onto the floor." She grinned and Drew laughed. "I . . . don't usually . . ."

"Make love on the first date?"

"That sounds immature, but yes. I'm usually more careful."

"About sex or your emotions?"

"Both. Drew, I haven't done one thing I would normally do since I came to Wallace. It's most disconcerting." He was going to kiss her, and she jerked her head back. "Please don't kiss me. It'll only confuse me more."

"Are you embarrassed by what happened between us?"

"No. Puzzled."

"Why?"

How could she tell him that the strength of her emotions, the uncontrollable intensity of her own desire was something she'd never felt before, and it scared her. "I don't know why. It's just one more strange happening in a strange few days."

Drew wrapped his arms around her and held her closer. "Tell me this. I know I'm supposed to look a little like Andrew Joshua—"

Sydney snorted. "Like you were hatched out of the same pod."

"I saw the look on your face," he said. "We all did when you talked about him. No matter how much you deny seeing Andrew Joshua, you and I know you did, and you're connected to him now. What I'm trying to say is, you're not mixing the two of us up, are you?"

"What a ridiculous thing to ask."

"Is it?"

"Yes. Andrew didn't kiss me. I didn't make love to him on a hard floor with a yellow-eyed dragon watching."

"Come out to the house tomorrow," he said, then glanced at his watch. "I mean today."

"I can't, Drew. I've still got an interview and a story to complete. The senator is expecting me, and from what little I've done since I've been here, I imagine I'll be there all day."

"Then the evening, or as soon as you finish. Come out and I'll cook you dinner." She nodded, and the back of his hand caressed her cheek, then his fingers slipped under her chin. He tilted her head back and kissed her deep and long. "That was just so you'll remember. Now, go inside." He set her aside, got into the car, started the engine but refused to move until she shut the front door behind her. He glanced up at the sky, the stars as bright as jewels on a queen's necklace, and said, "I hope you know what you're doing, Andrew, and since you brought her here, maybe you should figure out some way to make her stay."

Inside the house, Sydney leaned back against the door and closed her eyes. She didn't even feel like the same person anymore. Sighing in defeat, she pushed away and called for Emma.

"I'm up in my room," a voice floated down.

Sydney trudged up the stairs and walked into Emma's bedroom. At least whoever had broken in hadn't wrecked the whole house. "Let me help." She immediately rounded the other side of the bed and grabbed the end of the sheet, tucking in the corner. They quietly remade the bed and started picking up the few items of clothing from the floor. "Emma, if it really was Andrew Joshua who rescued me, why do you think he picked me?"

Emma was quiet for a few minutes as she worked, quickly hanging up her clothes. "Fate. Destiny. I believe you were meant to be on that road at that time for a reason, maybe not just for Andrew Joshua, either."

"Okay, say I go along with that. But what reason? There's nothing in those court records that changes anything. I can't prove that Andrew Joshua didn't kill Mary."

"Maybe that's not it. Wasn't the last thing he said, 'Tell them I found Mary'? What if he's trying to tell you where Mary is? If you find Mary, maybe she'll show you who the killer really was."

Sydney squeezed her eyes shut and sighed despairingly. "Are you telling me that I'm going to come face-to-face with another ghost? This is all crazy. You know that, don't you?''

''Yes, but it's so wonderfully romantic.''

They finished up in Emma's room and walked down the hall to the one Sydney was using. She glanced around at the malicious destruction. ''You know this wasn't necessary. Whoever wanted the information in my computer did this partly to try to cover up what he was after and partly out of plain meanness.'' Once again they began picking up clothes and remaking the bed. ''I know that the Wallaces pull a lot of weight around here because they're founders of this town, but do they have any financial interest here?''

Emma stared at her as if she'd lost her mind, and Sydney thought she'd offended her. ''I'm not asking if they're rich for my— I mean, I just wondered, with the lumber mill and the wonderful house Clay and Rosa live in . . . Oh, dammit, Emma. In these days of economic decline, the lumber and sawmill business has got to be hurting, and Drew let something slip that made me think he was almost broke.''

Emma sat down on the edge of the bed and laughed. ''I don't know about the economic climate of lumber, but the Wallaces are the richest people in town. They probably rate among the top ten richest families in Texas. They have scads of money.''

''Oh. How?''

''Land, Sydney. One thing none of the Wallaces would ever let go of is land. I've heard stories of them going hungry to pay the taxes on all that land. You see, the land was what the Wallaces first came to Texas for. Eventually, it paid them back in lumber, cattle-grazing leases, some oil, but what's most important now is the natural gas.''

Sydney sat down beside Emma. "I just assumed that from what Drew said and the way he's living—"

"Oh, Drew. The Chinquapin House is a prime example of their obsession with land. Since that run-down place and its land were originally owned by a distant Wallace cousin, none of the Wallaces would ever consider parting with it. As for the lumber mill, from what I've heard, the original Wallaces were cabinetmakers by trade, so I think they all have sawdust in their veins. When you get time, drive over to Preston Street. There's a big shop there that creates only handmade furniture the old way—no nails, no power tools. Clay Wallace is a master craftsman, and there are about five apprentices working in the shop year round and a long list of eager young men and women just waiting for the chance to work with him."

Emma shook the wrinkles out of a few of Sydney's blouses and hung them up. From the depths of the closet she said, "Clay's the one who encouraged me to start welding. Actually, he bought some of my first equipment and helped me renovate the room over the garage. He's a wonderful man—both the Wallace men are." Emma sat down beside Sydney again and pulled a corner of her lace collar from the back of her dress. She looked directly at Sydney, and just to reassure her friend, she said, "You know, I've been in love with Paul for years, though for a long time I had to keep my feelings to myself. He was married."

"Was?" It was all Sydney could think to say.

"She left him about two years ago. He says he's not ready to make another commitment." Emma smiled sadly and tried to pull the other corner of lace caught from the zipper, too. "My ma always had trouble with this collar catching. If you decide to wear it again, be sure to be careful with the lace."

It had been Emma she'd turned to earlier in the evening when she was dressing and couldn't get the zipper up. Sydney knew her cheeks must have turned as red as apples. There was no way around it. Emma knew all too well what had happened between her and Drew. Sydney's first instinct was to make an excuse. Her second instinct was to lie. She opened her mouth, but nothing came out. All she could do was stare.

Emma fell back on the bed and laughed. "If you could see your face! I swear you'd think I was your mother or this was the eighteenth century and you'd been caught in the haystack with the town rake."

She wasn't about to discuss Drew with her, not when she didn't understand what was happening herself. "I've got to get a hot bath and some sleep, Emma." When her friend stood up and was at the door, Sydney asked, "Is there a decent shoe store in this town? I can't afford to make a fool of myself again with the Fowlers. I've got to buy some shoes."

"Well, if you must, there's Ralph's, but I can't say you'll find anything your style. I don't even buy my shoes there. Actually, I do all my shopping in Dallas or Tyler."

"Anything, Emma. Anything would be preferable to pink tennis shoes or shoes a size too small."

"You might be better off once you visit Ralph's, and then again, you might not." Emma threw the statement over her shoulder as she shut the door. "So don't say I didn't warn you."

How bad could it be? Sydney wondered.

CHAPTER TEN

SYDNEY SAT IN EMMA'S CAR, glanced down at her new shoes and began to laugh. She should have known. Ralph's turned out to be a boot and saddlery shop with a few women's shoes on display. At least she had her own clothes on. The brown linen slacks and matching blouse trimmed in turquoise gave her a small amount of confidence.

"I did try to warn you," Emma said with a chuckle.

There was a hysterical edge to Sydney's laughter from pure exhaustion, and she struggled for control. "Emma, my body requires eight hours of sound sleep for me to function like a normal human. I've had two, and you take me into that shop and try on boots while I hunt for a decent pair of shoes." She smiled, thinking about her diminutive friend in size thirteen cowboy boots stomping around the shop, making faces at old Ralph while she tried on almost every pair of women's shoes he had.

Sydney looked down at her feet again, leaned her head against the window, closed her eyes and laughed. She was sporting a pair of white flats that wouldn't have been so bad if they didn't have long leather ankle straps. The problem was the straps were so long that they wrapped around her ankles four times, and to keep the shoes on, the leather ties had to be tight. "If I lose all feeling in my feet and they turn blue from lack of circulation, it's going to be all your fault. Why the hell wouldn't Mr. Ralph cut them off?''

"And ruin zee design?" Emma asked in an outraged mock-French accent with an East Texas twang. "My dear Syd. Those are Mr. Ralph's creations. He used to be—''

"Don't tell me. I don't want to know about him."

"Well, at least they fit."

"Small favors," Sydney grumbled, and glanced at her watch. "I can't afford to be late for another meeting with the senator, so if you're finished getting your jollies for the day at my expense, let's step on it."

Emma, still chuckling, did as she was told. "What's this about two hours' sleep? I managed four. Ah, let me guess. When I went downstairs to make coffee this morning, I noticed that the box of Wallace papers was missing from the kitchen table. I did lock the front door before we went upstairs, so. . .''

"Yes, Sherlock."

"I deduced that you couldn't sleep, so you reread all those papers, and from that very fake, sincere look on your face, I'd say you found something." She pulled into the hospital parking lot, stopped the car and opened the door. "But, I can also tell by that very contrived frown that you're not going to tell me what it is. So, goodbye. Don't worry about picking me up. Paul will drive me home, or I can always walk." With that, Emma climbed out of the car and closed the door.

Sydney quickly scooted over to the driver's seat and stuck her head out the window. "Don't be mad. I'm not sure if what I found is anything important. I need to check a few things out first."

Emma smiled good-naturedly and waved, but Sydney sat there and watched until her new friend had disappeared into the building. Damn, when she left Wallace she was going to miss Emma. She slipped the car into gear and rolled out of the parking lot.

It didn't take long to reach Rosehill, but Sydney had been so lost in her own thoughts and her problems, that she was a little shocked when the long driveway appeared up ahead. As she got out of the car a moment later and walked up the porch steps, she gave herself a quick pep talk, reminding herself that this was the reason she'd come to Wallace. She'd damn sure better pay attention and do her job, or she was liable to end up without one. She pressed the doorbell, determined not to be distracted by thoughts of Drew, Clay's problems or the mystery of Andrew Joshua and Mary.

"Good morning, Sydney."

She jumped as if she'd been shot, then stared at the senator's aide. "Good morning, John."

"Looks like you were a thousand miles away." He held the door open wider and motioned her inside. "I'm sorry, but the senator and Lauren are still out riding. They should be back any minute."

"That's all right. I think I'm a little early." She followed him through the house into the senator's study and accepted the offer of a cup of coffee. It wasn't until John walked to the back of the room, where a coffee service was set up, that she noticed the other desk and computer. "Who uses the computer?" she asked.

"I do, mostly. But the senator certainly does, and of course Lauren has her own upstairs."

Of course, Sydney groaned to herself, nothing could be *that* easy. She accepted the cup and took a couple of sips as she watched John return to the senator's desk and shuffle papers. "Do they ride every morning?" She pulled out her tape recorder, and a notepad and pen and sat down.

"Yes." He gazed briefly at the recorder. "Is that on?"

"Not yet, why?"

John leaned forward, his hard, narrow face set in earnest, concerned lines that raised her hackles. "We've been hearing some pretty wild things in the past twenty-four hours. I hope you're not taking what some people say seriously, at least not before you run it by us first. I'd hate to see you get embarrassed."

Her voice was polite, soft. "Thank you, John. But I assure you I never write anything I haven't thoroughly checked out."

John visibly relaxed. "That's good to hear. There're a few people in this town who have done nothing but try to discredit and smear the senator." He took a sip of his coffee. "You know, we handpicked you for this interview because of your background. It could be a big boost to your career."

Sydney went cold all over. "Handpicked because of my background? That's a strange choice of words, John. I would have thought you'd have picked me because of my past work."

"Oh my, yes. That, too. But you have to admit that having a fellow Texan, a woman and topnotch journalist writing the article on James was very appealing. And, of course, who your father is made the deciding difference." He went on talking, never noticing the deadly spark in her eyes nor the way her cheeks has gone from bright red to white. "Surely you didn't think we would have invited you here without doing a thorough background check? It did throw us a little when we were told you were using your mother's maiden name. But I can't tell you how pleased we were when we found out that Tom Shannon was your father.''

If she could have leaped across the desk, wrapped her hands around his neck and choked off what he was saying, she would have. Instead, she sat there with every muscle tensed, her white-knuckled fingers curled around the arm of the chair, listening, forcing herself to keep quiet. The pompous ass didn't know he was digging a deep grave for himself and the senator.

''James Fowler will be president someday soon. Neither he nor I are the type to forget our friends—or enemies. James likes you. He respects what you write, and if you play your cards right, someday you could hold a position with his administration, like press secretary.''

Sydney made no acknowledgment of his not-so-subtle bribe. When she neither smiled nor spoke but continued to stare at him, her expression blank and calm, his compliments seemed to dry up and trail away like dust. She let the silence stretch while her white-hot anger cooled and she mentally gathered together the scathing remarks she'd planned. She was just about to voice those remarks in the most sarcastic tone she could manage without losing her temper, when the door opened and laughter broke her concentration.

They were an idyllic couple: beautiful, healthy and perfectly suited to each other. Neither one's good looks overshadowed the other's. She'd seen them so many times around Washington, at various political functions, when they were done up to the nines, that it was a pleasant surprise to see them windblown, scruffy, a little sweaty and sporting genuine smiles. John had said they'd been out riding. For some reason a picture of Lauren and the senator dressed in English riding attire had immediately popped into her head, but she was pleased to see the well-worn jeans, scuffed boots and dusty cowboy hats.

Sydney noticed the warmth of James's greeting and Lauren's coolness. As John hovered, getting them coffee and generally doing everything but drinking it for them, she had a chance to watch the happy couple as she herself was being watched. Lauren hadn't taken her eyes off her. Without knowing how or why, Sydney realized she had an enemy in Lauren. The thought intrigued her.

Sydney figured offense was the best defense, but her mind was working a mile a minute wondering what she'd done to cause that look of disdain in those arctic eyes. She turned the tape recorder on.

James Fowler eyed the machine. "Can I at least sit down first?"

"No time like now to get on with it. Tell me something, Senator, one of your election promises was to start an investigation into some of the outrageous government spending. But as yet I've seen no action on your part. Congress voted to spend two hundred thousand dollars on the study of the sex life of the Japanese quail, five hundred thousand dollars to build a copy of the Great Pyramid of Giza in Indiana, one hundred and fifty thousand dollars to interpret the Hatfield-McCoy feud. It goes on and on—three hundred ninety-four thousand dollars to promote the sale of bull semen and four hundred sixty-five thousand to promote the sale of fried chicken fingers and thirty-seven thousand to study the handling of animal manure in Michigan. Those are some of the ones the taxpayers shake their heads at in total disbelief.

"Then there are those little secret goodies, hidden in bills and budgets. The ones destined to make the voter pause before he votes for the incumbent. How in this volatile political and economic climate can Washington keep passing excessive expenditures? Three hundred and seventy-five thousand to renovate the House beauty parlor, twenty-five thousand to study the location of a new House gym, two million dollars for new office furniture for the Senate, two hundred thousand to determine the placement of television lights in the Senate committee rooms, eight million for new elevators for the Senate—can't you people walk?'

"Oh Lord, help us all," Lauren groaned. "You sound just like one of those horrid little people with those so-called political watch groups." She made the term sound as if something nasty had been shoved under her nose.

Sydney enjoyed watching the senator's and John's expressions change as Lauren put her foot in her mouth. "I write a quarterly column for *D.C. Watch,* Lauren. I have for a couple of years."

"I'm sure my wife didn't mean ..." James said, then let it go and laughed, knowing any explanation he tried would only make it worse.

Lauren Fowler was a powerful woman, shrewd and cunning. She didn't need to be attached to the senator's coattails to swing her influence and weight around. Any businesswoman able to hold her own not only in the Texas market, but on the international scene, as well, was not someone to waste her time and energy with an intense dislike for a reporter.

Sydney knew full well that Lauren shared in every decision John and the party made for the senator. And if the senator and John knew so much about her career and personal life, so did Lauren. The catty comment had been an intentional dig. She knew it, as did the senator and John. But where John appeared pleased with Lauren's remark, the senator looked genuinely puzzled.

"Until the president is given the authority of line edit veto," the senator said, "a lot of these unfortunate bills will slip through. That doesn't mean they should ever be allowed to get to that point. As you're aware, there are special interest groups and dishonest politicians—always have been, always will be. If anyone thinks one man, whether he's a senator or president, can keep the crooks out, he's dreaming. Remember, it's the voters who elect the politicians, and they have the power to vote them out."

"That's a cop-out, Senator, and you know it." She was profoundly disappointed in James Fowler. He'd started out so strong, so full of promise and promises. Now it looked as if the seduction of a higher office had corrupted the incorruptible. The realization made her sad. Was there never to be another Camelot? Was her world never to see peace and happiness again?

"You think I've sold out for a few pieces of gold," the senator said. "I haven't, Sydney." He folded his arms on the desktop and leaned forward. "I've only been in office a couple of years. Some of my cohorts have been there, literally, all their lives. You're a realist. You know you can't rush in and buck the system and expect to survive. I have some good people in Washington who are willing to put their heads on the chopping block because they believe in me, what I stand for and my word. Those things you listed, I've been quietly investigating them, finding out who's responsible. Give me some time, a chance to make the changes I've talked about. I've preached until I'm blue in the face that a change is coming, that the American people are going to rise up and strike back. Someday, soon, I'll be in a position to make those changes. They will come, I promise.''

The sincerity was real, but could he survive the political machine? Sydney wondered. They talked for almost three hours, their time broken only occasionally by Lauren or John adding their thoughts or answering a question she'd asked them directly. She decided the interview had gone so well that she'd venture to change the subject.

''You've taken a controversial stand for the American Indian and his bid to reclaim some of his land. You know everyone is always empathizing with the Indian's plight—giving lip service is always politically correct— but you've taken a public stand that has angered the Bureau of Indian Affairs to the point that they've come out and condemned your plans and made some pretty wild accusations of their own.''

''You mean they've trashed my plans at every turn and called them un-American. What the bureau is hot under the collar about is that I want to return some public lands to the Indians. You'd think from the uproar that I was talking about stripping whole communities from their homes. What I'm proposing is returning national parkland, not all of it, but a small portion. Listen, if our Indian problem existed in another country, don't you think the U.S. would be outraged at their treatment? We've gone to war for democracy and people's freedom. It's time our country honors its heritage and faces up to what we've done to the first people of this land.''

Sydney nodded, liking what he had to say; realistically, though, she was doubtful. ''It's a noble cause, and I don't mean that sarcastically. I admire it and you,

Senator. But others have tried what you're doing and haven't gotten any further than you."

"Thank you." He leaned back, relaxed and pleased with himself. "But I expect to come out the winner. Now, may I ask you a question?"

"Of course," she said.

"Off the record, and will you turn the recorder off?"

She did as she was asked and waited.

"Sydney, you can't live in a small town without hearing about everything that's going on. I understand Emma Paulson's house was broken into last evening, but nothing was stolen."

She was pleased to hear that, small town or not, the local police were not inclined to tell tales. Howard had kept his mouth shut about the raid on her computer and the missing diskettes. "That's right. As far as Emma can tell, nothing was taken. It looks like a case of vandalism."

The senator shook his head in disgust. "Since you came here, this place has been a hotbed of gossip. Mainly about what happened on Piney Creek Road the day of your accident, then last evening at the restaurant . . . I don't know if Drew was just trying to kick up more dust or if he was serious. You can never tell with his sense of humor. What's all this about Andrew Joshua?"

She had no reason not to tell them, yet she hesitated, and she immediately felt the change in the room—a growing tension that hadn't been there before. Lauren looked nervous, John was definitely uncomfortable, the senator a little strained. Then she realized that if they'd already heard the story, even just parts of it, it was no wonder they were anxious. Most people she knew didn't believe in ghosts, including herself.

Sydney told her story, surprised at their total silence and rapt expressions. When she finished, they stared at her for a long moment. It was Lauren who spoke first.

"Of course it was Drew. Who else would have done it? Besides, from what I've seen and heard, he's the spitting image of Andrew Joshua. He's the only one who could pull it off. But why wouldn't he admit it?"

John Laker's head bobbed vigorously in agreement. "A better question is why would he be so adamant about it being Andrew Joshua?"

"I don't think it was Drew," Sydney found herself saying. Lauren and John looked at her as if she'd just sprouted horns. "I've never had anything like that happen to me. At first I was sure it was Drew, then I tried to pass it off as a hallucination, but how would I know Andrew Joshua's name? I've never been to Wallace. Then there's the portrait of Mary Clayton-Wallace, the one you have hanging over your mantel. I saw that same portrait that night." She glanced at Senator Fowler. "You're very quiet."

"Puzzled. Why would he, or whoever it was, say he found Mary? You know her body was never found. Now, all of a sudden someone's claiming he found her. And if he did, maybe the mystery will be solved once and for all."

"James," Lauren said in a scolding tone, "surely you don't believe in ghosts. Andrew Joshua is long dead and buried."

"Stranger things have happened, sweetheart."

"Dammit, James. I'm sick to death of the Wallaces."

"Lauren . . ." the senator warned.

Sydney was fascinated by the interchange and would have loved for it to go on, but Lauren's mouth folded into harsh lines and she immediately shut up.

"I'm sorry, Sydney," the senator said. "but my father was constantly talking about the Wallaces and the Fowlers. He was a gentle, just man who never believed Darcy or old Judge Jacob gave Andrew Joshua a fair deal. After he stepped down as head of the family oil company, with lots of time on his hands, Dad took up genealogy. I guess you could say he became obsessed with the mystery. Dad did extensive research and organized the Clayton/Fowler papers."

"Clayton/Fowler papers?" Sydney repeated.

"Mounds of them," James Fowler said with a laugh, then sobered. "Land records, death certificates, marriage certificates, old letters, personal papers, old newspaper articles, tax records and every dry, uninteresting legal item that was ever filed. Remember, Samuel Clayton was Mary's father, and Darcy was a relation. I was never very interested in Dad's hobby and usually ignored his ramblings. I'm afraid Lauren was the one who always had to listen to his long-winded stories."

Sydney managed to hide her excitement as she remembered the one clue she thought she might have found in Clay Wallace's box of papers. "So you never read the Clayton/Fowler papers?"

"That's right, but I did read about the trial," he said. "And I must say I agree with Dad. Darcy and his father should never have been involved. They should have disqualified themselves."

"Senator," Sydney said, leaning forward in the chair, "Clay gave me a box stuffed with papers that contain information about Mary's murder—the trial transcripts, interviews with people who were alive then, and so on. I must tell you, I don't believe Andrew Joshua killed Mary." What was she saying? She could be ruining her career over a ghost story.

James gazed at her with a thoughtful expression. "You think Darcy did it, don't you?"

"I don't know. I'm just sure Andrew Joshua didn't do it. Do you think your father would talk to me?" She watched his expression shift from interest to profound sadness.

"My father has Alzheimer's. It started about five years ago and has progressively gotten worse. He remembers very little now, often not even me."

"God, I'm sorry," Sydney said. She knew she was being a little callous by asking, "Tell me something, Senator, do you keep a journal?"

"Yes. Why?"

"I find that most politicians do. Do you know if Darcy or the judge kept journals?"

The Senator laughed. "Volumes of them."

"Could I read through them?"

"Of course...if I knew where they were." He turned to Lauren. "Are they here or at the nursing home?"

Lauren had her back to them, pouring herself a cup of coffee. When she turned around, she rested her hand on James's shoulder, then patted it. "I have no idea, James. I haven't seen those old things in years."

Someone was lying; like a good reporter Sydney felt it in her gut. Either it was the senator's generous offer that was false or Lauren's statement that she didn't know where the journals were. She was trying to figure it out when the senator's next remark threw her totally off balance.

"Darling, perhaps you could go over to the nursing home and ask Dad's nurse if he's rational today, then see if he can tell you where the journals are. And we'll look in the attic, too. By God, I'd like to find out what happened once and for all. I..." He fell silent and stared out the window. "You know all this talk about the journals has struck a chord of memory. Dad used to have quite a few good days and was always harping about those journals, but I'd heard it so many times, I never paid attention. Still, there was something he kept saying about a volume gone or missing...." He shrugged and brought his attention back to the people in the room. "I don't remember anymore." He wrapped his arm around Lauren's waist and drew her close. "Don't look so glum, darling. Actually, this could be fun. We'll make it a kind of scavenger hunt."

They all jumped when the phone rang. John answered it and put the person on hold. "It's the Speaker of the House, Senator."

Sydney and the senator rose at the same time. She tucked the tape recorder in her purse and said, "I have to be leaving. Thank you for offering to look for the journals."

"Nonsense." He circled the desk and shook her extended hand. "Maybe we can clear up some of this ancient history. Are you coming back tomorrow?"

"I think so. Let me see what I have. I'll call."

"Fine, Lauren will walk you out."

Lauren trod silently behind her, and Sydney could feel the hostility radiating from her like heat. She was just passing the living room when she stopped and gazed at the portrait of Mary Clayton-Wallace. "May I?"

"Of course." The words were polite and brusque.

Sydney walked straight to the painting. "She was beautiful, wasn't she?" Odd, but those blue eyes of Mary's seemed to be smiling today, and Sydney could have sworn there was a secret little tilt to the corners of her mouth that hadn't been there before....

"Yes, she was. That glowing complexion." Lauren sighed. "Sydney, you know that the Wallaces are using you, don't you? They're manipulating you to dig into the death of Andrew Joshua to embarrass my husband."

"Oh, I don't think so, Lauren. The senator doesn't seem concerned."

"My husband believes in truth, Sydney. And I don't know how you can just dismiss what the Wallaces are doing to you. Don't you know they'd love nothing better than to get their hands on Rosehill?"

Sydney's head jerked around. "What are you talking about? They want Rosehill?"

"You see," Lauren said with a pitying expression, "they didn't tell you everything, did they? Rosehill might have been built by Jean-Luc Darcy, but remember, it was given to the Clayton family, Samuel Clayton, when he married the Darcy girl. When Andrew Joshua killed Mary, old Samuel went crazy. Clay Wallace would have been his only surviving, direct heir, and as irrational as it was, he hated that child. Hated him so much he wouldn't have anything to do with him, refused to take him in or even see him. Some distant Wallace relatives raised Clay." Lauren turned to stare at the portrait of Mary.

"Sad, isn't it? Before the old man died, he had a new, airtight will drawn up. That's when he left all of his holdings, including Rosehill, to his wife's sister—Darcy's mother—making sure no Wallace would ever get their hands on anything that belonged to a Clayton. For years those Wallace relatives who raised Clay filed lawsuits for the child's sake, but nothing ever came of them."

Sydney gazed up at the portrait of Mary without really seeing, but refused to let Lauren see her face. She knew she must have looked like the way she felt, as if someone had just kicked her in the stomach. Why hadn't Drew or his grandfather told her any of this? Her gaze focused on Mary's face, and she suddenly felt warm all over. She gathered her senses, mentally stiffened her backbone and turned to Lauren. "I don't think this has anything to do with land or greed. It's about love and justice, Lauren. Mostly, I think, about an undying love that deserves the justice of the truth. Maybe love does last forever. It's a sobering thought, isn't it?" Sydney glanced at Mary once more, smiled, then walked out of the room with Lauren at her heels.

The senator's wife opened the front door for Sydney and followed her down the porch steps to the car. When Sydney slipped behind the wheel, Lauren put up her hand to keep her from closing the door. "I like you, Sydney. When this interview is over, why don't you take some time off, come be my guest at my spa for a week. Relax. Think about your future. Surely you don't want to be a reporter for the rest of your life."

The anger bubbled up, and Sydney clamped down on it hard. First the offer of the press secretary position, now a gratis week at an expensive, very exclusive health spa. "Thanks, Lauren," she managed, "but spas aren't my thing." She tried to pull the door shut, but Lauren held on.

"Sydney, I love my husband. He's a good man, an honest man. He deserves to be president one day. He'll be a wonderful leader for this county. Please don't do anything to hurt him.''

Sydney realized that it must have cost Lauren dearly in pride to beg. She shut the door, then stuck her head out the window. "For what it's worth, Lauren, I think the senator would make a good leader, too.'' Though she wanted the theft of her computer disks kept a secret, her instincts told her this was a good chance to drop the bomb and see if maybe the enemy ducked. "But I've been lied to, had my friend's house broken into and something of mine stolen. I'm going to find answers regardless whose feelings and reputations might get hurt.'' She was disappointed; Lauren didn't so much as blink a long eyelash.

SYDNEY FLEW UP the driveway to the Chinquapin House, slammed on the brakes, marched up the rickety, creaking porch steps and was about to pound on the door when she realized that it was standing open a crack. When she pushed the door wide open, the blare of music, muffled a little by the solid wood, increased enough to awaken the dead. There was absolutely no use in announcing her presence, so she just walked in. She was hot, tired and angry enough to spit nails.

She found Drew in what she thought would be the living room. The walls were spotted with water stains and missing wallpaper in places. She noticed four square openings cut up high in each wall and the black boxes filling them, and realized that they were speakers. There were long strips of faded floral wallpaper dangling from the ceiling and a huge five-bladed fan hanging on a cobweb-matted chain. If the walls were in a tattered state, the floors were magnificent: beautiful, narrow strips of pine, waxed to a mirror shine. Still, it was the man standing in the center of the room, his back to her, who snatched and held her attention.

Bare flesh, lots of it, was the first thing she noticed. He was barefoot and wearing only a pair of cutoffs that hung low on his narrow hips. Those jeans, she thought, were just a hair short of being indecent. Her advantage gave her time to gaze her fill. The angry line of her mouth softened a little as she measured the long, shapely legs, the way his narrow waist veed out to his broad back. Her eyes caressed the muscular shoulders and arms. That this man had been the class nerd in his youth made her come out with an unladylike snort.

He must have sensed her, because he turned and she got a full blast of naked chest and a steady stare from those seductive green eyes. For a moment she let herself get lost in that look of hunger. There was something in those eyes that warmed her more than the outside temperature ever could. She didn't move, smile or welcome his approach, but just kept looking at him, taking in every detail from the ragged edge of his cutoffs to the smooth, hard line of him. He was saying something, moving his lips. She pointed to her ears and shook her head, letting him know that the music was too loud.

He paused beside the stereo long enough to lower the volume, then reached for her arm and pulled her up against his chest. She put out her hand to push him away, felt his warm skin and hesitated. She was too angry to be made love to. Then she realized that Drew wasn't trying to seduce her; he wanted to dance. She was stiff in his arms, wanting only to talk, to tell him what hell she'd been through. His arm around her shoulders pulled her so close that she was pressed against the length of his body as he moved off, slowly.

"Drew..."

He shook his head and pressed her face into the curve of his shoulder, then began massaging her scalp and neck. She'd never danced so close before. His hips stroked hers, and when she tried to inch back a fraction, his other hand slipped from the center of her back to her bottom and held her steadily in place. The music was slow and romantic. The singer's voice was deep, soft and hungry with love and wanting.

Her body turned traitor; it had a mind of its own and relaxed. She gave in and let the music soak away her anger. She closed her eyes, listening to the words. "Who is it?" she whispered in his ear. He could have kissed her then, kissed her until she couldn't breathe, but he didn't.

"Miss New Wave, That's Michael Bolton," he whispered back.

He could have kissed her ear the way he did the night before, but he didn't. "He's not from the sixties."

"No, but he sings like the sixties."

He could have kissed her eyes shut, sighed and murmured that she was driving him crazy, too, that he ached for her, but he didn't. "What's the song?"

"'How Am I Supposed to Live Without You.' Now hush, and listen to the man sing his heart out."

Sydney closed her eyes and did as she was told. His warmth was as seductive as his caressing hands, his male scent a soothing balm to her ragged nerves. He could have stripped her naked, teased, kissed and made love to her on the floor again. She wouldn't have resisted. He could have talked to her about love, about the yearning, the loneliness and the empty feeling she had when she kept telling herself she had to leave this place, go back to her own life. He could have asked her not to go, but he didn't.

The music stopped and the disappointment was visceral. The silence pounded against her eardrums. She thought she could hear both of their hearts beating, and waited. When he just kept holding her, she lifted her head and looked at him. "Does this place have a bed?"

"Five bedrooms." There was a smile in his voice.

"No. I said a bed. You know, those wide things that are soft, where people sleep and sometimes make love."

"Ah, yes, I have one of those. A big one, but I don't think that's really what you want."

Sydney wanted to scream that it was exactly what she wanted, but she bit back the words. She was suddenly insecure. Had he just been playing with her? Was she making a fool of herself?

"Stop that," he said.

"What?"

"What you're thinking. It's written on your face." He drew her to him, kissing her long and hard, deep enough to let her know how much he yearned for her, and if that wasn't proof enough, he grasped her hand and slid it between them. "Does that feel like a man who doesn't want and need you? Sydney, I'd beg, borrow and steal a chance to make love to you again. But you walked in here all ready to tear me apart."

"Music soothes the savage beast, or something like that, right?" she asked, and firmly pulled away from him.

"When you're all teeth and claws, yes. I wasn't about to be on the receiving end of them. Now, tell me what's set you off." He glanced at the peeling ceiling and said, "And please, God, don't let it be something I've done."

Damn, he had the most annoying habit of making her laugh . . . and mostly at herself.

CHAPTER ELEVEN

SYDNEY TOOK a deep breath. "Did you do this?" she asked, gesturing to the room.

"That's a nice safe subject, but don't you want to tell me what happened?"

She smiled. "Let me cool off some.... Tell me about what you're doing here. Are these the original floors?"

He decided not to press her. "Yes, after a lot of work. I was just admiring my handiwork. The last of three top coats. They're beautiful, aren't they?"

"That's an understatement, but why did you do the floors first?"

"Because they required the least amount of work, and I hate putting up Sheetrock and taping walls." He slung an arm around her shoulders and led her from the room. "Let me show you the rest of the house—only the remodeled rooms. You'd probably faint at the others." He guided her down a long hall and pushed on a heavy swinging door, holding it wide while she passed him. The sudden blast of cold air made goose bumps stand up on his arms. "I've only air-conditioned the workroom, kitchen and my bedroom. When the rest of the house is finished, I'll put in central heat and air." He watched Sydney as she came to an abrupt halt and then turned in a circle, taking in his work.

She couldn't believe it. The kitchen was huge, with a fireplace and seating area at one end. At the opposite end was a cooking island of restaurant quality, with gleaming copper pots hanging above it. "I hope with all this that you cook."

"One of my many talents."

"You did all this yourself?" she asked in awe.

"Clay all but raised me, and the Wallaces have always had a love affair with woodworking. Come on, I'll show you the upstairs."

She admired the beautiful curved stairway and the wainscot. When she followed him into the equally frigid bedroom, she could only stand and gape while Drew quickly rounded the room picking up discarded clothes. The king-size bed was unmade and rumpled, and her heart kicked up its beat. She forced her gaze away from the bed and glanced around.

Drew's craftsmanship was as much in evidence here as in the other rooms. The abundant wood trim around the wide windows and doors was painted a glossy bright white, and each window had plantation shutters instead of curtains. The walls were the shocker, and it took a second to become used to the bright Chinese red. But after she'd blinked a couple of times, she realized she liked it. His bedspread was in bold shades of green. A comfortable pecan brown leather chair, love seat and a table were set off to the side in a sitting area. Drew was not only a genius but an artist. His combination of colors and textures made her feel dull and totally inadequate. "I'm impressed," she said with a gulp.

"Ah, but come see this." He pushed open another door and she walked through. The bathroom. It took a minute to take it all in: the shining brass, the white tile with ivy trim running the circumference of the room. Off to the side was a walk-in shower, and dominating the center of the bathroom was a hunter green whirl-pool. "It's spectacular, Drew."

"When Merlin and my games get to me, I work out my frustrations with physical labor."

She followed him out, speechless, and watched as he sat on the side of the bed, crossed his legs and patted the edge. She hesitated.

"This is the bed you asked for."

"I can see that."

He patted the mattress again. "A nice soft bed."

She smiled and sauntered over, then pushed down on it with her hand. "Yes, it's soft, all right."

"Inviting, too, don't you think?" He caressed the wrinkled sheets. "Guaranteed to make you forget your troubles and woes."

She flopped down, then fell back. "Do you have a knife?" When he paled a little, she stuck out her foot. "I tied these damn leather straps so tight I'll never get them off."

Laughing, Drew pulled one of her feet across his knees and began worrying the knots. After a few minutes of scowls, furious frowns and lots of mumbling, the second shoe fell to the floor. He massaged the red welts, then kissed them before he set her feet down and stretched out beside her. His fingers idly fiddled with the buttons of her blouse. "I like this." One finger traced the turquoise piping on the blouse. "But I like the flower number you wore with the pink running shoes yesterday." He began nibbling her earlobe.

"You would." She closed her eyes. The top button of her blouse popped open, then the second, then the third gave way, and the tip of his finger insinuated itself between her breasts.

"I like a free-spirited woman who doesn't believe in a bra."

"The only one I have that isn't East Texas red ended up in the wash this morning."

"Don't disillusion me. I like the image of the free-spirited woman better."

A tease was a tease in any gender. Sydney rolled onto her side, threw one leg over his hips, threaded her fingers through thick, curly hair, pulled his head to hers and kissed him long, deep and with the throb of passion that Drew seem to draw from her with a mere touch.

She loved the slow way he finished unbuttoning her blouse, the way his lips followed his hands. She caressed his bare chest, then slid her hands down to his cutoffs, quickly working the buttons. Cotton and skin—she'd never thought the textures could be so intoxicating.

For a minute they struggled with her slacks until she lay back and kicked both legs in a scissor motion. Drew began to laugh as he worked her slacks and underwear off. Then she molded her body to his and wrapped her arms around his neck, and their lips met with equal hunger.

She should have known this time wasn't about to be a replay of last night. He was slow, sometimes painfully so, until she urged him to go on faster but he would only chuckle. He drove her crazy, his mouth and hands everywhere, and just when she thought he was going to give her some release from the roaring in her ears and the ache below, he would slow down again, let her breathe, then take her back up to the brink. She couldn't stand it any longer and told him so. Then all she saw or heard was the light behind her eyelids and his voice in her ear.

They lay panting, drenched with the sweat of passion. After a while, when their breathing slowed and their heartbeats calmed down, he asked, "Can you move?"

She kept her eyes shut, totally spent. "Don't ask me to." Drew eased away, and she felt the cold draft, then the warmth returned, but it was only the covers. She sighed, too limp to move or protest. Then she realized she must have fallen asleep, because the next thing she knew, Drew had her in his arms and was carrying her somewhere. She was lowered into velvet warmth, and she jerked fully awake.

"Careful," he said from behind her. He settled her body between his spread legs and pulled her head back on his chest.

Bubbles tickled her nose and warm water lapped at the tips of her breasts. "I've died and gone to heaven?"

"That's a close description."

She snuggled against him and eyed her surroundings, taking in the television on the pedestal, the cordless phone that sat on the shelf within easy reach, and the remote control. "Do you live in here?"

"Sometimes, when Merlin has driven me crazy because I can't get his head to move naturally, or I've spent too many hours drawing on the computer or working on the house. It's nice to come in here, turn on the whirlpool, the music or television and relax." His arms tightened around her waist. "But I must say, you're much more comforting than all those things."

Sydney's head was resting on his shoulder, and she tilted it back so she could see his face. "Has your family been trying to get Rosehill?"

"What?"

"Rosehill. It once belonged to Mary's family. If by some miracle Andrew Joshua could be cleared beyond a doubt of Mary's murder, would that leave a legal opening big enough for your grandfather to sue the Fowlers for possession of Rosehill?"

"That is the craziest thing I've ever heard. Clay has never tried to reclaim Rosehill or any of the other Fowler properties. Where in the hell did this come from? Better still, who did it come from?" He still held her, but he twisted her around a little so he could see her better. "I think you'd better tell me what happened to make you come here ready to kill me." She opened her mouth and he gave her a quick kiss. "From the beginning."

"They tried to bribe me. Can you believe that?"

"Who? Not James?"

"No, of course not, but I don't know for sure if he knew anything about it."

"Well, there's only two others left—Johnenstein and his trusty sidekick, the only walking, talking ice sculpture, the Queen of Chill." Sydney began laughing so hard that he had to grab hold of her slipping body.

"Johnenstein is too short to make a good Frankenstein's monster. Why do you do that?" she asked, trying to sound stern. "Always making me laugh when I want to be angry."

"Never mind. What did Johnenstein offer you?"

"A job as James's press secretary."

He whistled. "With his career potential that could be a plum position." He raised an eyebrow when she didn't respond. "And the Queen of Chill, what did she drop on you?"

"I'll have to say her offer was a little more subtle. She decided I'd been working too hard, and an all-expense-paid week at her spa would be just the thing." She drifted off into thoughtful silence, then continued. "When she was sure I wasn't going to bite, she turned human and begged me not to do anything to ruin the senator's political chances."

Drew snorted. "She just wants to be First Lady."

"Probably, but she does love James, Drew. She also believes in him and wants the best for him. It's a little sad, I think." Sydney shivered, and Drew readjusted the hot water.

"I was leaving Rosehill, but I wanted to see Mary's portrait one more time. That's when Lauren reminded me that Rosehill used to belong to Mary's family. Then she told me that old Samuel had cut Clay out of his will and wouldn't have anything to with him."

"That's right, and as far as I know, only one suit was filed against the Fowlers on Clay's behalf, and that was right after old Samuel died." He wiped a glob of bubbles from Sydney's cheek. "I wonder why Lauren brought that up? She knows better." He leaned his head back on the edge of the tub and closed his eyes. "Maybe she's trying to send you off on a wild-goose chase."

"You mean a red herring? I don't know. Why? Why would she want to keep me busy researching something else? If they know as much about me as they say, then they know full well that I'm not about to drop the story on the senator."

He raised his head and stared at her. "What do you mean, they know so much about you?"

"Oh hell, I haven't told you that part. John made a point of telling me he knew who my father was, that it was a big factor in picking me to do the interview."

"Jeez, they seem bent on ticking you off, don't they? That's not politically smart, Sydney. And if anything, they are a smart and savvy bunch. Something's funny, and I don't mean ha-ha."

"Come to think of it," she mused out loud, "you should have seen their faces when I mentioned the journals."

"What journals?" he asked.

She dropped into a thoughtful silence, playing the scene over in her mind. "Surprise—that was the senator's expression. John looked sick and Lauren... I think she paled a little."

"What journals?" Drew demanded.

"Oh, I didn't tell you? After you left Emma's this morning, I reorganized the Wallace papers by date and reread them. I found something that struck me. In one of the interviews, the old woman who was the daughter of Darcy Fowler's cook and a child then, remembers, and I quote, 'them men reading and scratching in those books.' I assumed scratching was writing." She pushed away from him and sat up straight. "Drew, politicians are notorious journal or diary keepers, though God only knows why. These books usually end up being the ruin of their careers when they fall into the wrong hands. Still, politicians seem to have some egotistical craving to leave their thoughts and deeds in writing. That's human nature, and I don't think human nature changes. I took a wild stab and asked if Darcy or Judge Jacob had kept journals, and James immediately said they had. He even offered to find them and let me read them."

"Tell me, did Lauren's bombshell about Rosehill come before or after the offer to let you read the journals?"

"After." She gazed off into the distance. "The red herring . . ."

"As Emma would say, neat."

"Right."

She was angry all over again and without thinking, she quickly got out of the tub. It was only Drew's loud protest, his demand to know what she was going to do that made her realize she didn't have any idea. "Do? Now? I haven't the foggiest." She climbed back into the tub. "I hate being taken for a fool," she grumbled.

"I can see that." He waited until she'd settled down beside him, then picked up the remote control. Music flooded the bathroom. He began to hum, then said, "That's 'Cover Me' by Percy Sledge."

"Another great flash from the past?"

"That's right," he said with a laugh.

She'd been waiting for this. "Wonderful lyrics."

"The best came out of the sixties."

This was too easy, she thought. He was falling right into her trap. "I seem to remember a song from the sixties with lyrics better than that."

"Name it."

"'Purple People Eaters.'"

"That's from the fifties." He stared at her.

"Oh, yeah." She was going to have to have a talk with the music feature editor at the paper about his filing. Before she'd left Emma's house, she'd hooked up her phone modem to her computer and accessed her newspaper's music archives, requesting a list of sixties rock and roll songs and artists. "What about 'My Ding-a-Ling'?"

"What?" He sat up so fast that the water in the tub came precariously close to splashing over the edge.

"Or the unforgettable words of 'Yakety Yak'?" His mouth fell open. "The sensual language of romance of 'Charlie Brown,' 'Little Egypt' and 'The Streak.'" The look on his face was priceless, then he started to laugh and she had a hard time keeping her own expression somber. "I mean, I'd be all over a guy if he sang 'Poison Ivy' in my ear."

When he could talk, Drew said, "All right, I concede some of the songs don't have the most tender and endearing lyrics. What I'd like to know is how someone who doesn't know squat about rock and roll knows about those?"

"I'm turning into a prune," Sydney said, neatly evading the question and his sudden lunge for her as she stepped out of the tub, wrapped herself in a towel, then headed for the bedroom. She quickly rounded the bed and was picking up her discarded clothes from the floor when Drew padded in.

"Do you have go back to the Fowlers' today?"

She shook out her linen slacks. "No."

"Good." He slipped on his Jockey shorts, then stepped into his cutoffs.

Though there had been an earlier invitation to stay for dinner, she didn't know how he felt now and didn't know how to ask to stay. "I guess I'll go back to Emma's and write some of my story." She wasn't enthusiastic about the thought of work, and he must have noticed.

"Why don't you stick around here?" He started digging in the bottom drawer of a chest, pulled out a faded pair of jeans and threw them at Sydney, smiling when she managed to catch them before they wrapped around her head. "I'll fix us a late lunch, then put you to work helping in the living room."

Sydney held up the jeans. "What are these for?" She caught the cotton shirt he pitched over his shoulder.

"Work clothes. You can't very well tear down Sheetrock in those." He nodded to her own clothes, then held up a handkerchief. "This should cover your hair."

She hesitated momentarily. "I don't know, Drew. Emma's kindness might just run so far. I don't think she really planned to work all day, and I have monopolized her car lately."

"I'll tell you what. Get dressed. I'll go start lunch and call Emma. Maybe she and Paul will come by for dinner. I'll fire up the pit and cook steaks."

Lunch and dinner. It was an offer she couldn't refuse. He was almost out the door when she said, "I've never done any remodeling."

"That's all right. All you have to know how to do is use a crowbar and hammer."

He was gone before she could say anything more. She stood there a moment staring at the empty doorway, then started dressing, taking time to inspect herself in the full-length mirror. The handkerchief made her look like a scrubwoman. The shirt with rolled-up sleeves hung down to her knees, and the jeans...she had to do something about the jeans. They were too long and too big in the waist. When she leaned down to roll up the legs, they actually fell down around her feet. She looked around for a belt, then shrugged, grabbed a handful of material, glanced once more in the mirror and frowned. Well, she wouldn't win any beauty contest.

Sydney walked into the kitchen, holding on to the waistband of the jeans. "Do you have a belt or something?"

Drew set down the head of lettuce, tomato and jar of sandwich spread he'd been balancing on the granite island counter. "Sure." He disappeared through the butler's pantry, then returned with a length of rope and handed it to her.

Sydney threaded the rope through the belt loops, tied a knot in front, then climbed up on a stool and eyed the array of items strewn across the counter. "What's all this?"

"A Drew special. Now, watch a master at work and don't ask questions." He slid a cutting board over to her, then the lettuce and a big vine-ripened tomato. "Slice the tomato, not too thin, though, and shred some lettuce. By the way, Emma and Paul are going to come for dinner, so you don't need to worry about keeping her car."

"Good." She almost cut her finger as she did her task while trying to watch him out of the corner of her eye. He was putting together a mammoth poor boy sandwich. He split a loaf of French bread, liberally spread it with what she guessed was his own secret spread, then began piling on slices of different cheeses and meats and dill pickles. Her stomach growled, and she shoved the tomato and lettuce closer so he could reach them. But Drew picked up the plate, placed it in the refrigerator, then wrapped the sandwich in foil. She looked at the sandwich, then at Drew, and hinted just how hungry she was in case he had missed her drooling. "I'm starving, Drew."

He shook his head. "A little hard labor will enrich the flavor and make you appreciate the chef that much more."

She gave a longing glance at the wrapped sandwich and stood up. "What you're saying is, I have to work for my supper?"

"Oh, no. Supper's free. It's lunch you have to work for."

She grumbled under her breath all the way through the butler's pantry and into the living room. When he placed a crowbar in her hands, she weighed the idea of a forced escape to the kitchen. She was giving it more than a passing thought when Drew disappeared like magic once again. This time when he returned, he was carrying a couple of pairs of heavy socks and a beat-up pair of loafers.

"You can't walk around here barefoot, especially when we start knocking down Sheetrock. There're liable to be nails."

She laid down the crowbar, sat on the floor and pulled on the socks, then stuck her feet into the over-size shoes. "Yours?"

"Yes." He held out his hand, hoisted her up and watched as she tested the fit and feel.

"They'll do, but I wouldn't want to take a hike." She put on the plastic safety glasses he handed her, tied a dish towel around her face to keep out the dust, then picked up the crowbar and smacked the end in the palm of her hand. "Show me what you want me to do." She waited while he quickly spread canvas drop cloths over the floor and set up the ladder, explaining that he'd take the high-wire act. She glanced up at the twelve-foot ceilings and the shaky ladder and nodded. Anxious to get started, she listened to his instructions.

She never realized destroying something could be so satisfying. It gave her a gut-level, primitive feeling of power. Every swing of the hammer was a strike against her problems, real or imagined. She attacked her ene-mies and watched them crumble in the chunks of Sheetrock and dust.

Drew propped his elbows on the top of the ladder, smiling and watching. "We're destroying the Sheetrock, Sydney, not the whole living room."

Sydney glanced up and laughed. "I tell you, Drew, everyone should do this. It's wonderful therapy. Works out all your frustrations and anger."

"I know. It's also great when I can't make Merlin do what he's supposed to."

She wedged the curved end of the crowbar into her hammered-out hole and popped a large piece of Sheetrock out.

"Tell me something, Sydney. What do you want to do with your life? Will your career as a reporter still be satisfying years from now? Do you want to work on a newspaper forever?"

She worked the crowbar, grunting when more leverage was needed. "I love journalism, and I especially love writing about politics. Maybe because politicians are from so many walks of life. What they do and say, the laws they pass, are our future. They affect our everyday life, what we do and say and how we live." She set the crowbar down, picked up the hammer and began knocking large holes in the Sheetrock, all the while talking and punctuating each word with a slam of the hammer. "No other occupation affects the American people and economy so much. Politicians are a great contrast. They're a mystery, yet they're predictable. There's great compassion in them, greed, evil, intrigue and goodness, too. I've never felt more alive and active than I have the past couple of years writing my column for the *D.C. Watch*. But—" she reared back like a batter at the plate, the hammer even with her shoulder, then swung at the wall "—this trip has made me homesick. Homesick for Texas."

"All those things you love and hate in politics aren't exclusive to the Capitol or Washington, D.C. Texas politics are pretty varied, too. So why don't you move back?" he asked.

"And do what? Work for my father? Work for another newspaper that hired me because they're either friends of my father or an enemy and want to use me as a burr in his backside?"

"What's the *D.C. Watch*?"

"A quarterly newspaper that reports on the politicians, how they voted, what their expenditures are. We compare their campaign promises with what they're doing. We watch what special interest groups are wining and dining them, what lobbyists are trying to seduce them. It's like a quarterly report card. I'd love to start one here for Texas politicians. Shake up the wheelers and dealers of the state."

"Then do it," he said.

"Sure, Drew," she said sarcastically. "First I'd have to find a paper that'd be willing to print it for me. And do you know any paper or its owner that's not tied in some way to a politician's purse strings? I don't know of many."

"Dreams are made to come true, Sydney," Drew said. "You just have to help them along a little. Let me see what I can come up with."

They worked along the wall, with Drew on the ladder and Sydney below, until they'd finished the room. Drew glanced at the ceiling and asked Sydney if she was ready to tackle some real work. Sydney slid the safety glasses onto the top of her head, pulled the dish towel down off her nose and mouth and stared up at the ceiling. "I will not climb that ladder."

"Okay. I'll knock it down, you drag the rubble out of the way and help me move the ladder."

He was a relentless slave driver. By the time they'd done about half the ceiling, she was ready to collapse from fatigue and hunger. So when the doorbell rang, she dropped the Sheetrock she was holding and dashed out of the room.

The caller was so unexpected that she could only stand there and stare. The senator was getting an eyeful, too. He threw up his hands and yelled, "I give up." Sydney laughed and yanked off her dish-towel mask.

The senator leaned forward and squinted. "Sydney?"

Sydney copied his expression and movements. "Senator?" And she wasn't just trying to mock him, either. The usually immaculate, well-groomed, Ivy League senator was dressed in loose-fitting, plaid Bermuda shorts, a knit golf shirt that was at least ten years old, faded and stretched out of shape, and badly weathered Top-sider deck shoes. Sydney noticed that the toes turned up and the right shoe had a hole where the stitching had broken, so she could see his little toe.

"I called Emma to find out where you were," James said. "I hope you don't mind my tracking you down."

"No, of course not. What can I do for you?"

"Well, if you'll let me in, I'll tell you."

They laughed and Sydney stepped aside. Drew walked into the hall and stopped, then headed for James with an outstretched hand. "Damn, Chunky, you mean Lauren let you out in public dressed like that?"

"She's at the nursing home visiting Dad." He shook hands then moved past Drew, stopped at the open doorway to the living room and whistled. He looked at

Drew over his shoulder, then glanced at Sydney.
"Cheap labor?"

Drew chuckled. "No, I have to feed her lunch. Want
to join us?"

"No, thanks. But I'd like to talk to both of you."

Drew brushed at the white powder covering his bare
chest, then looked at Sydney. "Go on into the kitchen,
Chunky—" he pointed the way "—while we wash up."
He grasped Sydney's arm and led her to the back of the
house, pushed open a bathroom door, peered around
the corner, then firmly closed it. "I wonder what he
wants."

"I take it he's not a regular visitor here?" she asked
as water sputtered and spit from the old faucet. Drew
kicked the pipe underneath the chipped porcelain sink,
and the water poured out in a steady stream.

"As far as I know, he's never been near the property. Did you take in his appearance, and I don't mean
his clothes."

"Looks like he's been doing a little remodeling himself." Sydney took off Drew's shirt and shook out the
dust, then slipped it back on. She washed her face and
arms, then hurriedly dried off while Drew cleaned up.
When they had finished, they stood staring at each
other, then they both laughed. "We can't find out what
he wants in here," she said.

Senator James Fowler was sitting on one of the tall
stools in front of the kitchen island, eyeing the long,
foil-wrapped package. Drew headed for the refrigerator. Sydney took the stool next to the senator. She
looked at the sooty smudges on his forehead and one
cheek and the patch of cobwebs matted in his hair. "Is
something wrong, senator?" she asked.

"Please call me James, and no, nothing's wrong."

Drew set the shredded lettuce and sliced tomato on the counter. "Sydney, do you want a soft drink or a beer? James?" Both said beer, and he returned with two icy long-necked bottles. James lifted his up and took a long drink.

"Man, that tastes good." He watched as Drew unwrapped the poor boy sandwich, opened it up and liberally spread on the tomato slices and lettuce.

Sydney recognized the sign of a man ready to fight for food. "There's plenty, James."

"Well ... I've heard Drew makes a mean sandwich." He took another, more modest sip of his beer. "You can cut me off a small piece."

Drew divided the sandwich into thirds and added a heaping mound of potato chips to each plate, along with a big dill pickle. James didn't wait for the others but bit into his like a starving man. He could only nod his agreement for another beer.

"Jeez, James," Drew said, "doesn't Lauren feed you properly?"

He swallowed, then took another sip of beer. "She keeps me on a damn diet. You know how I put on weight, Drew. I exist on rabbit food most of the time." He held up the bottle and gazed at it with a glazed look of pure pleasure. "Do you have any idea how many calories beer has?" He eyed Drew and Sydney. "What do you care, you're both trim."

Sydney was glad Drew was keeping him entertained; she was so hungry, the sandwich so good, the beer so cold and refreshing that she was beyond polite conversation. When they finally finished their feeding frenzy, she wiped her mouth, drank the last of her beer and looked at the senator. "Why did you want to see me,

James? And why do you have cobwebs in your hair?''
Her curiosity had gotten the better of her.

He laughed and wiped his mouth, too. ''I almost
forgot.'' He swiped at the top of his head with his napkin. ''Lauren, John and I have been crawling all over
Rosehill's attic.'' He smiled, crossed his arms on the
granite counter and leaned forward. ''Believe me, that
sucker's bigger than you think, and there's everything
imaginable stuck, stacked and pushed together. I don't
know when we've had so much fun. Like a damn scavenger hunt.'' He paused at the puzzled look on Drew's
face. ''I told Sydney I'd see if I could find Darcy's and
Jacob's journals. Well, that's what we've been doing,
crawling all over that cavernous attic. I swear I'm going to have a garage sale and clean the mess out.'' He
lifted up the beer bottle and finished it off, then set it
down reluctantly. ''Among a mountain of deeds, wills,
letters and newspaper articles, we found the journals.''
He looked at Sydney. ''You're welcome to come over
and read through them. Maybe they'll shed some light
on this Wallace thing.''

''I'd like that. Was there a journal that covers the
time of Mary's death and Andrew Joshua's hanging?''

The senator shook his head. ''That one's gone.
Strange, don't you think? That out of about twenty of
Darcy's journals only one is missing? And it seems old
Jacob kept only intermittent entries, maybe because of
his age or self-preservation, but around the time of the
trial there was nothing in his. You know, I could remember Dad saying there was one journal gone, then I
realized that wasn't what he'd said at all. He kept saying it was *hidden*. I sent Lauren over to the nursing
home to visit Dad. Sometimes he has lucid moments.''

Both Sydney and Drew thought about what he'd said. She hadn't expected the openness, the honesty. She realized by Drew's slight frown that he hadn't, either. "Did you read any of the journals, James?"

"I skimmed over every one. Handwriting is a little awkward at times, but after a while you get the hang of it. I was fascinated, even enchanted at times. But I'll tell you, I wouldn't want to have lived back then. Too damn uncomfortable."

Drew collected the plates and set them in the sink. "So you didn't read anything about the trial?"

"Not in the journals, but I've read about the trial before." He knew what was coming and didn't wait for Drew to ask. "No, I don't think Andrew Joshua got a fair trial, Drew. Hell, man, there was no body. All the evidence was circumstantial. If anything, Darcy and the judge were criminal for allowing it to go on."

The telephone rang and Drew went to get it. Sydney asked, "You sure you wouldn't mind my reading through them?"

He was going to answer, but the tone of Drew's voice stopped him. They both listened. James was more puzzled than alarmed, but Sydney knew from Drew's stiff stance that something was wrong. She tried to eavesdrop, but Drew had lowered his voice, so she glanced at James and shrugged. They waited for him to finish.

When Drew hung up, he pulled up the stool, sat down and began to laugh. It wasn't the reaction either she or the senator expected.

"That was Rosa. She called to tell me that Clay has spent all day out at the cabin, walking around, trying to conjure up Andrew Joshua's spirit." He started laughing all over again. "I'm sorry, but I keep having a vision of that bullheaded, crusty old man chanting and shaking bones on the ground.''

"He didn't do that, did he?" Sydney asked, and James laughed, too.

"No. But if the old fool had known how, he probably would have. Rosa says he's become obsessed with finding out what Andrew Joshua wants. He's convinced that his father's appearance is proof that he didn't kill Mary. Of course, he doesn't think about anyone but himself. Rosa's worried to death he'll fall or have a stroke. After all, Clay's ninety-three years old, and it wasn't exactly a spring day today." Drew's laughter had given way to concern, and he got up and retrieved three beers. "He told Rosa that if Andrew Joshua appeared at the cabin once, he may come back."

"You know, Drew, the old man may be right." James held up his hand and began ticking off the points he was making on his fingers. "Say he didn't kill Mary. Her body was never found. Andrew Joshua was hanged—a violent death. His spirit, or whatever, can't rest. Now I know this sounds crazy. But along comes Sydney and he sees, senses, knows—whatever a ghost does—that this is his chance to make contact with the real world. I'd bet my life that if Andrew Joshua says he's found Mary, then he's doing exactly what Clay says. He'll return to show him the way."

Sydney's gaze bounced from one man to the other. From Drew, she expected it. James had hinted that he believed, but to actually hear the words spoken by a United States senator, a man who could very well be president one day, it was a shock to the system—her system. She gaped, then said, "You believe in ghosts? In Andrew Joshua?"

James looked bewildered that she'd even asked. "Of course. Don't you?"

"Of course," she mocked, and glared at Drew. "No...I don't know, maybe."

Drew bit his lip to keep from smiling. "She's a hard-headed realist, Chunky. Not like us." He took a sip of beer. "Clay says he's going out there tomorrow, too. Same place, same time as your car accident."

James stood up and stretched. "Next town you go to, warn them first, Sydney." He thanked Drew for the food and beer, then extended his invitation to Sydney to return to Rosehill tomorrow to read the Fowler journals. They were all at the door when the senator paused. "The anniversary's tomorrow, isn't it?"

Drew nodded. "Hey, James, come back when you need a sandwich and a beer."

The senator laughed and waved.

Drew shut the door, and Sydney followed him back to the kitchen. "Whose anniversary is tomorrow?"

"It's the day they hanged Andrew Joshua. Ninety-three years ago."

She wished she hadn't asked.

CHAPTER TWELVE

A GOOD NIGHT'S SLEEP made all the difference in the world. The hard work, good food and wine had also worked their beneficial magic. Of course, the fact that she'd spent half the night laughing at Doo and Emma had helped, too. Sydney reached for her coffee cup, took a sip and looked around the silent kitchen. She'd awakened early, just before dawn had split the sky, had slipped downstairs with her laptop computer and worked on her story about the senator while Emma slept.

Now, as the morning sun jostled the darkness away and she could hear Emma moving around, she shut off the computer and leaned back. Except for a few more questions that really weren't essential, she was finished. The thought was depressing.

She rose, poured herself another cup of coffee, then stood staring out the kitchen window. When, she asked herself, was the last time she'd enjoyed herself so much? Sydney couldn't think when that was. She'd become a workaholic, and for what—a good job, recognition? It certainly wasn't the money.

She'd been chasing her father's shadow for far too long. Where had it gotten her? Time was slipping by with horrifying speed. Maybe it was time to stop running and find out who Sydney Tanner Shannon was and what she wanted for the rest of her life.

"Good morning," Emma said. "You're pretty deep in thought there for so early." She poured herself a cup of coffee and slouched down in the nearest chair. "My head is killing me. How about yours? No," she went on without waiting for Sydney to answer. "You didn't drink but two glasses of wine, did you?"

Sydney chuckled and pushed over the bottle of aspirin. "Right, but I'd had a couple of beers at lunch."

Emma eyed her. "How are you this morning—sore?"

Sydney flexed her right arm, rolled her shoulder and winced. "A little."

"I tell you, I couldn't believe the amount of work you and Drew did before we got there. You make a good team."

Sydney ignored the hint. "Yeah, but if it hadn't been for you and Paul helping us clean up the room and haul out all that trash, we'd still be at it. You two make a damn good team, too."

"Hey, it was the least we could do to be wined and dined like that." She shook her head, moaned and propped her forehead in the palm of one hand. "Drew never ceases to amaze me. Is it right for a man to do everything so well?"

"No," Sydney said, and laughed. She noticed that Emma was dressed in sweats, also, and asked, "Going to play hooky today?"

"I have the next two days off. I need to get back to my welding." She nodded at the computer. "What about you? You finished with your article on the senator?"

"Yes and no."

Emma grinned. "That's a decisive answer for this morning. So, when are you leaving? Not that I'm trying to get rid of you."

Sydney moved away from the window and sat down opposite Emma. "I have a few more questions."

"From the way you said that, I take it they're not that important. Maybe you're just trying to come up with reasons not to leave at all?"

"Emma, Darcy and Jacob Fowler kept journals, and James has offered to let me read them."

"When did you become obsessed with history? You made it clear last night that your article won't have anything to do with the Andrew Joshua thing. Come on, Syd. You've been bitten and you know it."

"Bitten?"

"Don't play dumb, you're too smart for that. You've fallen in love with Drew, haven't you?"

"That's crazy. I haven't known Drew long enough to fall in love."

"Puh-leeze! What does time have to do with anything concerning love? Tell me this, can you walk away from Drew, never see or talk to him again and still be happy?" Emma raised her hand to stop Sydney's quick answer. "No, don't say anything now. Just remember Mary and Andrew. If their story taught you anything, or made any impression on you, it should be that the only thing that lasts forever is love."

Sydney blew her bangs off her forehead in disgust. "Don't confuse me any more than I already am."

Emma smiled. "Well, that's a start. Now, I want to show you something before the town wakes up." She took one last sip of coffee, rose, grabbed her purse and headed for the back door. "Come on, get up."

Emma's surprising resiliency forced Sydney to her feet, but her steps dragged all the way out to the car. The morning sun was already beating down on them with the promise that the day was going to be a real

Texas scorcher. They both groaned then laughed while the car shimmied to life. Emma held her head with one hand, the other pawing at the dashboard for her elusive sunglasses. Sydney just covered her eyes and moaned.

Within minutes they were in downtown Wallace. The main street was quiet and still with only a few cars parked in front of the local café. The town square came into view. Emma pulled into a parking slot and stomped on the brakes. "Out, out. I want you to see this before anyone else gets here."

Emma jumped out and Sydney followed more slowly, shaking her head, wondering how her friend could bounce back so quickly. The dappled shade from the big oak trees worked like magic, shutting out the sun and cooling the motionless air. The morning was so hushed that Sydney could hear their footsteps on the soft, thick grass. "Where are we going?" she whispered, then halted behind Emma when she stopped.

"Look," Emma said.

The hanging tree. The half-dead tree where Andrew Joshua had died. Sydney waited for the chill but sensed only warmth. She felt tears well up in her eyes and blinked. The grass around the base of the tree was covered with a rainbow of flowers. "Who did this?"

Emma shrugged. "Every year on this day, someone places flowers here. It's not Martha's doing—she's the local florist—and she swore to me no one orders them from her."

"Come on, Emma. Please don't tell me they just appear here out of nowhere. Someone brings them. Someone must see, must know who it is."

"I'm sure you're right. But over the years it's just become a happening. No one wants to find out now.

Besides, even though it's a tribute, it's also a yearly reminder, a slap in the face, that the ancestors of the townspeople took the law into their own hands and hanged a man." Emma lowered her voice and said, "Can you imagine the shame Wallace will bear if Andrew Joshua is ever proved innocent of killing Mary?"

Sydney swallowed the lump that had lodged in her throat and nodded. She reached out and touched the tree, feeling the cool roughness of the bark against her skin. "Emma... Emma, do you feel it?" she asked, an astonished look on her face. She waited until her friend was standing next to her, her hand inches away from the tree, then Sydney screamed. Emma immediately screamed, too, yanking her hand back as if it had been stung and jumping away from the tree.

Sydney started to laugh. "I'm sorry, I'm sorry. But the spooky tone of your voice... I just couldn't help myself."

It took a minute for Emma to catch her breath before she started laughing. "You've got a mean streak in you, Syd. I swear you do."

Both women screamed when a voice from the tree said, "You shouldn't try to fool the spirits." Drew stepped from behind the trunk. "What're you two doing here so early?" He set down a vase of fresh flowers then stood waiting, amused to see that he'd put a real scare into them.

"Damn you, Drew," Emma snarled. "Come on, Syd, let's go home."

Sydney ducked her head, hid her grin and trailed rather meekly behind Emma. She figured she'd done enough teasing and had better just go along with whatever Emma wanted.

Drew slipped into his Chevy convertible and followed Emma's car. When they reached her house, he beat them to the front door, holding it open as the silent twosome entered. "Okay, I'm sorry. But it was just too good to pass up. Speak to me. Please."

Sydney watched as Emma stomped off in the direction of the stairs, feeling guilty. "She takes this ghost thing very seriously, Drew. You shouldn't tease her."

"Me? You were doing a good job of it, too."

"I know and I feel awful." She started laughing, tried to sober up, then lost it when Drew began laughing, too.

"I hear you," Emma yelled from the top of the stairs, then stomped down and past them to the kitchen door. "I'm going to my workroom."

"Emma, Emma," Drew said, "I'm sorry."

Emma stopped and sniffed. "If you truly are, you'll make it up to me by telling me who puts all the flowers around the hanging tree."

"Come on, Emma. Why the townspeople have made it a dark secret, something to talk about, beats me. You, like everyone else, know very well there are only two or three people in Wallace who have a greenhouse big enough to raise all those fresh flowers.... It's my grandmother."

"Rosa?" Emma smiled. "Well, well, well," she said, heading for her workroom. "I swear I never guessed."

Drew glanced at Sydney, then quickly away, afraid he might start laughing again. "I could use a cup of coffee."

"Have you eaten breakfast?" She was suddenly starving, and when Drew agreed that he was also hungry, she led him into the kitchen. Within minutes she was frying bacon, scrambling eggs and making toast. "A nice low-cal meal," she said with a grin.

As Sydney was cleaning up the kitchen after they'd eaten, she thought about how quiet Drew had been throughout the meal. When she'd left him the night before, he'd said nothing about seeing her again. As a matter of fact, she remembered being a little hurt that he'd just stood on his porch steps and waved her off as she drove away. "Is something wrong, Drew?"

"No, not really. I was just thinking that I shouldn't have let you go last night. It would have been wonderful waking up with you this morning."

"Then why didn't you ask me to stay?" She put the last of the dishes in the dishwasher and began wiping off the counter.

"I guess I didn't want to put you in an embarrassing position in front of Emma and Paul."

"You think they don't know what's going on between us?" She picked up his cup and wiped the table in front of him.

"I'm sure they think they know, but it's another thing to openly admit it. I wasn't sure how you'd feel."

She was standing beside his chair, and without thinking, she reached out and smoothed back his hair. "I wouldn't have minded."

Drew smiled, his heart beating faster than usual. "Then you like the idea of sleeping in my bed, do you?"

Sydney returned the smile and moved away. "Yes."

"That's a step in the right direction." He eyed Sydney's laptop computer on the kitchen table. "Are you through with your article on Chunky?"

"Just about." She hung up the dish towel, returned to the table and sat down.

"So... you'll be leaving soon?"

"Yes." The word stuck in her throat.

"I see. You'll be going back to Washington?"

"No, actually I have some vacation time to take." She searched his face, hoping for something—a sign, anything—then realized she didn't have the foggiest idea what she was looking for. But Drew's expression was noncommittal and her own confusion made her nervous. She began picking the lint off her sweat suit.

"You know, I never asked you if there was someone special in D.C. Someone who makes you smile and laugh? Someone you love..."

His gaze was intent on her face, his green eyes as bright as emeralds. She couldn't have looked away if she'd wanted to. "There's no one."

"Then why go back at all?" He reached over and grasped her hand and held it. "From what you said, what you haven't said and a little reading between the lines, I get the impression that you could use a change. Why go back? Why stay where you're not happy?"

"Because I don't have anything else." She slipped her hand free and sat back. Maybe it was time to be honest, not only with Drew but with herself. "Drew, until I came here I thought I was happy." She saw the quick smile, the way the corners of his eyes crinkled, the dimple that came and went in one cheek.

"I hope I've had something to do with this revelation."

"You have."

"So, what're you going to do?"

Damn him, he wasn't going to give an inch. She couldn't figure out what was wrong with her. She'd always been direct and honest in any relationship; she was not one to pussyfoot around when stating the way she felt or what she thought. But this was different. Never at a loss for words, she found it difficult now to say what she was feeling. It was a new and puzzling experience, this indecision and uncertainty, and not on the whole a pleasant one. Her heart told her to take a chance, yet there was that inner voice, one reflecting deep insecurity, fear of rejection, that warned her to keep quiet. Her heart won out, and she took a breath and asked, "Don't you mean, what're we going to do?"

Drew laughed, delighted with the way she turned the tables on him, wanting him to make the first move. "Well—" he let the word stretch out "—you could stay here."

"And do what?"

"Whatever you want."

"That's easy for you to say. You have your work, your world. Our lives are miles apart, you know that. This whole affair has been crazy. Hell, ever since I stepped foot in this town, my life has been turned inside out and upside down. I'm a little scared. Every time something good has come into my life, it has never lasted. As cynical as it sounds, I've come to believe that nothing lasts forever in this world."

"You're sure of that? Absolutely sure?"

"Of that, yes." Sydney sighed. "Oh, don't pay any attention to me. I'm just a little confused, and you're not giving me any help here."

"Do you want words of commitment, of love? Because if you do, you'll have to be ready to take the responsibility and return the feelings."

"No." Damn him again. How had one man become so wise? "Not yet. They'd only confuse me more."

Drew thought he'd gone about as far as he dared for the time being. He leaned across the table and kissed her lightly on the lips. "Are you ready to go? Maybe you should change clothes."

She was startled by the abrupt change of subject, relieved and disappointed at the same time. "Where are we going?"

"Just go put on something casual, cool and comfortable."

When Sydney returned she was dressed in a pair of her own jeans, a brown scoop-neck tank top with one of Emma's mother's white linen and lace blouses over it, the sleeves rolled up and the shirttails tied at the waist. She sat down to tie her ruined pink running shoes and said, "Now, where are we going?"

"To Chunky's." He handed Sydney her purse, grasped her elbow and led her out the back door. "Remember he said we could read the Fowler journals?"

Sydney stopped dead in her tracks. "No. He said *I* could read the journals. I don't remember him extending the invitation to you, a Wallace."

Drew tugged on her arm. "I don't think he'll say no. After all, I have something on him."

"What?"

"Three beers and a poor boy sandwich."

Sydney shook her head and slipped into the front seat of Drew's car. They drove off and were about a mile from Rosehill when they saw the senator on his morning jog. Drew slowed down and Sydney said, "Hot morning, James."

"You can say that again," he huffed.

"Mornin' Chunky," Drew said.

"Drew." He tried to nod, but the only movement he could managed just made the sweat roll down into his eyes. One hand automatically went out to hold on to the side of the car. "What brings you out here so early?"

Sydney wasn't about to let Drew and the senator play her game out. "I'm taking you up on your invitation to read the Fowler journals."

"Good," the senator puffed. "And Drew?"

"He says he's going to blackmail you into letting him read them." Drew had slowed the car a little more, and the senator was walking fast beside it.

"Threatening to tell Lauren about the beer and food, is he?" The senator grabbed the side of the car and vaulted into the back seat. "Home, Drew," he demanded regally. "But I want you to know I'm giving in only because it was worth it and not because I'm scared of my wife's wrath. She's very understanding when I fall off the diet-and-exercise treadmill. She picks me up, dusts me off, reminds me no one will trust a roly-poly politician, then she hands me my daily ration of rabbit food."

Lauren's expression when they all walked into the senator's study minutes later was a classic mixture of surprise, shock and dismay. That expression turned into an angry mask when James told her that he was about to share the Fowler journals with them.

"James, you better clean up," she said, and was hot on his heels as he left the room.

"I don't think she's too pleased to have me as a guest, Sydney," Drew said when the door was firmly pulled shut.

Sydney shrugged. "Don't feel too bad. She wasn't all that glad to see me, either. You know, Drew, it's one thing to be protective of your husband and his career, but I think Miss Lauren's going just a tad too far."

Drew picked up a faded, obviously old, red leatherbound book and opened it to the first page. "Isn't there something about protesting too much?"

"As in, she's hiding something? I don't know. She's been like this from the first day I was here." She glanced at what he was reading and looked at the rest of the journals piled on the floor and stacked on the senator's desk.

Drew sat down in the nearest chair and glanced around. "I wonder where Johnenstein's gotten off to. He's usually hanging on Chunky's shirtsleeve."

Sydney sat on the floor next to Drew's chair and picked up a leather-bound journal. "Why do you associate John Laker with Frankenstein?"

Drew was already absorbed in the writing of another period and said, "Actually, he's more like Frankenstein's monster. Just watch him. He's got these big feet and makes it worse by wearing those heavy-soled shoes. He clomps, Sydney. Plods along two paces behind Chunky with that slow-clomping, rather stiff-legged gait. Don't you dare tell anyone, but I modeled Olf, Morgana's henchman, after John."

Sydney bit her lip and forced herself to concentrate on a journal. She was so engrossed that she barely heard the door open. It was the scent of expensive perfume that finally made her glance up and catch the unguarded look of hostility on Lauren's face. Then she noticed the very casual way Lauren and the Senator were dressed. He was wearing a bright orange sweat suit and Lauren was in shirt and jeans. After a second glance she realized that even though the Queen Bee's attire was casual, the blouse, an elegant yellow-and-white stripe, was silk and the jeans were designer. The big silver-and-turquoise medallion concha belt was probably worth more then some people make in a year.

The senator tapped his wife on the shoulder, and she murmured something under her breath before moving aside. John Laker followed the senator, and Sydney's gaze immediately fell to his feet. God, she thought, Drew was right. She felt Drew's leg moving gently against her shoulder, knew he was watching her and didn't dare look at him or she'd start laughing.

"We took you at your word that we could read these, James, and started without you. I hope you don't mind."

The senator surprised Sydney by sitting down on the floor beside her and picking up another journal.

"Of course not." He tipped up the book she was reading to check the date. "That one doesn't have much. Here." He handed her a different one. "This is the journal before Mary's disappearance."

"Did you ever find the missing journal?" Drew asked.

"Not yet, and it's not missing, it's hidden. Probably somewhere in this house. Lauren didn't have any luck with Dad yesterday, so she's going back to visit him later today. Maybe he'll have a lucid hour or so and be able to shed some light on the mystery."

Sydney noticed that Lauren and John had made themselves comfortable, but they weren't taking any interest in reading the journals. She was beginning to get the feeling that they were there merely as guards, silent and disapproving. Their silence and nonparticipation didn't seem to bother the senator.

"Darcy Fowler wasn't just in love with Mary Clayton-Wallace," Drew said. "He was obsessed with her. I've read ten pages and all he talks about is 'his Mary.'"

Sydney was half listening as she read Darcy's journal. "Here he keeps mentioning Andrew Joshua's coin. He seems particularly pleased with it." She turned the page. "Here it is again, but listen to what he has to say this time. 'Dad said it was unsporting to keep wearing the coin to remind Andrew that he lost to me.' ' "

Sydney glanced at the Senator. "What's he talking about?" She sensed that Drew was about to say something and leaned against his knee to warn him. Family stories had a way of being embellished; she wanted to see if the Fowler story about the coin was the same as Clay's.

James chuckled. "There was a county fair, and like at most fairs, the men drink their homemade brew and show off their prowess. From what I've read and the story passed down through *my* family, Andrew had been beating Darcy at the shooting contest. Darcy lost his temper and challenged him to shoot the center out of a gold coin. Andrew lost and Darcy never let him forget it. He even took to wearing the coin on a leather string as a constant reminder. I'll tell you what I think. It seems that was the only thing Darcy could best Andrew Joshua in, and I have a feeling from all I've heard about Andrew Joshua that he either let Darcy win or something distracted him."

For the first time, Lauren involved herself in the group on the floor. She slipped down beside her husband, leaned against his shoulder and directed her question at Sydney. "Surely you don't really believe Andrew Joshua was your rescuer, do you? I mean, you don't believe in ghosts?"

Sydney felt that Lauren was honestly trying to extend the hand of friendship. "If you'd have asked me that question before I came to Wallace, I would have told you no. Now, I just don't know. Do you believe in ghosts or spirits, Lauren?"

"Heavens no." She laughed, glanced at her husband, then Drew, then back at Sydney. "Goodness, you all think what she's said is true. Why?"

John Laker had had enough nonsense. "I think you're all crazy, and if Miss Tanner decides to print that a presidential hopeful believes in ghosts, it could ruin your chances, Senator. Unfortunately, the public and the press have long memories. Whatever you say here today could come back to haunt you."

"What a bunch of rot, John," the senator barked.

"Besides, John," Sydney said, "I'm not here today as a reporter." She was surprised when John Laker responded with a rude, ugly word. The senator immediately lost his temper, calling his right-hand man down. After he'd sent John out of the room to search the attic again, he turned to Sydney.

"I'm sorry, Sydney. Intelligent, loyal, totally dedicated people like John are rare. They also get so wrapped up in the process, protecting me from scandal or unscrupulous people, that they lose sight of the fact that I'm a man. I can think for myself without speech writers, I can make decisions on my own without a committee, and I can fight my own battles."

Lauren broke the tension silence by saying, "Just for the sake of argument, say what Sydney said she saw is true. Why would Andrew Joshua appear to only her, and what does he want?" No one offered an answer, and she gave them all a knowing, superior smile.

Drew set the journal he was reading across his thigh. "I don't know why he would appear to Sydney. Maybe it had something to do with that freak storm. You know, the old-timers in town have been talking about nothing but that storm the other day. Jim Ransom says—"

Lauren interrupted him. "Jim Ransom is crazier than a bed bug. He claims he's a hundred years old, and that's probably right. But my heavens, he also tells anyone who'll listen that he fought in the Civil War. If he can corner you long enough, he'll even tell you which battles he fought in."

"He's just a little confused at times, Lauren," James said. "It was his daddy that fought in the war. Jim's just repeating those stories." He kissed Lauren on the cheek. "Go on, Drew, what did Jim have to say?"

"That he was a boy back in 1900, but old enough to remember that storm. It made quite an impression on him, and if you take the time to weed through his wandering thoughts, he'll describe it exactly the way it happened. This week's storm scared him so bad, brought back all those memories so vividly, he called Clay and talked for an hour without rambling or losing his train of thought. He said the storm the other day, the one Sydney got caught in, was just like the one on the day Mary Clayton was murdered. And remember, Lauren, Andrew Joshua, like Sydney, was caught in the same freak storm on the same road while he was trying to get back to the cabin and to Mary."

Sydney couldn't believe that four intelligent adults were sitting around telling ghost stories. And at least two, the two most unlikely, seemed to believe what they were saying. She looked at Lauren and smiled. Lauren smiled back and shook her head as if she were thinking the same thing.

"They think we're crazy, Drew," the senator said. "Let me tell you something, ladies. If you've ever hunted in the piney wood forest or the marshes and gotten lost, you'd know that things happen out there.

Things that can't be explained. Tell them, Drew. You've hunted and fished around here, too.''

"He's right." Drew lowered his voice to a ghoulish growl. "I remember one story..."

Lauren clapped her hands over her ears and said, "I don't want to hear it."

Sydney laughed with the others but was in complete agreement with Lauren.

Drew was the first to stop laughing. "I'll tell you something. My grandfather believes that Andrew Joshua's appearance means something. He spent all day yesterday out at the cabin. He's going out again this afternoon, despite Rosa's protests. He swears that his father is trying to tell us something and using Sydney to do it. He believes that Andrew Joshua is going to show him where Mary is, and then we'll know who killed her.''

"That's the most ludicrous thing I've ever heard," Lauren cried out. "Ridiculous."

James was startled by his wife's vehement outburst. He stared at her for a second, then looked back at Drew. "Did anything strange happen at the cabin yesterday?''

"No."

Drew and the senator talked for a long time about the "what ifs" of the situation. Sydney was half listening, half reading, and she said without thinking, "Maybe he's going at the wrong time."

"What do you mean?" Drew demanded. "He'll be out there the same time of day as your accident, which by chance happens to be about the same time Andrew Joshua's wagon broke down."

The thought of the similarity gave Sydney the cold shivers. "But that'll be in the daylight, Drew. It was dark when I had the accident," She said. "Black as pitch, in fact, because of the storm. Maybe he should go at night."

"Of course, Drew," James said. "Whoever heard of a good ghost showing up in broad daylight? Tonight. Clay should go tonight. Not only because it will be dark, but tonight will be the actual anniversary of Andrew Joshua's hanging."

The sudden noise overhead—the thump of heavy, slow footsteps—made everyone jump. They were all craning their necks, looking up apprehensively at the ceiling, when the senator said, "Damn, John. I bet you he's doing that on purpose."

Like John earlier, Lauren had had enough. "You're all crazy. You're giving me the willies, and I don't want to hear any more about this." She jumped to her feet, dusted her designer jeans off, tucked in her silk blouse, then straightened her hair. "I'm going back to the nursing home and visit with your father, James, since you seem so determined to find out about the Fowlers. But this is the last of it. You've spent entirely too much time on this whole, ridiculous piece of history. Let it be."

The senator followed his wife out of the room, and Sydney returned to her reading.

"Which one of them do you think broke into Emma's house and pinched your disks?" Drew asked.

Sydney kept her head down as if still reading, but she was smiling. That exact thought had been running through her mind. "My bet is John."

"Mine, too," Drew said, and set down the journal. "Of course, the Ice Queen—" he saw Sydney's frown "—or Queen Bee, if you like, has a pretty good motive. As you can see she's very protective of Chunky."

"Maybe, but I don't think she's the type to deliberately tear someone's house up. It's too menial for her. What about the senator? Would he be so curious about what I was writing that he'd do it?" She set aside the journal she'd been reading.

"Not likely," Drew said, then thought about it again. "No, I don't think it's Chunky. Of course, that doesn't mean he didn't ask someone else to check it out."

"I guess we'll never know, and you know, I think I'd like to keep it that way. I'd just rather not know." She stood up and stretched, then began straightening the stack of journals. "This has been fascinating, and I've enjoyed reading about the Fowlers and the Claytons, but it isn't leading us anywhere. What we need is the missing journal that covers the time of Mary's murder."

"Hidden," Drew corrected. "That's what Chunky's Dad said." He stood and stretched, too, then glanced at his watch. "Let's go con Rosa into some lunch and have a chat with Clay."

They waited for James to come back, and as he was walking them through the house to the front door, Drew paused at the entrance to the living room to stare at the portrait over the fireplace.

James stopped, too, and followed Drew's gaze. "You've never seen her portrait, have you?"

"No. A few old photographs, but nothing like this." Like a man lost in a dream, he walked toward her, with Sydney and James close behind. She was beautiful. Her half smile captivated him, seduced him. Her eyes, so blue. The eyes of... He felt dizzy for a second, then spun around and stared at Sydney. "The eyes of Sydney," he said.

Sydney jumped. "What are you talking about? My eyes are blue. Hers are more aquamarine."

"The shape. It's the same."

"Dammit, Drew. Shape doesn't count," she said, and began walking out of the room.

"Sydney, he's teasing you," James said. "Or I think he is."

"Stop it, you two." She didn't wait to hear any more. "I don't think it's one bit funny." She could never make them or anyone understand that Mary had become important, special. She could joke, deny, even get angry about Andrew Joshua, but Mary was different.

From the first moment she'd seen the portrait of Mary Clayton-Wallace on the cabin wall, she'd been touched by the sadness in her eyes. She wondered why no one else had commented on the pitiful expression. Didn't they see? Sydney suddenly realized that they didn't, she was the only one who saw the difference. Mary had become as real, she thought, as Emma was. Her spirit was probably more tangible than Andrew Joshua's. Maybe it was because Mary, like so many women, had been the innocent victim, caught between the jealousies of two men. Two men loved her, and because of their love, one destroyed her and one paid the price with his life. It was Mary who needed her help, not Andrew Joshua. Mary had to be found, and Sydney knew she would do whatever it took to put an end to the mystery.

CHAPTER THIRTEEN

THE SUN BEATING DOWN on the top of her head was so intense, Sydney thought her brains might fry. The hot wind in the open convertible tugged at her hair and nipped like needles at her face. But she was lost in the numbing nothingness of deep thought and ignored the discomfort.

Drew glanced at the back of her head as she continued to pretend an interest in the passing landscape. "You're still angry with me. Why?" She didn't answer him, but turned her head and stared straight ahead. It was then that he saw the tears rolling down her cheek. Drew pulled the car over onto the shoulder of the road and stopped. He scooted across the bench seat and cautiously slipped his arm around her shoulders. "Sydney? Please don't cry. I'm sorry."

The lack of motion snapped her out of her reverie. She looked in his face, saw the lines of worry, the bright emerald eyes clouded with concern and the beautiful mouth turned down at the corners. "Why are we stopping?" She was shocked when he wiped her cheek, then held up his finger, showing her the wetness of her tears.

"Why, Sydney?"

"I don't know." She could see he didn't believe her.

"It's what I said about the resemblance between you and Mary, isn't it? It freaked you out."

She couldn't stand to see the wounded look in his eyes and rested her head on his shoulder. "Drew, I was thinking about her, wondering what could have possibly happened that day. She was alone with her new baby during that awful storm. Can you imagine how scared she was?" Sydney shivered in the noonday heat as though the temperature had dropped to freezing. "I don't know who killed her, but in those last moments she had to be thinking about Clay and Andrew Joshua."

"You really don't think it was him, do you?"

She closed her eyes to remember and replayed her experience in the cabin. "When I was with Andrew Joshua, I could tell he was a hard man, but fair and honest. Drew, there was so much love and tenderness in him, such a sense of compassion. No one will ever make me believe he killed Mary."

Drew was relieved he hadn't been the cause of her tears, and he certainly liked having her in his arms. But the side of the road on a hundred-degree Texas afternoon was no place to park. He slipped his arm from around her shoulders and slid back behind the wheel. "I think it was Darcy."

"Or a passing stranger?" she said, playing devil's advocate.

"If the killer was a stranger, then why would he bother to hide her body?"

She thought it was Darcy, too, but she was willing to give a Fowler the benefit of the doubt. The sudden movement of the car began to stir up the hot wind. It was almost refreshing after sitting in the still air. She wiped her damp cheeks with her shirtsleeve.

"Did you read the last journal James handed you?" Drew asked. "The one that was supposed to be written before the critical missing journal?"

"Yes, and I know what you're going to say. Darcy was a man violently obsessed with Mary. He couldn't stand the thought of her being with another man, especially Andrew Joshua. He wrote that the idea of Mary having her husband's baby made him physically ill. Could he have killed her? Oh, yes, I think he could have, but why? Why not kill Andrew Joshua, instead? If he did kill her, he destroyed the one person he loved."

They arrived at Clay and Rosa's home and were getting out of the car when Sydney said, "Do you think we'll ever untangle what really happened? Drew, I don't think I can leave here without solving this thing."

Drew looked up and spoke to the sky. "Thank you, Andrew Joshua." He grabbed Sydney's hand and together they ran up the steps. Drew opened the door and, loudly enough to wake the dead, called out for Rosa and Clay.

Rosa Wallace trotted from the kitchen, wiping her hands on her apron. She halted, frowned at Drew, spotted Sydney and broke into a beaming smile as she pushed an errant strand of gray hair off her forehead. "Must you yell, Drew? He wasn't raised in a barn, Sydney." She turned her soft cheek and accepted her grandson's kiss, then glanced at her watch. "Ah, I know why you're here, it's lunchtime."

"Got enough for us, Nana?"

"Of course, I was just putting a chicken potpie in the oven."

Drew smacked his lips, then ducked his grandmother's playful slap. "You're in for a treat, Sydney. Nana makes the best potpies in the world." He sniffed the air like a bloodhound on the scent of a raccoon. "And you made bread today."

Rosa Wallace threaded her arm through Sydney's. "Come along, child, you look like you've had enough of Drew for a while." They marched off toward the kitchen.

Drew was not to be left out and followed close behind. "Where's the old man? He didn't go back out to the cabin in this heat, did he?"

"Your grandfather," Rosa said, "is out in the garage hunting up a pair of pliers. He swears he's either going to cut that cast off his leg or cut his leg off." She started laughing. "He spent half of last night watching television and scratching his leg with a straightened coat hanger. You know what a baby he can be. Says the leg's itching so bad it's driving him crazy. As if he had far to go. Drew, you have to stop him from going to the cabin. He'll suffer heatstroke today."

Sydney realized that Rosa, though she was smiling and laughing, was worried sick about Clay. "Go tell him about tonight, Drew."

Rosa clucked her tongue in amazement as Drew left the house. "I usually have to tell that boy ten times to do something before he'll move." She stared at Sydney. "You're good for him. I don't believe I've seen him this happy in a long time." Rosa opened the back door and motioned Sydney through. "That pie's going to take an hour, so why don't you come with me to the greenhouse while I cut some flowers for the table. You can tell me what's supposed to go on tonight."

Rosa Wallace was a good listener. Sydney found herself talking about her and Drew's earlier visit to the senator's house as they walked along a shaded flagstone path.

"So you think that by going after dark something might happen?"

"I don't know, Rosa. I still don't know if I truly believe that a ghost rescued me. I mean, it's pretty far-fetched, isn't it?"

"I don't think so, dear. Andrew Joshua must have been a tortured soul. He couldn't have rested in peace—I wouldn't have. But, I agree it's Mary that I'm worried about. I'm a mother and a grandmother. If something violent had happened to me, and during that act I was scared for the safety, for the life of my child... Well, I'm older, I've seen and heard more than you have. Somehow I'd find a way to settle the score."

"Then you don't think I'm nuts?"

Rosa stopped and looked Sydney straight in the eye. "Child, if you're crazy, so are millions of others who believe in spirits. Just do what you feel, accept what your womanly instincts are telling you."

Sydney felt as if a heavy weight had been lifted from her mind. She sighed, nodded, and they started off again. She started looking around, taking in her surroundings with interest. The farther they got from the house the thinner the trees became. Sydney noticed a wire fence enclosing a beautifully tended vegetable garden off to their left and commented on it.

"I love fresh vegetables and herbs, love to can and cook and take care of my husband and home. I'm not very progressive, I'm afraid. Actually, I'm very old-fashioned." She eyed Sydney sternly, and when the young woman blushed, she gave a delighted laugh. "You're too easy, Sydney. We're big teases in this family, and you have to learn to roll with the punches, so to speak. Doesn't hurt if you can give back as good as you get, either."

Sydney was about to answer when the sight of the three greenhouses stopped her. She didn't know what she'd imagined, but certainly nothing like this. The smallest of the three was as big as average-size house; the other two were huge glass-and-steel structures.

Rosa explained, "I call the small one my spring flower house, because I have to keep it cool to grow tulips, daffodils and hyacinths. The other two are for various flowers, roses and some vegetables that do better in a controlled environment. Then, of course, during the winter we can have all the lovely summer vegetables we want."

"Surely you don't do all this by yourself?"

"Heavens, no. I make Clay help me, and Drew when I can catch him. They say they hate farming, but don't let them fool you. There's something very therapeutic about getting your hands in the rich earth. When Drew came back after his divorce from Ellen, I used to find him out there sometimes in the middle of the night. Then when he took over the old Chinquapin House and started remodeling it, I knew he was all right." Rosa opened the door to the smaller greenhouse and motioned Sydney in. "But I didn't think I'd ever see him like his old self again . . . not until you came."

Sydney heard her but couldn't say anything as she gasped at row after row of spring flowers. Brilliant colors filled the greenhouse, shining in the hot summer sunlight like sparkling jewels. "These are the flowers that I saw around the hanging tree this morning."

"Yes. I love fresh-cut flowers. They don't last long in the heat, but they do make a spectacular, eye-catching sight for a while, don't they?"

"A reminder, beautiful though it is," Sydney said.

"Exactly. My little poke at the town. It's fun. Clay gives all his employees the day off with pay, too. He's always done that, won't let them forget." Rosa picked up a pair of scissors from a shelf and snipped off several tulips before turning back toward the door. "You must think we're all a little dotty."

Sydney laughed. "Yes, as a matter of fact, I do. The trouble is, I think it's catching. I'm as dotty as all of you."

Rosa was laughing and took Sydney's arm. "Let's go back to the house. Drew's had enough time to talk Clay out of his foolishness—mind you, not without an ear-splitting argument, I'm sure. We can only hope they've settled down to merely growling at each other like a pair of pit bulls."

Drew and Clay were sitting at the kitchen table, glaring at each other. Drew stood up when Sydney and his grandmother walked in. "As you can see, the cast is still on."

"Yeah, sure, brag to the ladies about how you arm wrestled a pair of pliers out of the grasp of a ninety-three-year-old man in a weakened state." He shoved the coat hanger down between the cast and his leg and worked it up and down. "Rosebud, I think ants have made a nest in here."

Rosa bit her lip. "Don't think about it, dear heart."

"I never thought my own wife would turn on me. I'm in mortal agony here. Call that damn Dr. Doolittle and have him send out something." His glare turned on Sydney. "What're you smiling about?"

"I guess you're suffering too much to go with us to the cabin this evening?" For a moment she thought she had gone too far and offended everyone. There was a sudden silence. She felt the others freeze in place. Clay

Wallace's face turned red, his white beetle brows clashed together. Sydney quickly glanced at Rosa, saw with relief that the woman was staring at the ceiling, her shoulders shaking with suppressed laughter. She shifted her gaze to Drew and saw his head bend, his own gaze fixed on the floor.

"Rosebud, did you hear the gal just try to blackmail me?" Clay demanded.

"Yes, Clay, and it worked, didn't it? Your leg stopped itching."

"Damned if it didn't." Clay winked at Sydney, then laughed a deep, rumbling sound of delight. His amusement and any retaliation he might have had in mind were interrupted by the ringing of the telephone. He snatched it up. When Drew started talking to Sydney and Rosa, Clay hushed them with a hiss and a wave of his hand then said, "Hold on a sec, Sally." He covered the mouthpiece. "Sydney, go pick up the extension in the living room. Keep quiet, though, and just listen."

Drew showed her where to go and stood there watching her expression, trying to listen by putting his ear next to hers. When Sydney gently hung up the phone, he asked, "What's going on?"

"I don't know exactly, but that was a woman and she was reading a story..." They reached the kitchen in time to see Clay hang up.

"Well, what do you think, gal? Did what she read sound familiar?"

"Could be from the stolen disk," Sydney said. She sat down opposite him and asked, "Who was that?"

"Hell and damnation," Drew muttered. "What's going on?"

Clay chuckled. "Sally Pearson over at the *Wallace Morning Sun* was reading me part of Buddy's feature story for tomorrow's edition. It's a story about a certain Washington, D.C. reporter, an accident on Piney Creek Road, the Wallaces and the Fowlers. Sally was pretty sure you didn't talk to Buddy, and she said that's what bothered her—he had a story on the computer that didn't look like his work. Everyone might think Sally's just a society busybody, but she's not dumb by a long shot. She knew about the break-in at Emma's house, and Howard's her second cousin and he told her about the theft of the computer disks, and she put two and two together."

"You're saying Buddy was the culprit who broke into Emma's house?"

Clay looked at Sydney. "Well, was what Sally read your words?"

Sydney thought a moment. "Maybe. I'd hate to accuse anyone without seeing the complete article, but from what I heard they were very close. But it wouldn't make sense for Buddy to use my words. Surely he'd rewrite the story in his own words?"

Clay chuckled. "Buddy hasn't got enough common smarts to look down in a rainstorm."

"But why the hell would he take the chance?" Sydney asked.

Clay leaned back and gave them all a smug smile. "It's a last-ditch effort to save the paper. One big story. Maybe big enough to be picked up by other papers... say, Sydney's father's."

Sydney groaned. "Just what I need. My father calling me to confirm that I'm chasing ghosts."

Drew was watching his grandfather closely. "What have you done, Clay?" he demanded. "You're just a little too pleased with yourself."

"Oh, well, I guess you'll find out soon enough. Buddy will probably find out tomorrow when the bank demands payment on his last note."

"Clay," Rosa said, "what's going on?"

"Rosebud, haven't I always told you there's more than one way to skin a polecat? Buddy Hilton made our William's life hell. I'm not saying William was lily-white, but Hilton was vicious. He's always hated the Wallaces and made no bones about it. He's a hypocrite, a bigot, and if you read some of his articles really close you'll see what a racist he is. Last year I found out, and no, I'm not going to tell you how, but I found out he was a card-carrying Ku Klux Klan member." He thumped the table with his fist. "Wallace doesn't need him or his kind to influence the young."

"So, you wily old coot," Drew said, "what have you done?"

"Not much." Clay looked around and smiled. "Just put him out of business."

Drew glanced at Sydney. "He's very proud of himself, and he's going to draw this out, so just sit back and relax."

"No, no. I just made a decision to stop him, and what better way than to take his voice away from him. You see, about nine months ago, Buddy wanted to borrow a considerable amount of money from the bank to update his operation—computers, printers, that sort of thing. You know how John Marsh at the bank hates Buddy. So John and I worked a little deal, maybe illegal as hell, but who's going to prove it?"

"Clay," Drew groaned, "get on with it."

"Don't rush a good yarn, Drew. Always in a hurry."

"Clay, dear." Rosa gently placed her hand over her husband's and patted it. "If you don't stop your dithering, I'm going to make you sleep in the guest room from now on.''

Sydney had to duck her head and stare at the floor to keep from laughing. She didn't know when she'd had so much fun, nor had she ever been around such a caring, fun-loving family. She envied them their closeness.

Clay cleared his throat and sat up straight. ''You know, Drew, Buddy Hilton may not have been directly responsible for your father's death, but he contributed to it. There was no sense in him writing all that trash, then when he started in on you, well, I made up my mind that he was going to pay, and this is payback time. I told John to give Buddy the loan, then I bought the paper from the bank. In other words, I hold the mortgage on the *Wallace Morning Sun*. I've been fair and allowed Buddy to miss two payments. Now, I've instructed John and the sheriff to foreclose in the morning, early, before the next edition can come out.'' He was pleased at the three shocked faces and stunned silence. ''We're all starving to death, Rosa. Where's lunch?''

WAITING FOR TIME to pass. Waiting for the sunset. Waiting for the dark to come. She wasn't good at waiting. The anticipation mixed with excitement and dread wore on the nerves. This waiting was the hardest thing she'd ever done.

After lunch they'd all converged in the living room, talked until they were all talked out, then ended up sitting in a nervous silence. Sydney had looked through the old family pictures, asking questions, forcing the others to contribute so they wouldn't end up snapping at each other. She'd played peacekeeper between Drew and his grandfather until she was exhausted. Too late, she realized that they enjoyed sniping at each other, but by then she had a headache.

She finally ended up sitting next to Rosa, away from the men, thumbing through magazines, pretending to read. A thousand times she replayed her rescue over and over in her mind. A thousand times she heard Andrew Joshua say, "Tell them I found Mary."

The sun was setting, drifting in and out of view between the clouds on its way down. Suddenly a sharp light, the last ray, struck the surface of the window-pane at just the right angle, sending one blinding shaft of brilliance into the living room like a lightning bolt. Sydney jumped. She felt bathed in the brightness. She covered her eyes, but the moment was gone as fast as it had come, leaving the room in semidarkness. It was time to go.

SYDNEY SAT BETWEEN Drew and Clay in the front seat of Clay's pickup truck. They were all quiet, as if afraid to speak, afraid to hope what the night might bring. The tension in the cab was palpable.

"What was the road like yesterday, Clay?" Drew asked.

"Good enough for the pickup."

"What about the old logging road? Would that be better?"

"No. Hasn't been used in years. Probably take a four-wheel-drive vehicle to use it." Clay tapped his cane against the cast on his leg. "Did you remember all the flashlights?"

"Yes."

"The mosquito repellent?"

"There's a wind," Sydney said, just for something to say. "Maybe the mosquitoes—"

"I brought it, anyway."

"The thermos of cold tea? Liable to be hot tonight."

"Yes," Drew said, and gripped the steering wheel until his knuckles turned white.

Sydney closed her eyes, wondering if this was how the rest of the evening was going to go. She felt edgy, nervous and twitchy, as if she were ready to jump out of her skin.

"What if he doesn't come?" Clay asked. "Or what if he comes and I can't see him?"

Sydney heard the longing in the old man's voice and forced herself to relax. She felt Drew do the same and knew he had heard it, too. "At least there's a full moon," she said. "I don't think we'll need flashlights."

"Maybe Sydney is the only one who can see or talk to him."

"Clay," Drew said, "if he comes, you'll see."

"Hope so." Clay cleared his throat. "It would be..."

No one said anything else until Drew turned off the highway onto Piney Creek Road, then made another turn onto the lane that wound its way to the cabin. Sydney expected to feel something, but there was nothing but the memory of a hazy gray morning, of the canopy of trees and droplets of water that had splashed against her face. She remembered the pain in her head as the horse plodded along, the feeling of warmth from the quilt and the security of strong arms around her. She waited for a sign, a touch, anything to let her know that she wasn't chasing a dream. But there was only the night, the sounds of the truck and the presence of the two men beside her.

A tree had fallen across the lane, so Drew pulled onto the shoulder and stopped. "We'll have to walk the rest of the way."

Both men got out, but Sydney stayed were she was. It was Drew, his hands full with two flashlights and the thermos, who noticed Sydney wasn't with them. He told his grandfather to go on, that they'd catch up in a second, then stuck his head through the passenger window. "What's the matter, Sydney?"

"Your grandfather seems to think I can conjure up Andrew Joshua like that," she said, snapping her fingers. "He's trying to hide how excited he is, but he can barely sit still. Drew, what am I supposed to do? Call Andrew Joshua's name? Pray?" She slid over to the door and whispered, "I don't know if I really want to see him again."

"You're scared," He opened the door and she reluctantly hopped out, then pulled out one of the flashlights he'd stuck under his arm. "I don't blame you. I'm not exactly calm myself." He held out his hand and his flashlight shook.

"Right. But you're excited about this. It's an adventure, a glimpse into the unknown. For me, I think I've seen enough."

"Sydney, if you really don't want to do this, I'll take you back to the house. Just say the word."

She glanced around, seeing nothing but trees, the sky full of bright stars and a moon that was as brilliant as the sun. The air was hot and still. A bead of sweat rolled down from her temple to her jaw. She wanted desperately to leave and desperately to stay. Sydney closed her eyes and took a deep breath. "Let's go." A sudden steady breeze touched her face, ruffled her bangs. The leaves in the trees rustled like a sigh.

They picked their way over fallen tree limbs, around holes and rocks. The narrow beams of yellow light danced over brown patches of grass and thick ferns before picking out the deteriorated perimeter of the cabin. Their footsteps were muffled by the thick carpet of leaves. Clay called out that he'd found a good place for them to wait, and Drew and Sydney made their way over to a moss-covered mound.

Sydney glanced around before she settled down between Drew and Clay on the pile of fallen stones. They were inside the ramshackle cabin. The huge log walls, after years of deterioration, were now only mounds of wood scattered here and there to remind the visitor of the outline of the cabin. The roof had fallen and decomposed many years ago. The night closed in around her; the dry wind and the darkness made her tense. A sound from the shadows, like the frightened squeal of a woman, made her jump, and her heart skipped a couple of beats. "What was that?"

"Animals," Drew said.

Sydney raised the flashlight, but Clay gently took it away from her. "Nothing's going to bother us."

Another sound came out from beyond the grasp of her imagination, and she cringed. "I don't like the dark," she mumbled, and could have kicked herself for allowing her childish fears to surface in front of an audience.

Clay sighed loud enough to let her know what he thought of her declaration. "Moon is as bright as a spotlight. The noises you're hearing could be miles away from here."

In the widening gulf of quiet between them, she became sensitive to the life of the night, the animals that crawled and stalked and were poised for attack. Were these creatures watching them, she wondered? And if they had thoughts, did they think what fools those humans were, perched on stones waiting for a ghost? She couldn't stand her own thoughts or the silence and asked, "After Mary died, did the sheriff or someone do a search of the area, a thorough search?"

"Yes," Clay said. "As to how thorough, I don't know. I do know they searched as far as the lake, in the marshes, bottom thickets and the caves."

"What caves?" Sydney latched on to anything to keep a conversation going and fend off the uneasiness and the knot of disappointment beginning to form in her stomach.

"Indian caves down near the river. There's one about a mile or so from here. When I was a child, my friends and I used to explore them, until we got caught. There are deep tunnels that go back so far I never had the courage to find out just how far they went. There are also Indian burial grounds all around here. Some bigwig archaeologists from the University of Texas wanted to dig in the burial grounds and explore the caves, but I wouldn't give them permission. That stirred up a hornet's nest of righteous indignation from the *Wallace Morning Sun* until I made it clear to Buddy and the people from the university that I was part Indian myself, and the sites were not only sacred to the Indians buried there but also to me."

It was the end of conversation for a while. What little they indulged in came in fits and starts, a half-asked question, half answered with grunts and nods. As time slipped by, Sydney thought she might go crazy. She was terrified of what lurked beyond her vision, the unknown presence that hunkered down in the darkness. She knew she was being silly and unreasonable, but she couldn't help it. Her heart was pounding in her ears like a drum. "How long have we been out here?" she asked.

Drew turned on the flashlight to look at his watch. "An hour."

"Maybe if we hold hands...?" she suggested, and wanted to hit Drew when he laughed. After a little while she slipped her hands free of theirs and wiped the sweaty palms on her thighs. The quiet of the night had become her monster, and she started talking nonstop about anything and everything she could think of. She babbled until her throat was dry. Without a word, Drew handed her a cup of cold tea.

Clay twisted on his stone seat and said, "If you want to start this political-watch paper but don't want any affiliation with anyone who might try to influence what's being reported, why don't you just start your own?"

At first Sydney was totally baffled by his comment. Then she realized that during her ramblings she must have talked at length about her work, goals and dreams. At any other time she would have been appalled, but now she was just happy to have something to talk about. "I've looked into private publication, but it's awfully expensive."

"I just happen to know of a newspaper that's going to be for sale tomorrow." Clay chuckled. "I'd even co-sign a loan."

Sydney was speechless. She stared at Clay then turned to Drew and still couldn't say anything.

"Think about it," Drew said.

She tried, but as the conversation dried up like a well in the desert, all she could think about was the three of them sitting there waiting for Andrew Joshua and the fact that nothing had happened. The tension from the two men was as thick as frozen butter. It radiated from Clay in his very stillness, and she wondered when it would turn to anger. He was going to be disappointed and blame her.

Clay expected miracles and magic, but she could give him neither. She knew he'd thought all he had to do was drag her along and Andrew Joshua would appear. She'd even been naive enough to think the same thing. It wasn't working. She wanted to tell Clay she didn't have any control over what would or would not happen.

She was tired, depressed, and her backside was numb. Sydney placed her elbows on her knees, leaned forward, propped her chin on her fists and looked around. In her wildest dreams she never thought she would be inside these walls again, though they were now gone forever. The fireplace in the main room was just a heap of smooth round stones, and she realized they were probably sitting on some fallen chimney stones. It was a sad, forlorn place. A place of tears. But she remembered it differently....

Sydney could visualize it now, the wavering light from the fire and the yellow glow from the lantern. There—she could see the antique rifles over the mantel and the big stone fireplace with the rocking chair gently moving back and forth beside it. Sydney stared at the cradle beside the rocking chair and frowned, thinking that she didn't remember a cradle.

It was then that she felt the pain, intense and sharp. She glanced down at her hand, saw another holding hers, an older hand with age spots dotting the back. She raised her gaze to Clay's profile, saw the look of awe on his face, then she turned her head to Drew. He, too, was staring straight ahead with a rapt expression. As if in slow motion, Sydney followed their gazes.

The cabin appeared as it had been the night of her accident, but this time she wasn't alone. Beside her were Drew and Clay, and standing in the corner of the room was Andrew Joshua.

CHAPTER FOURTEEN

SYDNEY FELT A SUDDEN overwhelming sense of peace even though her heart was pounding. It was eerie how much Drew and Andrew Joshua looked alike, she thought. A ghost, he really was a ghost. It was the truth. She hadn't been lied to, hadn't had hallucinations—she wasn't crazy. Would anyone ever believe this, she wondered?

Drew reached for her other hand, and she squeezed it hard. He had seen pictures of his great-grandfather, but to see his very image right in front of him must have been spooky. She lifted her hand and pressed Drew's palm against her heart. No one spoke, afraid they might break the spell. Andrew Joshua was staring at her, smiling his sweet smile, and she nodded. He thanked her; though he never said a word, she felt it in her heart.

Clay's hand, still in hers, started to tremble. The movement broke the daze she was in as she realized that Clay was not a young man and the shock of seeing his father, a ghost, could give him a heart attack. Sydney tore her gaze from Andrew Joshua and leaned toward Clay, but the words of concern died on her lips. His head was held high and his shoulders shook as tears rolled down his cheeks and dripped off his jaw. He was smiling widely, his green eyes, so like Andrew Joshua's and Drew's, shining with so many mixed emotions.

What was happening hit Sydney so hard it took her breath away. Clay had been an infant when he lost Andrew Joshua and Mary. Now he was seeing his father for the first time. When she looked at Andrew Joshua again, she couldn't hold back her own tears. Andrew Joshua was staring at Clay, his emotions a mirror of his son's, his tears glistening on his cheeks.

"Dad," Clay whispered. "Dad."

Sydney gasped. The cabin seemed to darken. The only illumination came from a roaring fire. Suddenly there appeared a beautiful woman standing beside the fireplace, her long blond hair loose and tumbling over her shoulders. Her dainty floral-print dress almost touched the top of her high buttoned boots. She held a small bundle in her arms, patting and rocking it as she glanced worriedly toward the window.

Sydney saw Mary start, saw the surprise on her beautiful face as the cabin door blew open and a man dressed in a long slicker and a hat pulled down low over his face stumbled in, then struggled to push the door shut against the wind. Wet leaves danced over the cabin floor, then settled down. Mary relaxed and smiled slightly as the man pulled off his hat, shaking the water off. He slipped out of the dripping slicker, shook it and hung it up. When he turned around, Sydney saw a handsome man of medium height, with blond hair damp around the edges and light eyes. He was smiling, but Sydney knew and shivered. This had to be Darcy Fowler. She must have voiced her thoughts, because Drew whispered that it was indeed Darcy.

She glanced at Andrew Joshua. He was still standing in the corner of the room, but his attention was not on what was happening. His gaze was fixed on his son.

How many times through the years had Andrew Joshua watched his wife's murder and been unable to stop the scene from replaying over and over. How many years of agony and desperation had he endured?

She switched her attention back to the two people and saw that they were talking, yet she heard no words; the night was as silent as before. Mary pulled the baby's blanket away from the round face, then turned so the man could see the child. Sydney stopped breathing when she saw Darcy push the baby away. There was anger in Mary's face; her words were coming fast as she bent to lay the baby down. She gave the cradle a gentle push, and it began rocking.

Sydney wanted to close her eyes as something she'd thought of earlier came back to her. The jealousies of two men: one had died, the other had killed, and an innocent woman and child were their victims. Darcy grabbed for Mary, grabbed her hard and pulled her against him. He held her tightly and kissed her roughly. Mary was no weakling; she fought hard. She kicked out and her fingers curled into claws. Darcy shoved her away. Mary stumbled back and lost her balance. She grabbed at his clothes but her fingertips only managed to grasp a leather string. There was a flash of brilliance in the firelight as she grabbed again, but her backward momentum had taken her farther off balance and she fell, hitting the back of her head on the corner of the hearth.

Sydney sighed a long, shaky breath, trying to release the knot of pain in her chest. Darcy was on his knees beside Mary. His growing desperation was real, his agony an open wound when he realized she was dead. It was over. They'd found out who killed Mary, and even though it was an accident born out of obsessive love, it was no less tragic.

But it wasn't over. Sydney felt Drew and Clay tense. Andrew Joshua was motioning for them to get up, and all three scrambled to their feet. As Drew was shoving a flashlight at her, she realized what was going on. Darcy was picking Mary up in his arms. He carried her to the back door and, struggling with her weight, managed to unlatch it. The fierce wind slammed the door wide open, tumbling leaves across the floor of the cabin and making the lace curtains flutter wildly. The wind pulled at their clothes and blew Mary's long blond hair around the man's face until he was forced to shake his head to clear his vision. Then they disappeared into the darkness and the storm.

Andrew Joshua was right behind them, and Sydney quickly followed, amazed to see how the storm soaked Darcy and Mary to the skin, yet she stayed dry. The wind almost knocked Darcy off his feet, and he moved slowly with the limp body. But only a gentle breeze ruffled Sydney's hair. She'd forgotten Drew and Clay and stopped only long enough to see Drew helping his grandfather as the old man cursed and hobbled along on cane and cast.

"Don't worry about us," Drew yelled. "We're right behind you. Just keep as close to Andrew Joshua as you can."

She hurried to keep up, but her pace was slowed by the rough, uneven forest floor. "Please don't let me lose them, Andrew," she begged, then realized she'd shouted it. She was talking to a ghost again.

After a while—she didn't know how long they'd walked or where they were—she was exhausted and scared. Drew and Clay were no longer close behind her. The flashlight was now her only source of light. The moon was just a wishful thought as the trees became thicker, their leaves a tight canopy cutting out all light. She'd been so afraid to take her eyes off Andrew Joshua and lose the way that she'd tripped and fallen several times on exposed tree roots or broken limbs. Her clothes were filthy. Three times she paused, only long enough to call for Drew, but he answered only twice. The last time there was no answer at all, and she'd stood there staring back the way she'd come, trying to decide what to do. But the decision was taken out of her hands. Andrew Joshua was suddenly beside her, the weight of his hand on her shoulder. She looked into his green eyes and saw the urgency, the pleading.

"Please," he said.

She was off again. Slower this time and a little more careful about where she put her feet. Suddenly there was a muffled yelp—a human voice—the sound of something tearing across the ground, the thud of the same something hitting the ground hard, then the scramble of footsteps. Sydney began to run. Fear had snatched her breath. Andrew Joshua disappeared around a bend, and she lost sight of him. Determination drove her on, careless of the dangers underfoot. She rounded the bend, then skidded to a stop in a small clearing. The man carrying Mary was just disappearing through a solid dark wall. Andrew Joshua stopped, glanced back, then he, too, disappeared.

Sydney was panting with fatigue, shocked that they'd all vanished. Wearily, she lifted the flashlight to inspect the place where Andrew Joshua, Mary and Darcy had gone when she heard a noise off to her left. She

spun around, the light moving with her. In her frantic
search for the source of the noise, she caught a flash of
white, a glimmer of something shiny, then it was gone.

Sydney lowered the flashlight and turned back
around. She was exhausted, physically and emotion-
ally. Her arms hung limply at her sides. She was sweaty,
dirty, scared and heartsick. There was nobody there—
nothing. No Andrew Joshua to guide her or tell her
what to do. She bit her lip hard. Surely they hadn't
come this far just to have it end. There had to be something behind that wall or they wouldn't all have gone
through. Did Andrew want her to try to follow them?

She wanted to cry and scream at the same time, but
she was too damn tired to even move. Drew and Clay
were never going to forgive her. Her breath was coming so hard, her heart beating so loudly in her ears that
she thought she imagined hearing Drew call her name.
Holding her breath, she cocked her head and listened.
Her name floated on the night, eerie in the stillness, but
it was Drew. Sydney spun around and stared back the
way she'd come. She was about to answer the call when
she heard a noise she recognized. A feeling of uncontrollable anger overwhelmed her. Her body trembled,
and she stopped, listening for what she expected next.
A minute later the sound came.

"Sydney." The beam of Drew's flashlight caught her
standing in the middle of his path. As he came closer,
he saw how disheveled she was. "What the hell happened?" He could barely get the words out, he was so
weary. He lowered Clay to the ground, and then sat
down himself. He was physically drained and unable to
hold his head up. Coping with his grandfather had worn
him out.

After urging Sydney to keep up with Andrew Joshua, he'd stayed with Clay, helping him hobble along the uneven terrain. But Clay wasn't to be held back and had demanded that Drew carry him. They'd stood facing each other, tempers short, yelling and glaring. As usual, his grandfather had got his way. Drew couldn't believe he'd actually carried Clay piggyback all that distance. And to make matters worse, Clay wouldn't shut up. He'd kept yelling out orders to go this way and that way. Drew could still hear the old man's voice ringing in his ears.

Sydney was so happy to see them she flopped down on the ground, threw her arms around Drew and kissed him. She ignored Clay as he kept asking where his mother and father were and leaned close to Drew so she could see his face. "You look awful. What happened? I thought you were right behind me."

Drew glared at his grandfather. "For heaven's sake, Clay, please hush. I can't think." He took a couple of deep breaths, then answered Sydney. "I look like hell because I've been his—" he glared at Clay again "—beast of burden, his damn lackey, and because he's an ungrateful old coot."

Clay used his cane and struggled to his feet. "Where are they, Sydney? Where'd they go?"

Drew shone the light up at his grandfather. "Let us catch our breath, Gramps." He knew Clay hated the nickname and used it only when he was thoroughly disgusted. It galled him that the old man looked so clean and fresh, but then, of course, he would.

He turned to Sydney. "I think my back's broken. My legs feel like Jell-O. I've nearly been strangled to death, I've been yelled at until I think Gramps may have permanently damaged my right eardrum, and if he waves that damn cane one more time, I'm going to take the greatest pleasure in breaking it over his head."

Sydney wasn't feeling particularly sympathetic at the moment. "At least you had someone with you. I've been running around in the dark all by myself, chasing ghosts, for God's sake. I've fallen so many times my knees could probably take root and grow. Look at me," she demanded, and sat still while he shone the light over her. She took a closer look at him, too, noticing his scratches, the smudges and dirt. Sydney picked twigs and leaves from her hair and flicked them away, then in a delayed reaction, they both started laughing.

She sobered long enough to say, "I tell you Drew, if anybody finds out about this night, I'm ruined." She covered her face with her hands and giggled.

"If you two are quite through," Clay said, standing over them like an avenger, "I'd like to know what happened."

Sydney remembered. "I'll tell you what happened. Someone's been here, that's what. And I'm not talking ghosts. I'm talking about a warm-blooded human." When neither man said anything, but just stared as if she'd lost her mind, she said, "I was following Andrew Joshua through the woods near here—" she pointed back where she'd come from, "—when I heard a scream, then it sounded like someone was running through the bush. But I couldn't take my eyes off Andrew, Mary and Darcy." She took a deep breath and let it out slowly and loudly. "They all disappeared through a wall. Then a few minutes later, right when Drew started calling me, I heard the sound of a car door slamming and an engine starting up."

Clay thumped his cane against the ground. "What do you mean, they disappeared through a wall?"

"What wall?" Drew demanded.

Sydney sighed. Drew was more like his grandfather than he would have liked to have been told at this moment. They obviously didn't give a hoot about the identity of the person she'd caught a glimpse of, and she stubbornly decided she wouldn't tell them now even if they begged her to. Without a word to either of them, Sydney struggled to her feet, stood for a few seconds to test how much strength was left in her legs, then walked back toward the clearing. She couldn't have cared less if they followed or not.

Once she was back where she thought Andrew Joshua and the others had disappeared and shining her light at the wall of matted green vines, she wasn't so sure it *was* the spot.

"Is that the place?" Drew asked as he and Clay came up behind her.

"I don't know." Clay's light joined hers, moving quickly over the area. "Everything looks the same...."

Clay walked a little away from them. "I know what this place is. It's one of the Indian caves. Come over here, Sydney." When she was beside him, he shone his flashlight on what looked like a dark circle. "Is this where they went?"

She added her light to his and saw the yawning dark hole, a few feet wide and tall. She then turned her flashlight off, glanced down to let her eyes adjust to the darkness, then looked back at the cave opening. "No. There wasn't an opening. It was a solid wall of vines."

"Damn, the whole side of the hill is a mass of vines," Clay said. "It has to be here. This is the only opening to the cave."

"But Clay, you said they'd searched the caves," Drew reminded him. "And didn't you used to come here? You must have explored this cave."

Clay's shoulders slumped as he leaned all his weight on the cane. "You're right. There's nothing in there. If only we hadn't lost sight of them."

"If only I hadn't lost sight," Sydney mumbled, and walked off, shining her light over and up and down the hill as she went. She'd only gone a little way when she noticed a small pile of torn vines and leaves. She moved closer and recognized what it was. Someone had tried to tear away through the wall of vegetation. "Drew, Clay, over here." She dropped to her knees and started tearing wildly at the vines, yanking handfuls of leaves free and tossing the debris over her shoulder.

"What are we doing?" Drew knelt beside her, helping grapple with the thickest and toughest of the vines, pulling them away.

Clay came up behind them, staring in openmouthed amazement at the sight of them on the ground, like two dogs digging for a bone. "What's going on here?"

She was like a woman possessed and wouldn't stop. "This has to be where they disappeared." Her hands stung, her shoulders ached, but she couldn't stop.

"Are you sure?" Clay demanded, moving closer and aiming his light so they could see more easily what they were doing.

"This is where someone was working just before Mary, Andrew Joshua and Darcy disappeared."

Drew sat back on his heels. "What are you talking about?" He couldn't help grinning when she turned her face toward him. Clay's flashlight illuminated the smudges of dirt streaked across her forehead and one cheek. She was angry and it showed in the straight line of her lips and the hard gleam in her eyes.

"I'm telling you there was someone here, doing exactly what we're doing now. For whatever reason, Mary and Darcy disappeared and Andrew Joshua followed them. Someone knew this is where they were going before they vanished."

"What's the gal babbling about now?" Clay growled as he hovered over them like an aging bear. When Sydney explained in detail what she'd heard and seen, Clay said, "I don't understand. Who was it?"

Sydney knew, but she was in no mood to impart that information until she had proof. She wiped her hands on her jeans and started working again.

It wasn't much longer before they were rewarded for their exhausting work. Sydney grabbed a handful of vines and yanked hard—nothing happened. Her frustration made her careless. She leaned over, working her hand through the vines, reaching for a better hold, but she lost her balance and fell forward. The wall disappeared and she plunged into total darkness.

She lay still, afraid to move or even breathe until she realized that she wasn't hurt and had only fallen a little ways. She became aware of powdery dirt under her cheek, and raised her head. Then, like a trapped animal, she sniffed the air. There was a dry, stuffy smell to the place. Cautiously, she rolled over onto her back. She could hear Drew yelling her name and Clay talking. The darkness was so total, so overwhelming, she couldn't see her hand in front of her face.

Sydney sat up and faced the direction Drew's voice was coming from. "Drew, shine some light in here."

"God," he breathed in relief. "Are you all right? Where are you?"

"Haven't the foggiest idea. But please, some light." After a moment and some raised voices, a beam of light penetrated the darkness. Sydney crawled a few feet, stuck her hand out of the hole she'd fallen into, grabbed the end of the flashlight and yanked it through. "It looks like I'm in a cave." She moved the light around. "But it's not very big, just enough room for the three of us." He should have been tearing his way in by now. "You are coming in, aren't you?" When he didn't answer immediately, she moved closer to the opening and screamed, "Drew!"

"I'm here. Clay and I were just having a discussion as to who's going to try to crawl through first."

Sydney moved back as far as she could, sat down with her back against a rock wall, aimed the light at the opening and watched as Drew struggled, wiggled and grunted his way into the cave. He barely had time to get his feet on the ground, much less look around, when Clay started through and he had to help the old man.

Sydney sat watching their efforts as they grumbled and sniped at each other, then paused to catch their breaths. She smiled and stood up. With their three flashlights on, the cave was no longer dark and threatening, and she could afford to be amused. "If you two are quite through, there's an opening over here."

As much as they wanted to find where Andrew Joshua and Mary were, they were fascinated by the cave. They started off down a long, narrow tunnel. At times they had to double over, but eventually they emerged into a large chamber.

Drew shone his light across one wall, highlighting the Indian paintings. "Just look at this Clay."

"There's no telling how old this cave is, Drew. I know that as much as I explored the other caves, I never found this one." He moved away, looking around as he went.

Sydney shivered. There was something about the place she just didn't like. She shone her light slowly around, trying to find what it was in the dark shadows that was bothering her. As she was sweeping the light across the far side of the chamber, a glint of something bright caught her attention. She moved toward it, then stopped and closed her eyes when she realized what it was. "Drew. Clay."

It must have been something in her voice that warned them. They hurried over to her and added their light to hers. Clay gasped and Drew wrapped his arm around her shoulders.

"Mary?" she asked.

A few feet away were the skeletal remains of a woman. She was lying on a large flat rock, her arms flung away from her body. Parts of her dress still covered the bones. Tears filled Sydney's eyes and blurred her vision. "I saw something shiny. That's how I found her."

They moved closer, then Clay stuck his cane out to the side and in his haste nearly struck them in the chest. "Don't go any closer." He'd seen what they'd yet to see.

Sydney blinked away the tears. A wedding ring, a thin band of gold, lay in the dust near the body. It must have slipped off her finger and rolled away. But then Sydney saw something else and realized that was what Clay and Drew were staring at. In Mary's right hand, entwined around her bony fingers, were the remains of a leather string, and at the end of that string was a gold coin with a hole in the middle. Proof, she thought, indisputable proof that Darcy Fowler had not only killed Mary but had hidden her body.

Sydney glanced around, thinking how quiet it was and how beautiful with the paintings on the wall. It was Clay's howl of pain and loss, then his sobs as he fell to his knees, that grabbed Sydney's attention. She thought he was having an attack and went down on her knees beside him. Drew was on the ground, too, trying to hold his grandfather, but the old man shook his head and brushed them away with a swipe of his hand.

Clay rocked back and forth in his pain and despair, then he shuddered violently all over and forced himself to take a deep breath. He couldn't talk. It was as if his voice had dried up, and so he pointed, then hung his head.

Sydney didn't know what was going on. She looked in the direction he'd pointed, but still didn't know what was wrong. Drew made a sound like a growl, or was it a moan? "What is it?" she whispered.

Drew left his grandfather's side and walked over to Sydney. He put his arm around her shoulders and held her tightly. "Look beside her, about even with her elbow."

Sydney's legs went out from under her, and she sagged in shock. It was a good thing Drew had such a strong hold on her, she thought, or she'd have collapsed. Beside Mary's body, written in the dirt, was the name *Darcy*. Mary had been alive when Darcy left her in the cave. Maybe she'd come to in the darkness, maybe she'd never been totally unconscious. They'd never know how long she'd lain there, how long she'd lived, but it was long enough to name her killer.

Sydney couldn't stand it anymore. She pushed away from Drew and walked back toward the tunnel. She wanted out, away from the whole tragic affair. Yet even as she left, sensing that Drew and Clay were silently following, she couldn't get the horror of what had happened to Mary out of her mind. For the brief time she'd lived, she had to have known that she would never see her baby or her husband again. She had to have known that she would never rest beside her husband in death.

Somehow the freak storm the day of her accident, identical to the one that happened ninety-three years ago, was some kind of time warp, a release. Sydney knew she'd been in the right place at the right time for Andrew Joshua to make contact, and he'd left her with a message and a puzzle to solve. It was the only explanation Sydney could think of, one that she was willing to live with.

She came to the opening of the cave and immediately crawled through. It wasn't until she was standing up, breathing in the fresh air, that she saw them. Andrew Joshua and Mary, standing arm in arm, looking back at her. "Clay. Drew," she whispered, never taking her eyes off the couple a few feet away. "Clay, get out here now."

Clay was the first out, and as he stood up, his breath caught in a loud gasp. He stared at his mother and father, saw their longing and love for him but also saw their regret and sadness at having to leave him again.

"You're together at last, aren't you. Goodbye," he said, and his voice shook with emotion.

Like a puff of wind, they were gone. Sydney felt empty all of a sudden, as if she'd lost something precious. But she was happy, too. She looked up a Drew. "They're together forever now."

"Yes. That was really something, wasn't it? Do you think anyone will ever believe us?"

"They damn well better," Clay snapped, "because I have a body and the evidence. Drew I want you and Sydney to go back to the pickup and get to the nearest telephone. Call the sheriff. Make sure you talk to the sheriff and not that kid, Howard. Tell him to get the coroner and get out here fast." He hobbled over to the entrance and sat down. "It's about time this town knew the truth."

Drew hesitated. "We're not going to leave you here alone, Clay."

"Why the hell not? Don't you understand, there's nothing left here anymore. Everything's at peace, probably even old Darcy. Besides, if what Sydney says is true, that someone was here, I ain't about to leave and let them come back and destroy anything." He scowled at his grandson. "For once don't argue with me, Drew. I'm not going to leave my mother alone, not now that I've found her." He settled his back against the vines and crossed his arms over his chest. "Thank you, Sydney. Without you, none of this could have happened."

The lump in her throat felt as big as a baseball, and she could only nod. Sydney pulled on Drew's arm to get his attention. "Leave him be, Drew. We'll stop at Rosehill to use the phone." She hesitated a moment, debating whether to tell Clay what she planned to do.

"When you're through here, come to Rosehill, Clay. You'll need to speak to the senator." Clay looked at her hard for a second, then agreed.

Drew and Sydney were quiet all the way back to the pickup, each lost in thoughts. Once they were on the road, he asked, "Why Rosehill?"

"Because we have some unfinished business there."

"Don't be so damn secretive, Sydney."

"I'm not. I just don't want to say anything until I'm one hundred percent sure. But I'll tell you this—someone from Rosehill was at the cave site tonight. They knew Mary was there and exactly where the entrance was."

"How?" he asked.

"That's what I intend to find out."

"Maybe they've always known. Maybe with all this talk about you seeing Andrew Joshua, they were afraid he'd do just what he did tonight and lead us to Mary's remains."

Sydney kissed him on the cheek. "Stick to your fantasy world, Drew. You're no good at mysteries. If any of James's relatives had known where Mary's body was, they would have destroyed it long ago, along with anything that might implicate them."

Drew reached the turn to Rosehill's driveway. "Something's up. Look."

If she hadn't known better, she would have thought the senator was holding a party. Every light in the place appeared to be on. As they got closer, Sydney noticed the white Jeep parked at an odd angle, its front end a couple of feet on the grass instead of the driveway. Drew stopped the car and Sydney hopped out, running to the Jeep, looking it over. "See all the red dirt on the tires?'' She touched one, rubbed the earth between her fingers, then held them up for Drew to see. "Fresh," she said. "Come on. I think I hear raised voices."

The front door was standing wide open, and Sydney moved quickly through it, following the voices. When she came to the doorway of the senator's study, all conversation stopped. "Been ghost hunting, Lauren?"

The immaculate Lauren Fowler was as big a mess as she was. She was sitting down, her silky blond hair tangled with leaves and twigs, her face and clothes filthy. Sydney pointedly looked down at her own hands, then stared at Lauren's. They were both in the same shape: filthy, scraped and bleeding in places. "You should have stayed to see the finish. It was spectacular."

Drew went directly to the telephone and called the sheriff. No one made any pretense of not listening to the conversation, and when Drew hung up there was dead silence for a few seconds.

"Will someone," the senator roared, "please tell me what the hell is going on? My wife comes in looking like this, babbling something about seeing strange things. I can't even get her to tell me where she's been. Then you two barge in in the same condition as my wife, and Drew calls the sheriff. Whose body is the coroner supposed to pick up? Someone damn well better start explaining what's going on."

John Laker passed the senator a large glass of brandy, and James held it to Lauren's lips. "It's obvious, isn't it?" John said. "Whatever's wrong with Lauren is the fault of these two. I think you should let me call the sheriff back, James. Get him out here."

Drew smiled. "Shut your mouth, John, before I have the pleasure of shutting it myself."

Sydney knew Drew wasn't far from losing it. And if he did, John Laker was going to bear the brunt of too many years of pent-up hostilities. "James, I think Lauren's in shock," she said. "She was out at the cabin tonight. I think she saw something she didn't understand. It scared her." She told the senator what had happened at the cabin and the cave, dragging her story out, including every detail. While she was talking, the senator nudged his wife over far enough so he could sit down beside her, and began sipping at her brandy, listening intently.

Lauren's color began to come back. "You mean, I really did see ghosts? Oh, James," she wailed. "I saw him carrying poor Mary's body. He killed her and hid her body just like the journal said."

A dreamy look glazed the senator's eyes, and he surprised everyone by saying, "I wish I'd been there."

"For God's sake, James, don't be an ass," Lauren snapped. "It was awful. Just awful." She shuddered violently, snatched the glass of brandy from his hand, gulped it down, then held it out for a refill.

"What journal, Lauren?" At that point Sydney figured she could have dropped a feather and it would have resounded in the room like a brick hitting glass.

Drew pulled over a chair, touched Sydney on the shoulder to get her attention, nodded that the chair was for her, then handed her a glass of brandy. "You found Darcy Fowler's missing journal, didn't you, Lauren?" he said.

Lauren's beautiful, pouty mouth thinned into a straight line of defiant silence.

"Did you, Lauren?" the senator asked. "Did Dad tell you? And you didn't tell me?"

"You were busy, darling."

James scowled. "I see. You read the journal, found out the truth and went to investigate by yourself?"

"Yes," Lauren said.

"Where did you find it, Lauren?" James demanded.

"Your father told me about the dummy drawer in the rolltop desk in the attic."

"Tell me something, Lauren. What were you going to do if you had found Mary's remains? Were you going to tell me then?"

Sydney noticed how Lauren's much-needed color had drained away again, leaving her skin pale. "I'm sorry to say, Senator, but I think if she had found Mary, she would never have told you or anyone else. Would you have, Lauren?"

Lauren Fowler refused to look at Sydney or Drew, but kept her gaze glued to her husband's angry face. "They'll ruin us, James. Don't you see, I did it for you!"

"No, Lauren, I don't see. Please explain just how you think this could ruin me."

Sydney was beginning to feel sorry for Lauren. Whatever Lauren was, the Queen of Chill or Queen Bee, a corporate shark or a beautiful, talented social butterfly with aspirations of being First Lady, she loved her husband to the point that she was willing to do anything to protect him. Sydney looked at Drew, found him gazing at her, and realized that he, too, understood Lauren's motives.

"I just wanted to help you, sweetheart," Lauren pleaded. "They could ruin everything you've worked for. Your reputation, they could take Rosehill, everything."

"My reputation, Lauren?" James said. "For a murder that was committed by my ancestor almost one hundred years ago? I don't think so. As for losing Rosehill, why would you think that?"

"Your father said that was why he hid the journal. He was afraid what Clay Wallace would do about the will."

Sydney could see that the senator didn't understand what his wife was talking about. "Dammit, James, she's talking about old Samuel Clayton's will, remember? The one that was rewritten after Mary's murder and Andrew Joshua's hanging. He prevented Clay from inheriting any of his property, including Rosehill. She's afraid Clay will fight the will since it was made under false circumstances. But Lauren, Clay has a right to know what happened to his parents. An innocent man was killed for a crime he didn't commit. Mary was murdered and Darcy Fowler was responsible for both. I've come to know Clay, Lauren, and I don't think you or the senator have anything he wants."

James stood up and began to pace back and forth. "I just can't believe this, that my own wife would do such a thing. Lauren, where's the journal?"

"In the glove compartment of the Jeep."

"John, go get it."

Sydney leaned back and closed her eyes. She was so tired and the brandy Drew had made her drink was making her relax. So much had happened tonight, she felt drained. She'd been a witness to a love so strong that it had transcended the most enigmatic obstacle of all: time. There had been too many bitter years, too many memories of a love that was not to be.

Sydney could see now that her parents had married each other for all the wrong reasons. Her father had eventually found someone he truly loved, and even though it had torn his family apart, he'd walked away from those who loved him too much to let him be happy. He had walked away, but, she realized suddenly, not from her or her sister. That separation had been her mother's doing. God, she didn't want to end up a bitter woman like her mother.

She was confused about her own emotions and her life. Up until she'd come to Wallace, she'd thought she'd made all the right decisions. For the first time, she thought about growing old alone, and the idea wasn't one she wished to dwell on.

Sydney opened her eyes and sat up when she heard John's heavy footsteps as he returned to the study. Johnenstein, she thought, and glanced at Drew. They shared the thought and a smile.

The senator snatched the journal from John, opened it to the date of the storm and began to read aloud. It was a sad tale of a man obsessed with love and hate. Darcy hadn't been punished by the law for what he'd done, but he'd suffered for the rest of his life. Several minutes later, when the senator finished, he tossed the journal at Lauren. "Would you ever have showed this to me?"

Lauren was smart enough not to lie. "No, James. I would do anything to protect you from pain or embarrassment."

Sydney could see that James was speechless at his wife's declaration. Speechless and dumbstruck. For a politician, it was surprising that he could still be shocked. She had a feeling that things were going to change around the Fowler household. Maybe the senator would even gain a few pounds just to show his Lauren who was the boss. She was so lost in thought that she almost missed Lauren's next statement.

"We're going to lose Rosehill, aren't we, James?"

The senator sighed. "You don't see it, do you, Lauren? It doesn't matter. Rosehill is just brick and wood. It's just a place where we live."

If Clay Wallace wanted a dramatic entrance, he got his wish. He stormed in looking as if he'd been dragged through the bushes backward, then rolled in dirt. But his back was straight, his head held high as he hobbled across the room. "James Darcy Fowler, your great-granddaddy killed my mother."

"I know," the senator said.

If the wind had been knocked out of his sails, Clay wasn't about to show it. "Darcy was also responsible for my father's hanging."

"You're right. He planned it. I don't know what to say, Clay," the senator said, "just that I'm so sorry about Mary and Andrew Joshua."

"No need to be. They're together forever now. You had nothing to do with their deaths."

"Drew and Sydney told us everything that happened tonight. Is there anything I can do? Anything you need?"

"Yes, there are three things I want." Clay sat down on the edge of the desk, hooked his cane over one knee, and without looking at John, said, "Get me a glass of that brandy, John."

"God," Lauren cried, "what did I tell you, James. He's going to ruin us."

"Are you, Clay?" the senator asked, and even though he'd told Lauren it didn't matter, the thought that he might actually lose Rosehill and all the trappings that went with it was daunting. "Are you going to fight Clayton's will and try to reclaim what I guess should have been yours?"

Clay threw back his head and laughed. "James, Samuel Clayton hated my father before he even looked crossways at Mary, just because Dad was part Indian. From the moment he realized Mary was in love with a Wallace, he became like a man possessed with hate. He did everything to keep them apart, including disinheriting Mary when she married Andrew Joshua. He was a bitter, nasty, mean-spirited man. Mary knew it and was happy to get away from him."

Clay paused and looked at the senator, then at his wife. "There's not one thing, James, that I want of that old bastard's. And all I want from you are just three things."

"What?" James said.

"First, the Fowlers will attend Mary's funeral tomorrow. Second, I want the portrait of my mother."

"Of course, we'll all be there, and as to the painting, it's yours. After Drew and Sydney told me about Darcy, it was the first thing I thought of," the senator said. "And the third thing?"

"I want the people in this town to know the truth. I'm not looking for a big splashy story or to hurt your political career. With some experience you'll make a good leader, but I want the truth in the *Wallace Morning Sun.*"

"But Clay," Sydney interrupted, "there is no more town newspaper."

"What the hell . . . ?" James said, voicing his bewilderment while the rest only stared at Clay. It was John who finished the senator's sentence.

"What are you talking about? Of course, there's a paper, and Buddy—"

"Doesn't own the *Wallace Morning Sun,* boy. I do." Clay grinned at Sydney. "Will you write about finding Mary's body and the evidence of Darcy's guilt? You're the only one I'd trust with the truth without mentioning that we were out there chasing ghosts. You would know how to tell the story right."

Sydney glanced around the room, as if someone would have an answer for her. She finally looked at Drew, and for a moment they stared at each other, then he turned his head as though he couldn't bear to hear her answer.

"I'll write the story on one condition." She was her father's daughter, after all. . . . Suddenly, all she could see was Drew's face, the deep green of his eyes and, she prayed, the shine of love there. "Sell me the *Morning Sun.*"

"Done!" Clay yelped and laughed. "Told you I'd cosign the note."

"No, you won't have to. I have a trust fund my father set up for me, and this is as good a reason as any to spend it." Drew still hadn't moved and continued to stare at her as if he didn't believe what he was hearing. "One more thing, Mr. Wallace. I'd like to marry your grandson, if he'll have me."

Drew didn't wait for his grandfather to answer, but grabbed Sydney by the arm and hauled her out of the room. He was confused about where to go and first stopped at the living-room doorway, shook his head, then dragged her, protesting, all the way out the front door. The evening had cooled off; the breeze was refreshing and clean. The moon looked brighter to her.

Drew swung Sydney around to face him, holding her by her shoulders. "You're sure?"

She didn't want to hear what she thought he was going to say. "I'm sorry. I don't know what got into me. If I embarrassed you in there, I'm so sorry."

"Sorry? For what?" Drew gave a devilish chuckle. "I see. You're suddenly not so sure of yourself, are you, Miss Big-Time Reporter, Miss Realist?"

"Drew . . ."

"Sydney . . ." he mimicked her pleading tone. "All right, I won't tease. And to answer your question—" he pulled her close and touched her dirty cheek, then cupped her face in his hands "—I'd marry you this minute, but are you sure?"

"Oh, Drew. I'm not sure of anything. I've told myself that this is too soon. I keep hearing my mother say that love that comes too quickly leaves the same way. But my heart tells me differently." She threaded her fingers through his hair, loving the soft curls. "I think for the first time in my life, I'm just going to follow my heart."

"You believe in ghosts, goblins and things that go bump in the night?"

"Yes," she said laughing.

His lips were barely touching hers, just enough to feel their warmth, but he didn't kiss her, not yet, not until he had an answer to his last question. "You believe in love at first sight?"

"Yes." Sydney held tightly to his head, pulled his mouth to hers and kissed him deeply. "And I believe in dragons that talk, magic and rock and roll."

Drew glanced down the long, tree-lined driveway, saw the car headlights and said, "I wondered how long it would be until the town heard. Here comes the world, Sydney."

She recognized the car. "No, here comes Emma. What was it she once said?" She was quiet for a moment, her head resting against his chest. "'The only thing that lasts forever is love.'"

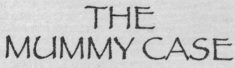

Take 4 bestselling love stories FREE

Plus get a FREE surprise gift!

Relive the romance...
Harlequin and Silhouette
are proud to present

A program of collections of three complete novels by the most-requested
authors with the most-requested themes. Be sure to look for one volume each
month with three complete novels by top-name authors.

In September: **BAD BOYS**

Dixie Browning
Ann Major
Ginna Gray

No heart is safe when these hot-blooded hunks are in town!

In October: **DREAMSCAPE**

Jayne Ann Krentz
Anne Stuart
Bobby Hutchinson

Something's happening! But is it love or magic?

In December: **SOLUTION: MARRIAGE**

Debbie Macomber
Annette Broadrick
Heather Graham Pozzessere

Marriages in name only have a way of leading to love....

Available at your favorite retail outlet.

REQ-G2

 HARLEQUIN®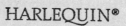

1993 Keepsake

CHRISTMAS

Stories

Capture the spirit and romance of Christmas with KEEPSAKE CHRISTMAS STORIES, a collection of three stories by favorite historical authors. The perfect Christmas gift!

Don't miss these heartwarming stories, available in November wherever Harlequin books are sold:

ONCE UPON A CHRISTMAS by Curtiss Ann Matlock
A FAIRYTALE SEASON by Marianne Willman
TIDINGS OF JOY by Victoria Pade

ADD A TOUCH OF ROMANCE TO YOUR HOLIDAY SEASON WITH KEEPSAKE CHRISTMAS STORIES!

HX93

When the only time you have for yourself is...

STOLEN *moments* ™

Christmas is such a busy time—with shopping, decorating, writing cards, trimming trees, wrapping gifts....

When you do have a few *stolen moments* to call your own, treat yourself to a brand-new *short* novel. Relax with one of our Stocking Stuffers— or with all six!

Each STOLEN MOMENTS title is a complete and original contemporary romance that's the perfect length for the busy woman of the nineties! Especially at Christmas...

And they make perfect **stocking stuffers,** too! (For your mother, grandmother, daughters, friends, co-workers, neighbors, aunts, cousins—all the other women in your life!)

Look for the STOLEN MOMENTS display in December

STOCKING STUFFERS:

HIS MISTRESS Carrie Alexander
DANIEL'S DECEPTION Marie DeWitt
SNOW ANGEL Isolde Evans
THE FAMILY MAN Danielle Kelly
THE LONE WOLF Ellen Rogers
MONTANA CHRISTMAS Lynn Russell

HSM2

 **WORLDWIDE LIBRARY**

HARLEQUIN SUPERROMANCE®

WOMEN WHO DARE DRIVE RACE CARS?!

During 1993, each Harlequin Superromance **WOMEN WHO DARE** title will have a single italicized letter on the Women Who Dare back-page ads. Collect the letters, spell D A R E and you can receive a free copy of **RACE FOR TOMORROW**, written by popular author Elaine Barbieri. This is an exciting novel about a female race-car driver, **WHO DARES ANYTHING . . . FOR LOVE!**

OFFER CERTIFICATE   O85-KAT

To receive your free gift, send us the 4 letters that spell DARE from any Harlequin Superromance Women Who Dare title with the offer certificate properly completed, along with a check or money order of $2.50 for postage and handling (do not send cash) payable to Harlequin Superromance Women Who Dare Offer.

Name: _____

Address: _____

_____

City: _____ State/Prov.: _____

Zip/Postal Code: _____

Mail this certificate, designated letters spelling DARE, and check or money order for postage and handling to: In the U.S.—WOMEN WHO DARE, P.O. Box 9057, Buffalo, NY 14269-9057; In Canada—WOMEN WHO DARE, P.O. Box 622, Fort Erie, Ontario L2A 5X3.

Requests must be received by January 31, 1994.
Allow 4-6 weeks after receipt of order for delivery.   R-085-KAT

Susan aqluecait

HARLEQUIN SUPERROMANCE®

HARLEQUIN SUPERROMANCE WANTS TO INTRODUCE YOU TO A DARING NEW CONCEPT IN ROMANCE...

WOMEN WHO DARE!
Bright, bold, beautiful...
Brave and caring, strong and passionate...
They're women who know their own minds
and will dare anything...for love!

One title per month in 1993, written by popular Superromance authors, will highlight our special heroines as they face unusual, challenging and sometimes dangerous situations.

The lady doctor and the sheriff are heading for a showdown in #574 DOC WYOMING by Sharon Brondos

Available in December wherever Harlequin Superromance novels are sold.

> ℛ **Collect letters.**
> **See previous page**
> **for details.**

WWD-DLR